PRAISE FOR
A DANGEROUS HEART

"This was a great story of healing, redemption and forgiveness. Secrets, regrets, and danger threaten to destroy the family and their legacy, but the strength of Isaac and Clare's love and their faith in God brings them through."

—ELAINE, GOODREADS

"This is a fascinating story! There's intrigue, deception, gunfights, and more. I love the McGraw family! They take care of each other and offer forgiveness and protection."

—JEANETTE, GOODREADS

"Action filled, emotionally charged, the contrast of grumpy and sunshine along with a faithful (and interfering) family are what makes this story great. A book I thoroughly enjoyed reading."

—CATHERINE, GOODREADS

"Loved, Loved. Loved this book. I enjoyed seeing the hearts of Clare and Isaac slowly changed. The bond of the family is one of favorite things in this series. The relationships with the next generation of McGraws is so much fun. Loved seeing how they cared for their new family. Once a McGraw, always a McGraw… blood or not."

—TERRI, GOODREADS

"A lovely grumpy/sunshine historical romance.. So enjoyed it. Sweet, romantic, and feel-good.."

—MARIANNE, GOODREADS

A Dangerous Heart

WIND RIVER MAIL-ORDER BRIDES

A Dangerous *Heart*

Lacy Williams
Wendy Galinetti

To my mother,
who loved a good romance and showed me
the joy of escaping into a book.

"A GOOD NAME IS RATHER TO BE CHOSEN THAN GREAT RICHES, AND LOVING FAVOR RATHER THAN SILVER AND GOLD. "

Proverbs 22:1 KJV

One

Y OU CAN'T CATCH ME!"
Shrieks and laughter from young voices carried on the early-autumn breeze as Isaac McGraw strode through the yard between the barn and the original family homestead—now his older brother Drew's home.

His six-year-old niece Tillie had sprouted up while he'd been gone on his last mission for the U.S. Marshals. Eleven-year-old Jo had grown lanky and awkward and looked more like her mother every day. But when Isaac looked at them, sometimes he saw the little tykes they'd been before.

Isaac's younger brother Nick trailed the girls toward the barn. He was within shouting distance but only raised his hand in a wave.

Isaac returned it half-heartedly and continued toward the main house.

He steeled himself and slowly pulled in air through his nose, the smell of damp hay and musky horses mingling in the fall air—familiar scents that now felt suffocating. A low-hanging fog clung to the grass and the bottom rails of the paddock as Isaac trudged through the mist and climbed the steps. The aroma of freshly brewed coffee greeted him as he crossed the threshold. He stalked to the dry sink, reached for a cup on the shelf above, and snagged the tin pot from the stove.

"Were you out all night, Uncle Isaac?"

Isaac had seen his nephew David stacking plates in the corner as soon as he'd come inside. It was too much to hope the fourteen-year-old would keep his silence.

Isaac nodded, setting the coffeepot down and turning to lean his hips against the counter. He lifted his cup to take a sip but avoided looking directly at the boy. It was too hard. David reminded him of another boy, one who hadn't lived to see his fourteenth birthday.

"Are you going again tonight? Can I come with you?"

David's questions tumbled over each other. The boy had idolized Isaac since they'd pinned the marshal's badge to his chest. And even now, when Isaac had given it up.

"No." Isaac hadn't meant to growl the word, but there it was.

David went quiet, subdued.

Drew hadn't asked Isaac to keep watch, but it gave him an excuse to keep his distance, and it felt like penance for not having been here when the well had been poisoned a few months ago. According to their middle brother Ed, the family had been so ill they might've died.

Voices carried from the adjoining living and dining

room, along with a husky laugh that belonged to his new sister-in-law Kaitlyn.

Moving to the doorway, he caught sight of Rebekah, Ed's wife of only a few weeks.

Two of his brothers had settled into marriage recently. It was another sign he didn't belong here anymore. He preferred the isolation of the hill country, his only companions a few varmints and a herd of cows.

But the ongoing feud with their neighbor made the solitude impossible. For now.

Isaac knew that any man willing to poison and kill wasn't going to give up easily. That's why Isaac needed to keep watch. Heath Quade wasn't going to give up, not when the McGraws owned the best water in the county. Quade had made that abundantly clear as he'd bought out two more neighbors over the past weeks. It wasn't enough for him to own the biggest ranch in the county. He'd bought or finagled nearly every piece right up to the McGraws' property lines.

Isaac's chest cinched tight at David's disappointment. He moved into the dining room to join Ed and Rebekah and Drew and Kaitlyn.

"What's this?" his brother Ed asked, bewildered. He was looking down at a white piece of paper on the table. Rebekah stood behind him, hands on her hips.

"It came to the mail-order bride postbox addressed to Isaac, postmarked a week ago. I found it in the mail when we were in town yesterday." She narrowed her eyes on her husband. "I thought I was the only one you were writing to."

Isaac watched color rise into Ed's cheeks, and a tiny part of him liked that his brother's new wife was sassing him. Months ago, Ed and Drew and Kaitlyn had cooked up a plan to find Isaac a bride—without bothering to ask him if he wanted one. The letters that were exchanged after the family had placed the mail-order bride ad on his behalf had caused a mess of trouble—and resulted in a match between Ed and Rebekah.

It gave Isaac a perverse kind of pleasure to see his brother squirming from the consequences of meddling in his life. Isaac was still angry.

"You are the only person I wrote to," Ed said.

Rebekah softened. "Then why does this Clare Ferguson say she's arriving on the train tomorrow?"

Isaac went still.

There was a jerky movement in the doorway at Rebekah's question.

"Hold up, son," Drew said at the same time as Isaac swiveled his head.

David stood in the open doorway, guilt written clearly on his expression. The kid had no poker face. He was trying to edge away unobtrusively, but Drew's focus was legendary.

"Why don't you come in here and tell us what you know about this letter." There was no room for disobedience in the command.

David hung his head, barely stepping inside the room. "Jo made me do it," he mumbled.

"Do what?" Ed asked.

Isaac's skin prickled at the sideways glance David shot him.

"Write a letter," the boy said hesitantly. He rubbed the back of his neck. "To get Uncle Isaac a wife."

Kaitlyn choked on her coffee.

It seemed that once he'd started, the words just tumbled out. "We heard you all talking at Uncle Ed and Aunt Rebekah's wedding. About Uncle Isaac. I told Jo it was a bad idea, but she—" His gaze flicked to Isaac. "We don't want Uncle Isaac to be sad anymore. So we picked one of the extra letters and wrote back to the lady who sent it."

Isaac's skin stretched too tight over his bones. No one in the family knew what had happened. There was no way David and Jo could know the well of darkness he'd descended into. But their innocent desire to help him—when he didn't deserve it one whit—hit like a punch to his solar plexus.

Isaac saw the guilty looks his brothers exchanged and Drew's glittering gaze.

"How many letters did you write?" Kaitlyn asked.

"Only two. Back and forth. They were good, long letters though. She's a really nice lady from a farm in Missouri. We paid for her train ticket from Jo's egg money and my savings."

"Why would you do that?" Drew demanded.

Ed had color high on his cheeks. Rebekah was hiding a laugh behind her hand.

David tilted his chin stubbornly. "Well, it worked for you and Uncle Ed."

Isaac turned to leave. He wanted no part of this.

But Ed said, "You'd better stay."

Anger flared. His brothers were still meddling in his life.

"I don't suppose you want to meet this woman?" Rebekah asked quietly.

Isaac ignored her completely.

Drew spoke to David. "Apologize to your uncle."

"You can't just mess with people's lives." Kaitlyn's words overlapped with her husband's.

David's chin was still jutting out. "Pa and Uncle Ed did."

Drew placed his hands on his hips and glared at his son. But he couldn't quite put any heat in his argument. "You're gonna have to fix this," he said. "You're gonna ride to town tomorrow and tell this woman to go back home."

"What? But Pa, she's coming to marry Uncle Isaac!"

The outburst was so unexpected from the usually even-keeled David that for a moment, the room went still.

Isaac felt the weight of the look Drew and Kaitlyn shared, the careful way Ed averted his eyes, Rebekah's hand on his arm.

"I'm not marrying anybody, kid," Isaac's voice grated. "Not ever."

David spun and ran from the room. The banging door punctuated the awkward silence that permeated the room.

Drew cleared his throat. "We'll make this right."

"You taught him to meddle," Isaac said coolly. "I want no part of this."

He left without looking back.

"Aunt Clare, are you really gonna get married to a cowboy?"

Get-ing marr-ied, get-ting marr-ied.

The train chugged and clacked, its wheels singing Clare Barlow's future.

She looked down at her eight-year-old nephew Ben, who gazed up at her with a wrinkled nose and an expression filled with curiosity. He had his mother's soft brown eyes and ready smile, always seeing adventure around every corner of life.

"What do you know about being a wife?" On Clare's other side, twelve-year-old Eli had his chin jutted at a stubborn angle and his arms crossed. His feet swung out into the aisle as if he couldn't sit still. A trait he came by honestly, from her side of the family. The Barlows were always on the run.

When he wasn't scowling, Eli was a handsome boy. Already more handsome than his father, with his intense dark-brown, almost black, eyes framed by thick lashes, and a square jawline that hinted at the man he would become. Not like his father, if she had anything to do with it.

Noth-ing, noth-ing.

Clare found a reassuring smile for both boys. "Yes, I'm really getting married. And he's a rancher, not a cowboy."

She would have to be enough. She'd gambled everything on this escape.

It wasn't the courtship most young women dreamed of—marrying a complete stranger. But Clare's belief in fairy-tale endings had been shattered years ago by her father. She'd learned a harsh truth that many girls never grasped: every fairy tale contained a villain, and sometimes that villain was a part of one's own family. A father. Or a brother.

"Can I be a cowboy too?"

Sweet Ben. Clare slid her arm around his small shoulders and pulled him closer. She whispered a reminder in his ear.

"Of course. And remember, you're to call me Ma."

"Okay," he whispered back.

She'd waited until now to tell the boys about the plan. Too much was at stake. She'd been too afraid of being found out before they'd left Missouri. She'd spent the first hours of their journey constantly looking over her shoulder, certain that Victor would find them.

Her outlaw brother would kill her for running away. Doubly so for taking his sons.

She knew what she'd done wasn't properly legal. She had no papers, no official claim to Ben or his brother. But she'd promised her late sister-in-law Anne in those last days before she'd passed. She could still hear her breathless plea. *Take them. Keep them safe. Make sure they don't grow up like him.*

And Clare couldn't break that promise.

The scenery out the window showed the Laramie Mountains in the distance.

Al-most there. Al-most there.

Calvin, Wyoming, was the next stop.

Absently, Clare noted the portly gentleman in the row in front of them getting up out of his seat. Before she'd fully registered it happening, Eli had slipped his scrawny arm between the seats and snatched it back with something clasped in his hand.

Clare caught his wrist in an iron grip.

"What is that?" Her whispered hiss and tightening grip had Eli revealing a fine gold watch with a broken chain.

She glanced over her shoulder at the man halfway to the hopper toilet at the back of the train. He hadn't even registered the watch was missing. No one else paid them a lick of attention.

It was a valuable piece—gold-plated and everything. It would be so easy to slip it inside her pocket. The man wore a fine suit. No doubt he could buy another. Clare and the boys had little funds. Her past whispered to her: easy pickings.

She took the watch from Eli's hand and dropped it back on the seat in front of them.

"We aren't Barlows anymore," she told him in a low, steady voice. "Remember the things your mama taught you. Thou shalt not steal."

Eli shoved back into the seat. He crossed his arms over his chest and jutted his chin in defiance. Gone was the older brother eager to help with his baby brother. Now she saw an echo of Victor, his father. Anne would have known better what to say, how to reach him. Clare didn't.

Her stomach clenched with grief over missing Anne. Through every hardship, Anne's faith had been a beacon. She'd changed Clare, brought light and truth into the world of darkness Clare had been born into. Clare had to continue Anne's legacy for her boys.

"Calvin, Wyoming!" the conductor announced as he passed down the aisle. As the train slowed, Clare's heart pumped faster. Ben sprang to his feet, gripping the seat back in front of him and lifting his boots off the floor to get a better view through the window of the row in front. Eli remained affixed to the seat, his mouth screwed tight.

She prayed he would keep his mouth shut and not give them away the first moment off the train.

The train braked and rolled to a stop. Clare rose from her seat, heart pounding, knees trembling. She smiled tightly at the boys.

At the front of the train, the steel-haired man with a wide, neatly trimmed mustache, around the same age as her pa, was the first passenger to stand. After a grand stretch, he donned his fancy black Stetson. She'd made him when he'd first entered the compartment. He had the sharp eyes and that certain shrewd manner of a man who lived outside the law.

Ben's hand slipped into hers. She dropped her eyes, turning her face away from the oily gaze that made her skin crawl and focusing on keeping the boys at her side as they disembarked.

A brisk breeze swept over the boardwalk, stirring up dust as Clare stepped off the train. Her skirt flapped against her legs as she surveyed the town. Behind the rooftops, the hills were dotted with trees, their green leaves on the verge of turning gold and amber with the cooler fall weather.

The streets were wider than the ones back home. Wide enough for two large wagons to pass. Wide enough for the herds of cattle that ranchers would drive into town and load onto trains headed for Chicago. Isaac had written in his last letter that she would arrive in time for the roundup. And wouldn't that be something?

She passed a young woman, carrying a toddler on her hip, who seemed to all but disappear into the arms of a hulking man in overalls. Clare froze and pressed sweaty hands together, struck by the realization that she hadn't considered how to greet her new groom. Would he anticipate a warm hug?

Where was Mr. McGraw?

She scanned the area and caught on a lone cowboy near the corner of the platform away from the rails. Dressed in dark trousers and a light-blue canvas shirt topped with a black vest, he stood rigid, shoulders squared, chin slightly lowered. He had that watchful look—steady and unblinking. His fingers even twitched at his side, a gunman ready to draw.

For a moment, she recoiled. Then she noticed what was missing—no gun belt, no pistol. Still, he glanced around, alert as any lawman.

No one else waited on the platform. Other folks were walking away. This had to be Isaac McGraw.

She took a few steps in his direction, her breath catching at the heat of his intense stare. If this was him, then her intended groom was an exceptionally handsome man, with his high cheekbones, vivid green eyes, and square jaw softened by a dimple. But why was he scowling at her?

They met at the far corner of the platform. She was aware of Ben and Eli trailing behind her. Eli muttered something to his brother that she didn't hear.

"Mr. McGraw?" Was that her voice? Breathy and trembling?

She saw the minute flare of his nostrils. Other than that, he was totally unreadable. He nodded.

"I'm Clare."

Ben shifted his feet, and the handsome cowboy–rancher's eyes flicked over Ben and moved to Eli. His frown tightened.

Her stomach dropped. She hadn't told her intended groom about her nephews. She hadn't wanted to give him any reason to reject her.

She glanced away. Saw the train porters unloading wooden crates. One crate caught her attention with the flash of a familiar name—*Hercules Powder*. Explosives?

She blinked, drawing her gaze back to the rancher, who didn't look any happier to see her. This man was nothing like the man in his letters, who'd written so fondly of the ranch and his family. Unease twisted in her belly, like when one of Pa's plans went awry.

She put a hand on Ben's small shoulder. "This is Ben. And this is Eli." She raised her other hand to Eli's shoulder.

Isaac's scowl deepened, but he didn't outright reject them. His gaze traveled to the street, past the crowd on the boardwalk, and landed on the man in the Stetson, standing several yards away, still on the platform. Stetson was talking with two other men who must be in their forties, wearing dusty trousers and vests over their shirts. Ranchers?

Isaac McGraw stiffened, and his eyes narrowed. She needed him to focus on her.

"Will we be going to the parson's house first?" Clare pressed, trying for a soft smile. "Before we go to your ranch?"

Isaac's eyes snapped back to her, distraction gone. "Miss—there's been a mistake. I didn't send for you, and we are not getting hitched."

His words didn't register at first. When they did, she felt

that knot in her belly twist tighter. "What do you mean?" she asked. "A mistake?"

He didn't answer directly. "It would be best if you got on that train and went back where you came from."

Ben's hand fisted in her skirt. Eli made a scoffing sound. She could feel the boys' nerves ratcheting higher. Or maybe it was her own.

"That won't be possible." There. She'd kept the tremble from her voice.

But Isaac didn't soften.

She was aware of curious gazes from people milling about the platform nearby. She couldn't afford to give Isaac more time to argue. "I don't understand. You sent for me so we could be married."

"I didn't send for you."

He'd said that before, but it didn't make any more sense this time. His voice was low and urgent and made her think he wanted her to be silent.

It only agitated her more. She reached into her skirt pocket and pulled out the folded envelope. "I have your letter right here. You promised we'd marry!" Her voice pitched higher and louder than she intended.

Heads turned from the crowd on the platform, especially Mr. Stetson and his two companions. Their gazes were like nettles on her skin. She and the boys were too exposed out here in the open. She stepped closer to Isaac McGraw. Close enough to see the tight lines around his mouth and hear his breath catch.

"Is there somewhere more private we could go to straighten out this misunderstanding?" she asked softly.

Ben chose that moment to yank at her sleeve. "I'm hungry."

Isaac glared at her. "We are not going anywhere," he ground out. "You're getting back on that train."

Her plan was unraveling before her eyes. Since she'd stepped foot off the train, nothing had gone right. Victor was behind her. There was no returning, not after what she'd done. She couldn't give up. "You gave your word. We're getting married."

A shadow fell over her. "Is there a problem here, miss?"

She didn't notice until she looked his way that it was sharp-eyed Mr. Stetson from the train.

She was close enough to see the subtle change in Isaac's expression, the way his back bristled. He turned a stony face to the interloper. "No."

The man ignored Isaac, his calculating eyes on Clare. He puffed out his chest and tipped his hat toward Clare. "Heath Quade, president of the Cattlemen's Association and a citizen of this fine town. And you are?"

"None of your business, Quade," Isaac growled.

Ben butted his head into Clare's side, jolting her. She'd been so caught up in the tension between the two men that, for a moment, she'd lost track of both boys. Panic flared as she turned—until she spotted Eli, quietly watching Quade. Relief rushed through her.

"I thought you were getting married." Ben chose the worst moment to pipe up.

Heath Quade's shrewd eyes darted between Isaac and Clare. "That true?"

The muscle in Isaac's jaw jumped, but he remained mute.

Quade turned a calculating glance toward Clare. "You one of those mail-order brides? The McGraws sure do like them."

Clare didn't know what he meant, but it was clear his words stirred up something in Isaac.

"This ain't your concern." Isaac stepped in front of Clare and the boys, partially blocking her from Quade's view. She was surprised by the protective gesture after his earlier scowl.

Isaac's head turned, and she realized the two other men had stepped over to flank their friend Quade. With her feet at the back of the platform, it felt a little like being trapped. Her gaze darted all around as she looked for an escape.

One of the men addressed her. "This man botherin' you?"

She shook her head.

Apparently, the moment of distraction meant Quade had stepped to the side, around Isaac. He addressed Clare.

"I couldn't help but overhear—"

"Stay out of it, Quade." There was something dangerous in Isaac's tone. Couldn't everyone hear it?

Quade didn't. "As an upstanding citizen of Calvin and a duly elected official, it's my duty to come to the aid of a lady who finds herself abandoned at the train station."

Isaac blocked Quade when he tried to step closer, keeping his lean, muscular body between Quade and Clare and her nephews. Almost like he was shielding her.

Her chest tightened. Had anybody ever stepped between her and danger? She didn't think so.

"Did I hear you say you had a letter? A written promise to marry could be considered a binding contract."

Clare's fingers gripped the letter tighter. She wanted to shove it back into her pocket. But that would be too obvious now.

Quade spoke to the man closest to him. "What do you think, gentlemen? It'd sure be a shame if one of Calvin's first homesteading families got sued for breach of contract."

Isaac's shoulders tensed, and his stance grew more rigid.

The other rancher looked uncomfortable. "If McGraw can't keep his word, the circuit judge can sort this out when he comes to town."

Something passed between Quade and Isaac. She wished she could see Isaac's face.

Quade said, "Maybe we should just walk over to the marshal's office and see what Marshal O'Grady has to say about this."

Eli, a statue throughout the whole exchange, began to shake. His fists were clenched at his sides, and he was standing on the balls of his feet, ready to run.

Clare gripped his sleeve. "That won't be necessary," she said quickly to Quade. "I'm sure Mr. McGraw and I can come to an equitable—"

Isaac turned toward her. He motioned to the stairs off the platform. "The wagon is thataway. Get a move on."

The command in his voice grated on her last nerve, but she also had a sense that this was the only offer he was going to make. And she needed to get off the platform, away from so many prying eyes. Eyes that could report back to Victor if he ever sent a scout looking for her here.

She grabbed Eli's arm with one hand and Ben's hand

with the other and followed Isaac's long-legged stride off the train platform.

Two

WITH HER FINELY TUNED INSTINCTS, Clare felt a prickling awareness of the curious gazes from passengers on the boardwalk and the men they'd left behind at the station as Eli and Ben scrambled into the wagon box.

The wagon itself was loaded with supplies and waited outside the dry-goods store.

A few feet away, Isaac and a boy with a similar stubborn jawline, a little older than Eli, were engaged in an intense conversation. Every line of Isaac McGraw's body conveyed suppressed anger and frustration.

The wind carried his last clipped words to the boy. "You ride ahead and start fixing this."

"I'm hungry," Ben muttered again.

Clare leaned over the wagon bed to pat his shoulder. "Try to take a nap," she urged. "We don't want to cause trouble in our first moments here."

"Too late," Eli mumbled.

Isaac stalked to the wagon, ignoring a lifted hat from a man passing by as he approached.

Clare quickly climbed onto the front seat. The trip would be tense at the start, just inches from him on the seat, but she knew how to calm angry men.

"You don't happen to have children?" she asked, a hint of honey in her voice.

The wagon shifted as he settled on the bench. His hesitation lasted so long, she thought he wouldn't answer.

"My nephew," Isaac finally grumbled.

"I thought I could see the family resemblance."

Another grunt, a flick of the reins, and the wheels began to turn.

"I know you weren't expecting the boys," she said with a tentative smile. "We hadn't really gotten that far in our letters."

They passed out of town as a lengthy silence settled between them.

"They're good boys. Growing up on a farm, they're no strangers to hard work. They can care for chickens or hogs. And they're fast learners."

Still no reply. It couldn't be more obvious that he didn't want to engage with her. And they hadn't been married before they'd left town. This wasn't a good start. At least the boys had settled in the back of the wagon, pulling their hats over their eyes.

From the corner of her eye, she took in Isaac's profile. A half-day's growth of dark-blond beard shadowed his hardened jaw. He kept his eyes fixed on the road ahead.

Her palms began to sweat. She rubbed them on her skirt, searching her mind for something from the letters to placate him. Yes. He had written he needed a cook.

"Your ad mentioned you were looking for someone to cook. I'm a great cook!" It was a slight exaggeration. Her mother had passed on when Clare was young, and Clare's early instruction hadn't been in cooking. It'd been pickpocketing.

"I didn't mention anything," he muttered.

He had. A whole paragraph listing his favorite meals. Didn't he remember?

The wagon rattled along the two-track road over a slight hill. Clare grasped for something to say as they rolled past the lodgepole pines and rocky outcrops that dotted the landscape. A slight breeze swept across the grassy prairie. The land was vast. She could see for miles in all directions. The McGraws owned several homesteads they had already proved up. From the few letters she'd received, she could tell they were proud of the land they owned.

"No wonder your family settled here. It feels like the land goes on and on forever."

His shoulders tensed even more, if that were possible.

Clare grew agitated. Every attempt to chip away at the man's icy demeanor failed. He remained as silent and unyielding as the distant mountains as he eyed a farmhouse set back off the road.

She breathed in a long, deep breath. Slowly released it. *He doesn't want you here.* But if he didn't want her, then why had he placed the ad? And written the letters?

She cast a glance at his grim profile again. Something Anne used to say passed through her mind.

Can't deny the sun's shining when it's right there in the noonday sky.

Fine.

She turned on the hard seat and confronted him head-on. "Why did you write the letters?"

He sighed and rubbed the place where his nose met his forehead. A fine blush bloomed at the top of his cheeks. "I didn't write any letters or place an ad. My brothers . . ."

"Your brothers?" Her voice had grown faint.

"My brothers cooked up a plan to get me a wife by placing one of those ads." The red on his cheeks deepened. "It didn't work out—for me."

What did that mean?

"Then my nephew"—he nodded ahead to where the lanky boy was just visible on horseback—"and my niece decided to write back to one of the letters. Your letter."

His nephew had written the letters. Everything she knew about him and the ranch, the life she had run to, had been written by a boy? Humiliation took root as she thought of the words she'd written back.

"I don't understand. Why would your nephew do that?"

She recognized the angry set to his jaw as he muttered, "It's complicated."

"You didn't put him up to it?" she pressed.

"I have no need for a wife," he growled.

This was all a child's prank? And she'd staked her future on it? She waited for more, but his mouth became a grim line.

"I'm real sorry," he said, but his words didn't make a real apology. He didn't sound sorry. He sounded annoyed. "David and Jo finagled a way to buy the train ticket with their own money and send it with the adults none the wiser." He shook his head with a humorless laugh. His eyes rested on her. "They shouldn't have done it."

Clare's stomach sank. She pictured the short advertisement Anne had circled in the newspaper. Anne had called the ad "God's providence." Looking back now, Clare saw it for what it was. Too good to be true.

Her thoughts whirled, trying to find a solution for this disaster. "You sure you don't want to get married?" Her mind went to the ads she'd scoured over and over. Men who listed ads seemed to want companionship and help with ranch work.

"No." The curt word left no room for argument.

"So what am I supposed to do?"

"That's not my problem."

"You came all the way to town. That shows a sense of responsibility," she argued.

"I came to make sure David didn't do something foolish," he snapped.

The words carried a sense of honor that she'd appreciate at another place and time—not when her careful plans were unraveling all around her.

"You can go back where you came from," he said.

"The boys and I can't go back. There's nothing left to go back to—no home, no family, no farm."

He glanced over his shoulder at the boys. Eli was awake, head propped on one elbow at the back corner of the wagon, staring at the passing scenery. Ben stirred from where he'd fallen asleep tucked between two crates.

The enormity of what she had done hit her.

Isaac let out a long-suffering sigh. "My brothers can re-group and help you figure out what to do, since David and Jo created this mess."

Isaac scanned the horizon with a level of attention she didn't expect from someone who claimed to be a simple rancher. That made her even more curious about him—more so than the dozens of little mannerisms she'd noticed during the past half hour. Her thoughts were interrupted by a small finger tapping her on the shoulder.

"I'm hungry." Ben had crawled over some crates stacked at the back of the wagon and tried to whisper in her ear. She'd pushed off his needs back in town. She had nothing to feed the boys.

Isaac leaned forward and reached under the seat, rum-maging. He pulled out a shiny metal lunch pail that was overflowing with so much food that the red-and-white cloth tucked around its top strained to contain it all. He handed it to her, his eyes on her only long enough for Clare to take it from him before setting it on her lap. Under the cloth, she found biscuits, thick slices of ham, and two ap-ples at the bottom.

"Looks like someone made fresh biscuits this morning. Would you mind if the boys shared one?"

"They can have all of it."

The quick act of kindness seemed to contrast with the gruff, angry man next to her, but she wasn't going to argue about this. Not when the boys needed food.

She turned to hand a fluffy biscuit to Ben. The wagon jostled, and her shoulder brushed against a hard, muscled bicep. A tingling sensation shot down her arm into her fingers. His jaw remained tight and his gaze miles ahead.

"What do you say?" she murmured.

The boys gave a chorus of awkward thank-yous.

No-no. No-no.

One of the wagon wheels squeaked. Instead of the hopeful message she'd heard on the train, worries cascaded in time with each turn of the wheel.

No husband.

No home.

No future.

What now?

Isaac shifted beside her. Suddenly, those sharp green eyes were turned on her, studying her. "I've got some questions of my own, you know." His voice was low and raspy and deceptively calm. "Like why a woman like you would need to become a mail-order bride."

She bristled, then caught herself. A woman like her. What did he mean by that?

In the back of the wagon, the boys were chattering in low voices. Something about a rabbit.

A woman like her would go to great lengths to protect the people she loved.

"What kind of woman is that?" She tipped her head artfully.

But his eyes were sharp, not curious. "You said you know about farming and cooking, and you have two boys to help.

And you're a looker. You couldn't find a man in all of Missouri to take you on?"

Clare felt a subtle flutter inside as Isaac's words registered. *A woman like you* and *a looker*. Her face warmed as she realized Isaac McGraw thought she was pretty.

"What happened to your husband?"

What husband? It was on the tip of her tongue, but she caught the words just in time. She flicked a glance back at the boys, who didn't seem to have heard.

"He's gone." She tried for a note of sadness and finality. It was true. Victor had left town on a job—she hadn't asked more. And when her brother returned to the farm, he would find her and the boys gone.

"Things were getting difficult back in Missouri—taking care of the boys on my own. I had nobody to help with the farm. Seems like I was always scrimping for food."

She was careful to tell the truth.

From under her lashes, she chanced a peek at him. He was watching her. His scrutiny was sharp, observant, and deliberate. A seasoned lawman assessing a suspect's sincerity?

Why had she thought that? She quickly cut her gaze away.

Her dress sleeve had pulled up on her left arm, exposing an inch of a white scar. She carefully slid it down to her wrist. She had one more card to play. And nothing to lose.

She turned and waited for him to face her. Looked at him from beneath her lashes. "I was lonely," she said.

The truth hit like a blow to her stomach.

For a moment, something sparked in the air between them. A shared recognition?

Was Isaac McGraw lonely too?

But then his eyes shuttered. "We're on McGraw land now. The homestead isn't far, and the whole family will be waiting."

Her face burned. All her charms fell flat on this rancher. She stole another glance at his profile. He was a complete mystery to her. But she would figure him out. She had to.

The sun hung low in the sky, casting a warm glow over the valley and the misty mountains farther away. From this distance, Isaac saw David disappear into the barn and had to quash a second bout of irritation toward the boy.

Isaac's instincts had sent him to the train station after Drew had talked Isaac into going to town for supplies.

His instincts had been right. David had ducked away and slipped into the crowd the moment Clare and those boys had stepped off the train. Isaac couldn't help being angry at the mess his nephew had created. David was usually a good kid. What had gotten into him?

The woman beside him had gone silent a few miles ago. When he'd informed her they were close to home, her eyes had devoured the landscape. He caught her short, sudden intake of breath followed by a faint "oh" as the wagon and its weary crew rolled up and over the last hill and the homestead came fully into view. Her shoulders straightened, fingers tightening around the edge of the bench seat. The youngest boy had fallen asleep, his head resting against a sack of flour. The oldest watched the scenery with careful interest.

Isaac hadn't let himself look at her full on since the train platform but couldn't erase the image from his memory. She was striking. Beautiful. The kind of quiet beauty that settled under a man's skin without him realizing it. His eyes swept over her now. Her brown work dress was plain, but it suited her. What caught him, though, was the shawl she'd draped around her shoulders. Soft brown with a wide stripe of cream and blue that wrapped around her like a protective arm. Its wispy fringe swayed with the motion of the wagon, brushing lightly against her creamy cheeks. The touch of it seemed to soften her face even more, drawing his eyes when he knew better than to look.

Their gazes caught for a moment. She had the kind of eyes that flashed warmth, and a wide, expressive mouth that could distract a man less cynical than him. Now those eyes shone with pleasure while her lips parted in awe.

"It's lovely," she said, barely above a whisper.

Her admiration sparked something inside him. How many times had he ridden up this road? With Clare beside him, he was seeing it with new eyes.

The barn, the bunkhouse, the fenced paddock where several horses grazed, weather-worn but well maintained by the labor and grit of three generations of McGraws. His chest tightened with both pride and the suffocating need to escape.

A thread of smoke drifted from the chimney of the main homestead, evidence that a fire still burned in the hearth. Drew and Kaitlyn sat on chairs pulled from the kitchen to the front stoop, mugs in hand. Isaac swallowed, almost tasting the strong brew.

A dog barked. A blur of tan, black, and white chased circles around Tillie. Her blonde braids swinging, she tried to pivot but tumbled to the grass. Isaac saw a flash of her as a toddler, when he'd catch her from falling and swing her into his arms.

"Stop." Tillie shrieked and giggled as his brother Nick's shepherding dog furiously licked her face.

Isaac blinked and looked away. He'd had nowhere else to go when everything had fallen apart. He needed the seclusion of his cabin to hole up, lick his wounds, and try to find a way forward. And to keep his eye on Quade.

He assessed the pretty woman sitting next to him. She'd come here as a mail-order bride. Why? He pushed aside his natural curiosity. Clare Ferguson was not his responsibility. But he couldn't shake the nagging feeling that she might bring trouble.

Isaac pulled the reins taut, and the wagon rolled to a stop. Drew and Kaitlyn were already off the porch, walking hand in hand. Jo appeared from the barn and sprinted to the wagon. David dismounted and tied his horses to the corral fence before returning to the wagon.

"Uncle Isaac, you brought her home with you!" the girl exclaimed. Her eyes, wide with excitement, flitted from him to Clare and to the back of the wagon. Her brow wrinkled.

Isaac fisted the reins, his gaze tangled with Clare's. She lifted her eyebrows. He dipped his chin. Vowing to ignore her, he slid from the bench and halted at the side of the wagon. He craved distance. Recalling the gentle brush of her shoulder, his bicep responded with a twitch, as if haunted by a phantom touch.

Clare's boys were already out of the wagon.

"Is that your dog?" Clare's youngest asked. She'd called him Ben.

Isaac gritted his teeth, hardening himself against the young boy's curious tone. He restricted his thoughts to the tasks at hand. Tend to the horse, unload the supplies, and fix the box staple that had come loose on the wagon. His meddlesome family could figure out the rest.

He was already running his fingers over the loose staple on the sideboard when he heard Jo say, "She didn't say she had boys."

Drew ambled to Clare's side of the wagon and offered a hand down, but he sent Isaac a side-eyed look over the wagon. Kaitlyn stepped forward, laying a gentle hand on Clare's arm.

"Welcome to the McGraw homestead, Miss…" Kaitlyn faltered, her forehead wrinkling as she took in the boys scrambling around the supplies while Jo unlatched the wagon back.

"Ferguson." Clare provided her last name.

A beat passed where Isaac expected Clare to say more. She didn't. Was this the same woman who had yammered all the way from Calvin?

There was a flurry of introductions and a mention that Ed and Rebekah were currently over at the Boutwells' place nearby. Nick was with the cattle.

Clare Ferguson was all smiles, the youngest boy glued

to her side. Eli and David stood a few feet from each other near the back of the wagon, eyeing each other awkwardly. Isaac moved to the back of the wagon, lowered the tailgate. He grabbed a large grain sack, hoisted it over his shoulder, and headed to the barn. Drew grabbed one too, following Isaac and leaving Kaitlyn with Clare and the children.

"What happened?" Drew asked when they were inside the barn.

"Quade happened." Isaac tossed the feed sack onto the ground. It landed with a thump that wasn't satisfying enough.

"What?"

"Quade and his cronies were on the platform at the depot. David disappeared." Isaac had seen David sneaking toward the wagon just before Clare had disembarked.

"When I met her"—he jerked his thumb back toward the wagon and the women's chattering voices—"she was spouting off about the letters. Quade was quick to offer to help her sue us for breach of contract. Said it would be a real shame if the family lost our homestead in a lawsuit."

"That skunk!" Drew's eyes narrowed, but his anger was banked.

After hearing about Clare Ferguson's hardships, Isaac couldn't really say whether she would do it or not. She obviously needed the money.

"Folks started gathering around. I thought it best to bring her here instead of making a bigger scene."

"This scheme of Jo and David's was foolish." Drew ran his hand over his face and blew out a breath. "Kaitlyn can buy her train tickets to go home. I'd take her back to town tomorrow, but I can't—not till after the roundup."

Kaitlyn's inheritance had helped the family out of a difficult spot earlier in the year.

Isaac's stomach growled, reminding him he'd given the boys his lunch. He thought of Clare, who'd only taken a few bites and given the rest to her boys. She had a mother's heart.

Drew must've heard. "Come on up to the house and eat."

As they walked, Isaac studiously ignored Clare walking with Kaitlyn toward the house. Drew glanced between them. "So, what do you think of Clare?"

Pretty. The word almost tumbled from his mouth. He pressed his lips together. Sure, she was pretty. Probably one of the prettiest women ever to arrive in Calvin, Wyoming. Her dark hair was pinned up, but a few tendrils had escaped, curling at her temple and brushing against her cheek. Her hazel eyes danced, and her smile was striking enough to land like a gut punch. Isaac still couldn't figure out why she would need to answer an ad.

He didn't think she'd throw her lot in with a man like Quade.

But she had traveled hundreds of miles to marry a stranger.

He took the two steps up the porch stairs, cracked the door open, and stepped inside. Drew followed, crowding in behind him. Inside, Clare stood with Kaitlyn in the hall, smiling one of her charming smiles and inspecting his grandmother's cross-stitch that hung in a wooden frame over the row of hooks near the door. A Bible verse they'd all had to memorize.

In all thy ways acknowledge him, and he shall direct thy paths.

He'd once believed that—that God was directing his steps. But God had abandoned Isaac. Or Isaac had gotten off the path somewhere.

Clare turned to Kaitlyn, eyes shining. "Your family must believe in the providence of God."

"Oh yes. It was God who sent me to Drew and the children."

Clare's voice softened. "I can't help but think that maybe those letters that got sent are kind of like the story of Abraham sending his servant to fetch a wife for his son Isaac."

The statement was so preposterous that Isaac sucked in air when he should have swallowed.

Drew stepped near and gave him a couple of slaps on the back, then removed his hat and dropped it over one of the hooks.

Kaitlyn smiled at Isaac's discomfort, but in a flash, she turned green and excused herself to run upstairs.

Clare's cheeks turned pink. Her eyes followed Kaitlyn up the stairs, then turned to Drew.

"She okay?" Isaac asked.

Drew ran a hand through his dark hair, releasing a sigh, but then his expression changed. The corner of his mouth lifted, and a gleam sparked in his eyes. "She's in the family way."

A beat of envy struck Isaac, followed by a piercing sadness. He hadn't known. He would be an uncle again, and he hadn't noticed. He'd been here. Home. But not truly engaged with his family.

Drew let out a sharp breath. "That's why I can't go back to town. Kaitlyn won't be able to go on roundup. We'll be short a cook."

Clare hovered nearby.

"I can cook for you," she volunteered. "The boys would love to ride out on a roundup."

"No." But Isaac's quick refusal went unheeded.

Drew's eyes had a considering look in them.

Clare barely glanced in Isaac's direction.

"I'll accept payment," she said to Drew. "If I'm not to be married, I'll need to figure out what to do next. And I'll need money."

Frustration boiled in Isaac's gut. Drew was the oldest brother. The one who felt responsible for the entire family.

How had Clare known just what to say so he would feel responsible for her too?

Isaac tried to catch his brother's eyes, shook his head. But Drew only sent him a regretful glance.

"My children created this mess. The least we can do is try and set things right."

Three

AGGRAVATION MOUNTED AS ISAAC whirled the roping loop over his head for the third time. His head pounded, and even his teeth ached. The dusty sweat on his open shirt chafed against his sunburned skin. The headstrong steer he'd chased up a ridge bawled, the sound grating on his last nerve. But what had really stuck in his craw the whole day? Running into Clare Ferguson at the crack of dawn before he could even drink his first cup of coffee.

The rope snapped, and relief flooded through him as it slipped over the animal's horns. The steer made a final attempt to escape, but with a tug of the rope, it became docile. Isaac's shoulders ached and his eyes burned. He blinked as the memories of the morning encounter flooded back.

He had rounded the corner of the chuck wagon and almost bowled her over. The unexpected surge of attraction took him by surprise. He'd caught her shoulders in his hands to keep her upright. Despite the drab work dress, she looked fresh and pretty in one of Nick's old cowboy hats. A nervous smile played on her lips, but her eyes drew him in as she greeted him with a surprised "Good morning."

"'Scuse me" was all he could manage. He tried to maneuver around her, but she sidestepped in front of him. Their gazes locked.

She didn't look away. Not like the rest of his family did when they came face-to-face with him. No, she held his stare, a silent challenge pulsing between them. He tried to go around her again.

"I need to talk to you," she said. "Drew and the other men are already gone."

He crossed his arms as she rushed on.

"I'm preparing to cook tonight's meal. Nick mentioned you like a good hot stew at the end of the day."

"Don't worry about me. I'll eat whatever's in the pot." Irked that his brother was wagging his tongue to her about his food preferences, he added, "If I'm around."

For a split second, her nostrils flared. Before he could blink, that sweet smile returned.

"I've searched the chuck wagon five times. There's no salt pork or beans. Your family is going to come back to camp hungry."

He sighed. "Kaitlyn's been tired lately—probably forgot to pack it." He pulled his hat off and clawed his hair back, racking his brain for a solution, but nothing came. He shoved his hat back on his head.

"I've gone through everything. Rearranged a bit."

It looked to him like she'd rearranged more than a bit. He'd never seen the wagon so neat and tidy.

"Like I said in my letters I sent you, I'm a good cook, but even I can't make stew without some kind of meat." A teasing smile offered him camaraderie. He didn't want it.

"You didn't send me any letters," he said coldly. "You said you were used to being on the trail. You'll have to figure something out." He stepped past her and strode out of the camp but couldn't stop himself from glancing back.

She stood watching him, scrutinizing him through narrowed eyes.

Clare Ferguson was a burr under his saddle.

He ruthlessly jerked his thoughts from her as he untied the steer and pointed the animal down toward the main herd, where David and Eli worked to corral the animals in a loose group. From his position at the top of the ridge, he saw movement across the river. The water divided the Mc-Graws' land from their nearest neighbor—Heath Quade. Only a sliver of Quade's newly acquired property near the railroad spur touched the river, hardly enough water for the cattle he aimed to run. Quade had feuded with Pa almost since he'd moved to Converse County. The feud had spilled over into his sons' lives.

Isaac squinted. Sure was a lot of activity. The river was a fair distance from Quade's barn and ranch house. What were they doing? He leaned down and reached for his field glasses in his saddlebag—only to come to himself and remember. He wasn't a marshal anymore.

He straightened in the saddle. He might not have a badge, but his job was to protect his family. He'd been at the winter cabin when the well had been poisoned at the ranch. Been isolated when Kaitlyn had been kidnapped a few months ago. Quade would not have a third go at harming his family. Not on his watch. He would check on the activity as soon as he could.

As Isaac rode in, a shrill whistle pierced the air. Nick, his dog Patch, and a herd of black and brown cattle, twice the size Isaac had managed to gather, poured down a neighboring hill. Drew drove another herd up a ravine from the opposite direction.

A blur of white, tan, and black wove around and between the moving cattle. Patch had more vigor than the three brothers combined.

"You good?" his kid brother called across the chaos.

He nodded. *Better than you.* The teasing words he would've once said got trapped behind his sternum. Nick frowned.

"It looks like your dog is a better cowpoke than you," Drew hollered to Nick from across the herd.

"That's my plan," he called back. "Patch makes my job easier." A smug grin lit up his face.

The cows moved along to join the herd, and that left the brothers riding side by side.

"You may have finally beat Isaac's roundup record," Drew said, tipping his hat back.

As they approached the camp, Isaac saw one of the boys, Ben, in the driver's seat of the chuck wagon. There were no animals hitched to it, but the boy was playing like he was driving the contraption. Clare neared, adjusted the reins in the boy's grip, and kissed his cheek. A wide smile split the boy's face.

"She drives a wagon like she was born to it, wouldn't ya say?" Nick prompted.

Was the offhand comment meant for him? Isaac ignored it.

Drew didn't. "Seems to know her way around a chuck wagon. Good with those boys too. I haven't seen David so excited for a roundup in a while."

Expectation hung in the air, but Isaac remained silent. They dismounted, the horses as dusty and tired as their riders.

"I'll take care of your horses," David said, breaking the silence to lead the horses away.

The men shuffled over to the crackling campfire and stretched out weary muscles. Eli and Ben argued softly near the chuck wagon.

Clare met the men with a pot of coffee in hand and a ready smile that turned a little stiff when she served Isaac. He looked away, his eyes settling on the flickering fire.

"Y'all look ready to drop." Her hair was pinned up so that the delicate curve of her neck was exposed.

Isaac sipped his coffee, telling himself it was the hot brew that warmed him, not his attraction to Clare.

The savory smell of sourdough and herbs had his mouth watering when he took his place in line behind Drew. What was in the cook pot? Nick, who was already seated on a fallen log and stuffing food in his mouth, groaned.

"Mmm. This is delicious."

Drew received his plate, piled with some kind of stew and biscuits, with a murmured "Thank you."

Without any other bodies between Clare and him, Isaac

had nowhere else to look but at her. As she ladled the stew, he kept his eyes on her hands. They looked even smaller lifting the large ladle. Her sleeve shifted up, exposing a thin white line stretching from her delicate wrist and disappearing into her sleeve. A scar? She caught him looking and wobbled the tin plate. His quick grasp steadied it before it could spill. She twisted her arm away, and his attention jumped to her face, where something he couldn't name sparked in her eyes. And now she was the one avoiding his gaze.

"Tastes like rabbit," Drew said as he spooned another bite into his mouth. "One of you shoot a rabbit I didn't know about?"

Nick scooted down the log to make room for Isaac. Isaac balanced his plate on his knees and shook his head. He glanced at Clare gathering dirty plates in a large tub.

"My ma shot it." Eli stabbed a long stick into the fire. He'd finished his meal but was hanging near the fire and listening to the conversation. "She couldn't find any meat or beans packed in the chuck wagon."

Drew looked to Clare, chewed, and swallowed. In the firelight, his cheeks turned ruddy. "Why didn't you tell me?" His voice was soft, but his shoulders tensed as he studied Clare across the fire.

"It wasn't a big deal." Clare hesitated, glancing at Drew. "I hope it's all right that I used the rifle."

"I wish I'd known," Drew said.

Isaac felt her quiet regard, but he kept his eyes on his plate.

"I mentioned it—"

Isaac lifted his head. She met his eyes across the fire.

Drew's attention swung to him. Isaac forced himself to take another bite of stew, though his brother's disapproval made the hearty meal taste bitter.

"Cl—Ma is a crack shot," Ben announced with pride as he rubbed Patch behind the ears.

"Nobody's a better shot than Uncle Isaac," David challenged.

"I don't know," Nick teased. "She might be a better shot than Swift Draw McGraw over there."

That stupid name. Isaac had once relished the moniker. Now he couldn't stomach hearing it. He wasn't that man anymore. Couldn't even wear his gun belt and pistols. Old memories surged, and the piece of sourdough bread he'd just shoved in his mouth turned to ash. He hauled himself to his feet and trudged away from the camp.

What would it take to win over Isaac McGraw?

Clare placed the towels on a flat rock at the bank of the river and carried the pail of dirty dishes down to the water's edge. Alone in the setting sun, she could let her guard down. Her shoulders slumped.

She drives a wagon like she was born to it, wouldn't ya say?

Seems to know her way around a chuck wagon. Good with those boys too.

Praise from Nick and Drew had stirred a momentary hope—one that had been dashed by Isaac's frigid silence.

The water from this little tributary off the river was bitingly cold as she scrubbed the tin plates. She didn't have to close her eyes to imagine Isaac sitting on the log near the fire with his face turned away. The man's rangy body might have been hunkered by the fire with his brothers, but his mind and heart had been miles away. Her hasty plan to prove her worth, to convince this McGraw brother to give her a chance, wasn't working. The man was immune to every smile she'd turned his way. While his brothers had downed heaping plates of her stew and bread, he'd only finished half his dinner.

Clare held the handles of three forks and wiped the water from the tines with a cotton cloth.

What was she going to do now? Her eyes moved along the river, taking in the pines and the rocky outcrops. She could grow to love this rugged land. She liked the McGraw brothers, who seemed to be caring and protective men, nothing like her brothers.

She bent to wash one last plate. A bright flash of sunlight over the mountain flared and glinted off a small copper tube half buried in the mud. Was that . . . An uneasy prickle climbed up her spine. She dug out the copper blasting cap and rinsed the sand off. What was a dynamite blasting cap doing here? She slipped it into her pocket. Abandoning the tub of clean dishes for the moment, she wandered along the water's edge, searching for more copper before the sun disappeared behind the mountain. She'd walked for several minutes when a boy's fearful shout echoed over the river. Clare froze.

"Eli!" she shouted. "Ben?"

Ben appeared, several yards upriver, his face filled with terror as his boots slipped on the wet stones and mud.

"Eli and David are—" He sucked in a shaky breath, tears brimming in his eyes. "There's a b-b-bear!" The sobs came hard and fast, choking off his words.

Clare gripped Ben's shoulders, her gaze jerking up at a sudden movement nearby.

Isaac. He appeared with a rifle in hand. Where had he come from? Without hesitation, he gave a quiet command.

"Ben, go find Drew and Nick. Tell them about the bear. Lead them to us," Isaac ordered. Ben's terror-filled eyes locked on Isaac, his head bobbing in obedient agreement. He pulled away from Clare and rushed toward camp.

Isaac jogged off in the direction Ben had come from. She followed, lagging as he traveled along the river and over small boulders.

"Climb faster!" Eli's cry came from upriver.

Clare's legs felt weighted as she trailed Isaac up a small slope. The rank stench of rotting fish and damp fur permeated the air, along with the low grunts, sharp snorts, and heavy breaths of the angry animal. David scrambled up a trunk just a few feet from a growling young grizzly. The bear rose on its back legs and extended its powerful arm to swipe at David's right boot.

Isaac raised the gun and pointed toward the sky.

Crack!

Clare recoiled.

"What are you doing?" she screamed, crazed with fear. "Shoot the blasted bear!"

But Isaac was frozen, staring at the bear. His ashen face was coated with a layer of fine perspiration. He drew the gun up into firing position, ready to take the shot, but his hands trembled so violently that the gun barrel swayed.

"Lift your foot!" Eli screamed from his perch several feet up the trunk. The paw clawed at David's boot heel as he lifted it to a higher branch. Enraged, the bear slashed at the branch where David's foot had been.

The thick lower branch of the tree snapped and hit the ground. The bear dropped to all fours for a perfect broadside shot. Why wasn't Isaac pulling the trigger? This bear was roaring angry and wasn't giving up.

Isaac lowered the rifle, a guttural keening tearing from his lips. There was no time. She snatched the rifle from his hands—he let her—and held it against her shoulder, sighting between the bear's neck and midsection, and pulled the trigger.

The shot rang in her ears as the recoil slammed into her shoulder. It knocked her back a step. She bumped into Isaac. The bear stopped, shook its head as if stunned. It opened its mouth and released a roar that ripped right through her chest and captured her breath. Then the beast dropped to the ground with a thud. Was it dead?

Someone was sobbing. Eli!

She shoved the gun at Isaac, didn't care whether he took it or let it hit the ground. She lifted her skirt and ran past the bear to the tree.

Drew, Nick, and the dog burst from the trees into the clearing. Nick carried Ben on his shoulders. Her nephew was still sobbing.

"Look." Nick directed Ben's attention to the fallen bear.

"You can come down now, boys," Drew said as he approached the tree where Clare was standing. The boys warily made their way down, branch by branch.

David stumbled when his legs hit the ground. His father caught him and drew him to his chest. The boy clung to his father. Eli climbed down. As soon as his feet touched the ground, he lunged forward, throwing himself at Clare. His head collided with her tender shoulder. He was shaking so violently she gritted her teeth and hugged him back just as fiercely. "You're okay now. You're a brave and smart boy, climbing up the tree so fast." She smoothed her hand over the back of his head and down his back and arms. He seemed fine.

"What were you boys doing so far from camp?" Drew demanded.

"We didn't realize—" David's eyes flew to Eli. He bit his lip. Was he hiding something? "We were playing a game."

Eli pressed his cheek into Clare's breastbone. His tears seeped through her dress. She glanced over to see Isaac watching them with shadowed eyes. He turned away before she could say anything.

Nick eased Ben from his shoulders but held his hand as they stood over the bear.

"Not a breath left in her. We'll put up the meat for the winter," Nick said.

Drew nodded, still frowning. "Let's get these boys settled."

They'd almost left the clearing behind when Clare glanced back to see Isaac still standing in place, staring at the bear, his shooting hand flexing at his side.

She wanted nothing more than to get away from the bear and this place. She'd almost lost Eli.

The boys were riled up after the bear incident. It took a long time before they quieted in their bedrolls. Clare was too anxious to sleep. Curled in her bedroll, she watched the flames dance as the men spoke in low tones from across the fire.

"I'll take the first watch," Nick said as he took his rifle and a sharp knife from the chuck wagon and disappeared into the night.

Isaac sat near the fire, slowly breaking tiny pieces from a stick and tossing them into the flames. Drew stood slightly behind the circle of bedrolls, and Clare saw how he watched Isaac, not the flames.

"That was a lucky shot," Drew said quietly. There was something behind the words, something between the two brothers she couldn't understand. Isaac hadn't looked her way once since they'd returned to camp. Until this moment, she hadn't realized no one had seen her take the shot. The boys had been too focused on the near danger, and Isaac had been holding the gun again by the time his brothers had made it to the clearing.

Isaac's gaze jumped to her, and for a moment, his mouth opened as if he might say something more—reveal the truth. But then he pressed his lips together, a muscle in his cheek twitching. His voice dropped, low and strained.

"Yeah. Lucky."

Drew's chin dipped. "If you hadn't been there, the bear might've killed the boys. I'm grateful today that you weren't away chasing some outlaw with the Marshals."

For the first time since they'd met, Isaac didn't look away. Something burned deep in his eyes. It wasn't anger but some other emotion she didn't recognize. Why didn't he tell Drew that he hadn't made the shot? Was he ashamed? Swift Draw McGraw. If Isaac was with the U.S. Marshals and was some kind of gunman, why hadn't he pulled the trigger? Why didn't he carry a revolver?

He'd nearly lost his lunch after the bear had fallen. She could still see him half bent over, his hands on both knees, shaken and terrified, just before his brothers had appeared. Now he lifted his chin as if daring her to speak.

The secret seemed to shimmer in the air between them. Clare didn't care whether anyone knew she'd killed the bear. It was Isaac's show of weakness that had her holding her tongue. And the knowledge that her instincts had been right. He was a lawman.

Finally, he swallowed hard and glanced away.

He rose. "I'll go help Nick," he said before disappearing into the night, leaving her unsettled and sleepless.

Isaac kept everyone at arm's length, even the family he clearly loved. Whatever demons were haunting him, they were his alone.

But now she and Isaac shared a secret.

Four

Y OU AREN'T STAYING TO EAT?"
Isaac shrugged in response to Drew's question. Two days after the run-in with the bear, two days spent pushing cattle into town, Isaac was covered in dust and craving some quiet. But with the bustling activity in the town square picnic area—farmers and ranchers from all over the county celebrating fall roundup—he wasn't going to get any peace here.

He caught a sidelong glance from Clare, unloading a picnic basket beside Kaitlyn only a few feet away. Two days of wondering when she'd spill the secret—he hadn't saved David and Eli—and he was strung tighter than a new barbed-wire fence.

"I'm gonna take a walk," he muttered, turning and heading down the street, weaving through the crowd on the busy boardwalk. A female voice snagged his attention.

"No, it was Isaac. I'm certain that's what I heard," said a

woman in a prim straw hat, red feathers jutting from the band, her voice dropping to a feigned whisper. "He tried to jilt her at the train station."

The hair on the back of his neck rose. Clare Ferguson had only arrived in Calvin three days ago, and already the town gossips were squawking.

"But she's right over there with his family," the shortest of the women, dressed in bright yellow, chirped and lifted her pointed chin. The group paused to crane their necks in the direction of the town square.

"She's a beauty. What I wouldn't give for all that thick dark hair." The woman's fingers patted a few thin graying wisps under her hat. The feather bobbed.

Isaac didn't want to think about Clare's glorious hair, thick waves flowing around her delicate shoulders. It had gotten mussed on the trip into town. She'd let it loose, fingering out the tangles before braiding it into a long rope. His stomach had stayed knotted the entire time. He blinked the memory away.

"Those her boys? Seems too young to have children that age," the tallest woman groused.

So, others had noticed too.

"Maybe she was a child bride." There was a harrumph, and all three continued down the boardwalk and out of earshot.

He'd best not go back to the family quilt. The train was coming in later this afternoon. Drew should put Clare and her children on it. Isaac thought about the activity on Quade's ranch and near the river. Maybe someone should be talking about that.

Guilt ate at him. Quade was spreading this gossip faster than quilts were multiplying in the patch of green across the street. Clare's reputation, along with the McGraw family name, was being sullied.

His gaze traveled across the street to Clare again. A full smile lit up her pretty face as Rebekah stood at her side and introduced her to several of the other ranchers' wives. Clare chatted easily with Mrs. Anderson, a local farmer's wife who'd emigrated from Sweden. Tilting her head to catch what Isaac knew would be broken English, she laughed with the older woman. Another genuine smile spread across her face and hit him like a slug to the gut.

He wasn't the only one affected. Her laugh drew the attention of a couple of young bucks loitering under a tree near the picnickers. A protective instinct welled up in him.

He pushed that down too as he marched down the boardwalk toward the general store. It wasn't his business who looked at her.

The bell jingled as he entered the store, the smell of fresh-ground coffee, leather, and spices filling the air. The chairs around the black stove at the center back of the long room were empty. A checkerboard with red and black checkers battle ready was laid out on a barrel between two chairs.

Mrs. Hyer stood behind the long counter, her pristine white shirt contrasting with the dark wooden shelves filled with neat rows of canned fruits, vegetables, and meats.

"Good afternoon." Her eyes flicked to him and then returned to the tall, rail-thin woman in a loose gray dress, purchasing a couple of spools of thread.

Isaac nodded and moved around a trio of barrels toward

the back of the store. Near the corner, he stopped to look at a display of coffeepots on the upper shelves. On the other side of the narrow store, Jakob Anderson and Mr. Hyer eyed the empty back wall, hands on their hips. Isaac kept his back to them, but his ears stayed attuned to their conversation.

"Quade's foreman came in less than a week ago and bought up all my shovels and pickaxes." There was a touch of bewilderment in the proprietor's voice. "Made a special order for dynamite too. Enough to blow the train it arrived on to smithereens."

Dynamite? Isaac's stomach twisted. His mind ran over the activity he'd seen by the river. What would Quade want with dynamite?

Isaac didn't wait to hear Jakob's response. He dropped the socks he'd been gripping back into the basket and strode to the door. Weaving through the crowd on the boardwalk, he rushed toward the town square, intent on finding Drew. As he crossed to the lawn teeming with picnickers—the last place he wanted to be—Isaac scanned the area. His eyes snagged on Quade, standing on the far side of the green square. The sidewinder's gaze was on Clare.

Isaac was still looking for Drew when he caught a flash of pink out of the corner of his eye and the faint scent of roses.

"If it isn't Calvin's own Swift Draw." Another Quade. Isabella, the oldest daughter, appeared before him, donning her charming smile. "I heard you were back." She tipped her chin. Her dark eyes sparked with—unease? Why? The petite, feminine woman had a rod of steel running through her spine and was as headstrong as the stallion she was famous for riding.

"Hello, Isabella."

"I also heard you killed a bear up near the ridge."

Isaac frowned. How had that news spread so quickly?

"You might want to be on the lookout for a rabid wolf too," Isabella said, the smile turning grim.

He studied Isabella's face. Saw the lines around her eyes now, the tightness around her mouth. Ranchers in the area kept each other informed about the wolf population. They were always a greater threat to the cattle come winter. Had the Diamond Q been losing cattle to wolves?

"Appreciate the warning," he said.

Heath Quade stepped in close and slid his arm around his daughter's shoulder. "This guy bothering you?" He shot Isaac a narrow-eyed glare.

"Of course not, Papa. I've known Isaac since our school days."

"Did you know he was in town just a week ago picking up his mail-order bride?" A cunning gleam lit Quade's eyes. "You marry the little lady yet?"

Isaac's skin prickled with awareness before he felt Clare's soft hand slide around his arm. He jerked slightly. She ignored his reaction and gazed up into his face. Her lips spread into a radiant smile. One that made his breath hitch.

"We've agreed to take some time to get to know each other before the wedding," Clare said easily, as if she hadn't just clubbed him in the head.

Quade's eyes glittered. "A sensible plan indeed. He's not

with the U.S. Marshals anymore, so he'll have plenty of time."

"I told you before, Quade, it's not your business," Isaac ground out.

Clare's fingers tightened on his bicep.

"It might be wise for you to take some time, miss, before you decide to hitch your wagon to the McGraws. They've had a bit of trouble lately. Couple of brothers in jail, bouts of illness."

Poison. Isaac gritted his teeth to keep from shouting. Or slugging the bottom feeder.

"Papa," Isabella cut in with a murmur. "I see Mrs. Wheaton."

He allowed her to tug him toward the street.

Quade sent him a final mocking look over his shoulder.

With Quade gone, Clare released her hold on his arm and stepped away, ending her charade. He felt the lack of her touch. The fact that he'd enjoyed her nearness annoyed him.

"When did we decide to have a wedding?" he growled.

She looked up at him through her thick lashes. He was close enough to see she had tiny freckles on the bridge of her nose and a touch of rose in her cheeks.

He inhaled and held his breath, bracing for her next words. A mistake. The scent of apples and warm sunshine invaded his senses and muddled his brain.

"You seemed upset when he confronted you at the train station. I thought I might head him off."

He was shaking his head at her reasonable words, but before he could demand she stay away from Quade, shouts erupted from near the schoolyard. Above the clamor, Ben's cry rang out.

"Eli, don't!"

Shouts and calls from numerous voices buzzed in Clare's ears as she pushed through the crowd, Isaac on her heels. Where were Eli and Ben?

The crowd parted long enough for her to see. In the center of the jostling crowd, a hulking man had clamped heavy hands on the shoulders of two boys. Clare's stomach dropped.

Eli.

His only good shirt was ripped at the shoulder. He wore his belligerence on his face like a shield.

"Let go of him!" she cried out.

"Hold on—" Isaac's fingers wrapped around her upper arm as they broke through the crowd and reached Eli and the others.

"This your hooligan?" the man demanded. "He started a fight with my boy!"

He shoved Eli in her direction.

Clare caught Eli by the shoulders. Eli threw off her hands and turned to lunge at the boy, but Isaac caught his arm.

"He's a cheater." Eli spat the words.

"Am not." The boy sucked in a swollen and bloody bottom lip. His cheeks bloomed with red blotches. He folded his arms across his chest. His father did the same. A matched set.

Clare's chest tightened. Eli's father would never stand

with him. Victor would thrash him for making a scene. Her nephew stood his ground, squinty-eyed, arms crossed beneath Isaacs's hand.

"I saw you."

Several more curious townspeople joined the onlookers. The whispers and murmurs in the crowd grew and surrounded them.

"You can't cheat in blindman's bluff," the boy scoffed.

Eli leaned forward. "You tripped Jo when she was blindfolded," he shouted.

Clare scanned the crowd and saw Jo and Ben huddled at one side. Jo edged through the crowd with a slight limp, Ben at her side, holding her hand. They joined Clare, Eli, and Isaac facing the accusers, like sides of a battle drawn. The bodice of Jo's pretty, flowered calico dress appeared no worse for wear. But the skirt had mud marks and a tear at the knee, while dusty brown splotches clung to the bottom ruffle.

"She's just a stupid tomboy who can't keep up with the rest of the boys." The witless boy fired another shot, this one aimed at Jo, but Eli reacted like he was the target. With a growl, he sprang on the boy like a wounded mountain lion. Eli landed a solid punch to his stomach before Clare threw her body between them, taking the brunt of a wild swing meant for Eli.

Pain exploded across the left side of her face.

Enraged, Eli tucked his head, a bull intent on driving into the boy. At the same moment, the boy lifted his elbow and jabbed Eli in the face. Eli's head snapped back, and his scrappy body staggered. The blow would have knocked him on his back, but in one swift movement, Isaac scooped him up.

Eli struggled and flailed.

Isaac ignored both Eli and the gawking crowd and stalked off, the boy tucked under his arm.

Clare watched his retreating form for a beat, then turned back to Jo. Her cheek throbbed like a thousand wasps had stung her. "Ben, you and Jo go back to Kaitlyn."

They would meet up there.

If Isaac didn't march them all the way to the train station.

Isaac set the still-struggling Eli down in a dusty alleyway. Clare pushed forward to get between the two. Isaac used his arm to block her.

"Don't hurt him." She braced for a blow, ready to take the fist that surely would be aimed in Eli's direction.

Isaac froze. Clare froze. Behind her, Eli must have been holding his breath.

Isaac's dark eyes searched her face, landing on her cheek.

She'd misread the situation. He saw too much.

"I'm not gonna hit him, Clare."

She stepped aside, but not before she widened her eyes at Eli, a warning to tread carefully. *Please don't give anything away.*

Isaac squatted in front of Eli, and she couldn't help but notice the way his muscled shoulders shifted beneath his shirt. He lifted his hand to touch Eli's swelling eye. Eli flinched but stayed rooted in place, his chin jutting up stubbornly. He was a picture of Victor daring their father to hit him.

"You've got a real good shiner blooming there. Doesn't look like the skin is broken though."

Eli's body remained tight, alert, like a caged raccoon's, his eyes darting to Clare and back to Isaac. *Stay calm*, she willed him.

"Must sting like the dickens." The soft drawl coming from this tough, impassive rancher thickened Clare's throat. It must have had a similar effect on poor Eli. His eyes pooled with tears that leaked and ran down his dirt-encrusted face. He swiped at them angrily.

"Well . . ." Isaac stood. He moved his hands to his hips and gave Eli's face one last perusal. "I reckon he's feeling worse than you, especially with that fat bloody lip. May have even bruised his ribs with the last walloping punch." He spoke evenly. "Much obliged to you for sticking up for Jo. Next time, get David first. McGraws don't confront bullies alone."

Eli's tight jaw slackened. When his mouth snapped shut, his eyes held a glint of admiration.

"Yes, sir," he croaked.

Clare's eyes stung with the threat of tears.

Isaac pulled a clean bandanna from his back pocket and offered it to Eli. Eli wiped his face with careful swipes around his blackened eye.

"Head back to Kaitlyn and get yourself some lemonade."

Eli inhaled and shuddered out a breath. He tucked his shirt in his pants and headed to the town square.

When Clare would have followed, Isaac said, "Wait."

She went still, her back to Isaac. Her heartbeat kicked up, pulsing in her ears.

He came up even with her, not quite shoulder to shoulder, at the mouth of the alleyway, watching Eli go. A long moment passed before he spoke.

"You wanna tell me why Eli cowers like that? Why you thought I was going to hit him?"

She bit her lip. No, she didn't.

"You've kept his pa out of every conversation I've heard." He was far too observant. His gaze shifted briefly to her cheek, and his jaw tightened.

"How long have you been stepping in and taking the blows for him?" His voice was calm, but there was an undercurrent of something—anger, maybe at himself for not being quick enough to stop her, or just at seeing Clare hurt.

Clare didn't want him asking questions about the boys' father. She'd prefer not to lie to him. *Lying just leads to more lies*, Anne would always say.

"Are we getting to know each other better now?" She tipped her chin up in challenge. "Because if we are, I have a question of my own I'd like answered. Why don't you carry even one pistol? And why did you leave the U.S. Marshals?"

She stared him down.

A muscle jumped in his cheek.

"Is it because you can't shoot?"

His eyes flashed like he was surprised, or angry that she'd said it aloud. His mouth opened, ready to snap back, but she cut him off. "I won't tell anyone."

She didn't have time to register the flare of emotion that passed behind his eyes before a voice called his name.

"Isaac! I need you."

Drew's angry strides hammered the boardwalk. His normally tanned face was white with fury.

"Quade's hired some men from out of town to reroute the river."

Five

I T'S CROWDED IN THERE," A BOY'S VOICE said.

For a brief second, the door behind Isaac opened wider, and the clink of dishes, along with Nick's soft baritone and Tillie's little-girl giggle, escaped onto the small stoop. The door closed and the quiet returned. But he wasn't alone. Isaac's shoulders tensed. He'd come out here to be by himself. Plunked himself down on the wooden porch steps, with his plate of biscuits and gravy balanced on his knees, to let his eyes roam the paddock and drift to the mountains beyond and breathe in the crisp early-autumn air.

Light steps approached him. He caught Eli's worn boot out of the corner of his eye. The kid needed new boots.

Not his problem.

Eli parked himself next to Isaac on the step and placed his elbows on his knees. He held a biscuit in each hand.

Doggone it.

"How come you sleep in the bunkhouse?" Eli said around a bite of biscuit. "Don't you got a house of your own?"

Isaac ignored the curious question and shoveled another fork full of biscuits and gravy into his mouth, letting his gaze drift to Bullet, loping toward the corral fence. He should saddle up right now, ride on out to his cabin. With roundup behind them, the cattle they'd culled all sold, and most of the hard work at the main house done for now, he could head out.

It had been late last night when the family had arrived home from town. Isaac had expected Drew would want to talk Quade business as soon as the kids had cleared out. Drew had been in such a hurry to get home last night that no one had said a word about Clare and the boys riding home too.

Clare's words from that first day echoed in his ears. *There's nowhere to go back to.*

Not his problem.

Eli examined him watchfully, flight-ready, the way boys did when they'd endured the company of mean and unpredictable men. Cody had never worn that look. Cody had trusted Isaac from the start.

Isaac swallowed hard, forcing down both biscuits and the bitter taste of regret. Cody had paid the ultimate price for it. His throat tightened.

Eli was oblivious to his inner turmoil.

"David said you're the fastest draw in three counties, maybe even the whole state." Eli barely paused when Isaac didn't answer. "My pa said Gideon Blake is the fastest in the West. Said he saw him once in Dodge City. I'd sure like to see you shoot. Maybe you could teach me?"

Isaac cast him a sideways glance and caught the challenge in the boy's face before the kid shoved the last of one biscuit in his mouth.

"Prob'ly not true anyways. Never seen you wear pistols," Eli muttered.

Isaac swiped the biscuit off his plate and took a bite, chewing slowly, ignoring the kid's taunt.

Eli played with his last biscuit, passing it from one hand to the other. His head swiveled to look at Isaac again.

"You gonna marry Clare?"

Enough.

"No!" he growled. "Get outta here."

At that moment, David banged out the door, jumped off the side of the stoop, and jogged to the barn. Eli sent Isaac one last wary glance, shot up, and ran to catch up to David. They met Drew riding up from the back of the barn. Drew dismounted, stalked toward Isaac while David led his horse into the barn, yammering with Eli.

"What's wrong with the dining room table?" Drew asked from a few yards away.

"Nothing," Isaac said as he set his plate on the step beside him.

Drew sighed and rubbed the back of his neck. There was something in his eyes. Concern yes, but more. Fear?

"I went scouting up on the ridge. Wanted to see for myself. Spied a plow hidden behind that outcrop of boulders near the bridge." Drew's lips tightened into a resigned frown. "More dirt's been moved near the bridge. Looks like that no-good conniving varmint really is aiming to divert our water supply."

"He should be behind bars," Isaac muttered, gazing down at his calloused hands.

After five years with the Marshals, dedicated to tracking the most notorious criminals, he found himself unable to protect his own family from one unscrupulous cattleman. He and the town marshal, Danna O'Grady, had spent hours trying to piece together evidence, to no avail. They couldn't prove that Quade had been behind the poisoned well or the bandit that had almost killed Rebekah.

"Quade's wily and knows how to keep his hands clean," Drew said.

Something was bugging Isaac. Images of dirt piles and shovels near the river surfaced in his mind, accompanied by Hyer's ominous words. *Enough dynamite to blow half the train to smithereens.* Or half the ridge. Breakfast turned to stone in his gut.

"He's not hiding what he's doing this time," Isaac said, his voice quiet, somber. "He doesn't seem to care that we know he's up to something on that ridge."

Drew's expression turned bleak, and Isaac saw the weight of worry in the slump of his brother's shoulders and the lines etched around his eyes and mouth. If Quade succeeded in taking their water, it meant their burgeoning herd would die off, crops would wither, and their entire way of life would dry up.

"I wondered why he rode John Braswell so hard to sell out. He wanted that plot of land to divert the water," Drew said.

"Braswell didn't have a choice. He couldn't prove up his land in time after his barn burned." Another crime they couldn't pin on Quade.

"He's not getting an inch of McGraw land. I promised Pa that I would protect the family legacy, but I don't know what to do anymore." Drew didn't usually make a habit of sharing his worries. Kaitlyn had softened him.

"What will you do," Isaac asked, "if it comes to a fight?"

"I'm praying it doesn't come to that. Nick wants to talk to an attorney and see whether rerouting the river and cutting off our water supply can be stopped with a lawsuit. I'd planned to ride into town today, but Kaitlyn was sick all through the night. I'd like to stick close to her and home."

Isaac stood, walked to the paddock fence, and leaned his elbows on the top rail. Drew joined him. Voices floated through the open kitchen window. Isaac was itchy. Couldn't sit still.

Drew pushed back off the rail. Let out another long sigh, this one resigned.

"I'll go," Isaac said. "I'll hunt down Frank Mecum. If he doesn't know, I'll push him to find out, quickly. Marshal O'Grady or Chas O'Grady might know something about water rights."

Drew nodded. "Fine. What about Clare?"

"What about her?" Isaac snapped.

"She's been a big help to Kaitlyn, especially since Rebekah can't be here," Drew said slowly.

"She can't stay. Not when Quade can use her as a threat to us."

Drew chewed on that for a minute. "All right. You can take her to town, put her on the train."

"I don't want to stay in town. I like the ranch," Ben whined.

Clare rested an elbow on the white cotton tablecloth, her head bowed over a steaming cup of coffee, wishing they were still at the ranch too. She forced herself to take a sip of the strong coffee and scorched her tongue. In her hurry to set the cup down, some of the brown liquid spilled onto the tablecloth. She quickly blotted it with her napkin. Now both the napkin and the tablecloth were stained.

She felt exposed sitting here at the hotel restaurant. This was different from the picnic while she'd been with the McGraws. She was right back where she'd started.

"I want to go back with Jo and Tillie," Ben insisted, his tone rising in pitch.

"We can't go back to the ranch," Eli stated. Throughout the journey to town, he had been mostly silent and taciturn, with only a muttered "Good, we can go back home" when they'd climbed into the wagon. Isaac had been tight-lipped and brooding too. He'd promised to come back to the restaurant after he'd handled his business at the lawyer's office.

The brown stains on the tablecloth mocked her. Maybe he wouldn't return, and they'd be left to fend for themselves. All her high hopes had crumbled. She prided herself on her warm demeanor and charm, but Isaac had stayed out of reach, avoiding any real conversation.

"Yes, we can." Ben's face scrunched, his eyes filling with tears. "Jo said—"

"You don't know anything. Shut your trap." Eli lambasted poor Ben, the acid in his voice so like his father's it rocked Clare. She put a hand on Eli's forearm and squeezed. When he met her eyes, she knitted her brows and formed a silent *shh* as the waitress approached.

She would have to get a job. Her mind ran through the limited options she and Kaitlyn had discussed. School teacher was out. She didn't have a formal education, although Anne had taught her to read and do simple sums. A seamstress? She could darn socks and repair tears, but that was the extent of her skill with a needle. Laundress seemed to be her only option. She would ask the waitress if the hotel was hiring. But where would they stay? A rented room? Even that felt too exposed. Anyone asking questions in town—asking for a woman and two boys—could easily track them down.

The waitress, a buxom woman with ginger hair and a no-nonsense way of serving, had introduced herself as Pearl. She removed an empty soup bowl one table over and stopped at Clare's table.

"Y'all want pie? Peach pie with fresh whipped cream today. I know for a fact that it's one of Marshal McGraw's favorites. Is he coming round here when his business is done?"

Ben's eyes widened. At the mention of Isaac's former job or the pie, Clare wasn't sure. Eli's gaze remained on his plate, but his face went pasty.

"We will take one piece of pie. Thank you, Pearl." Clare

threaded her fingers under the table. "I'm wondering if by any chance the hotel is hiring—a laundress or someone to work in the kitchen?"

Pearl tilted her head and pursed her lips. Clare's cheeks heated.

"I don't think so, dear. I'll just see about that pie." She bustled off.

"You can't marry a marshal. Barlows don't tangle with the law. That's what Pa always said." Eli's mention of Victor was like touching a cactus.

They couldn't stay in town. Isaac was no longer working as a U.S. marshal, but his reputation followed him, clung to him—just like her own.

"We will talk about it later," she said, as Pearl reappeared with the peach pie in hand. She served the pie, then busied herself clearing a table by the window. Clare's eyes trailed after her and caught sight of Isaac through the square panes of the front window. He stood on the boardwalk between the dance hall and the saloon. All the worries pressing in on her squeezed until she couldn't breathe. She had to try once more.

"Eat your pie," Clare told both boys. She set a firm hand on Eli's shoulder and waited for him to meet her eyes. "Watch your brother. Stay here. Understand?"

Both boys nodded, but Eli's expression was flat and unreadable.

Outside, a lively uproar spilled from the saloon. At the dance hall next to the saloon, someone plunked a tinny piano with a heavy hand. She made a beeline toward Isaac. He lifted his chin, and his gaze brushed over her. She slid her hand into her pocket and clutched his letter. She'd carried it with her to town as her backup plan, remembering that Quade had said it was a binding contract. What kind of person would use it against the McGraws? A Barlow. An evil person. She didn't want to blackmail Isaac. The McGraws had been good to her and the boys, opened their home, shared their meals. She liked them. Well, all of them except the enigmatic man now a few feet in front of her. Her feelings for him were . . . she didn't know. One thing was for certain: he'd be furious if she forced him into marriage.

The swinging doors of the saloon burst open. Shouts and commotion spilled out onto the street.

Bang!

A sharp crack split the air. Clare jolted, muscles tensing as her mind struggled to make sense of the chaos unfolding. A cowboy stumbled out to the edge of the boardwalk, teetered, then fell on his face. The gun in his hand discharged. The bullet hit the street, and a cloud of dirt erupted.

The echo of that gunshot gripped Clare's very core. The past seeped into the present and conjured up the painful memory she had tried so desperately to bury. Her brother Billy's face, frozen in time, materialized before her, his eyes wide with the same shock she felt now. Blood bloomed on his shirt. The street where he'd fallen, the shadows cast by the buildings—every detail was etched into Clare's consciousness.

Her breath hitched, caught in a stranglehold. Time stretched and a disorienting haze settled over her senses.

Every nerve screamed with the urge to run. Yet her feet remained rooted to the spot.

"Clare." A hand closed over her elbow, breaking her from the memory.

"Clare, look at me."

He'd finally said her name.

And she'd never heard his voice so gentle.

"How about we move across the street and away from this ruckus?" He didn't wait for an answer, just led her across the street with that gentle hand beneath her elbow. Her knees were wobbly, and as they crossed the street, she let herself lean into his warmth and strength.

Instead of going into the hotel dining room, he led her around the side of the building and off the street. Her back was to the clapboard siding of the hotel when he released her. She leaned against it for support and closed her eyes.

"I think it's time for you to tell me the truth about why you answered that mail-order bride ad," he said.

She slowly opened her eyes, bracing herself for an onslaught of harsh accusations. But instead, he looked at her with genuine concern.

"I already told you. The boys and I needed a fresh start," Clare hedged.

His eyes never left her face. "That was pure terror back there."

She couldn't hold his gaze. He saw too much.

"The boys are inside the dining room alone," she said, hoping to distract him. The last time they'd been left alone, Eli had ended up in a fight. "I need to check on them." She pushed away from the wall, but he boxed her in.

"What are you running from?" he demanded softly.

Another question she couldn't answer.

"My family has helped you. I think we deserve the truth. What are you running from?"

She didn't know what to do with this Isaac.

"My pa was a violent man," she blurted, closing her eyes against the memories. "I spent my childhood trying to appease him. He was not a good man. When he was home, he was mean and lazy. He seemed to delight in punishing every small infraction. An accidental spill could get me backhanded. Let the fire get too low? The whole day would be spent finding kindling and splitting logs. My best bet was to stay out of his way. Especially when he was drinking."

The memories and the constant fear echoed inside her. Tears pooled in her eyes and spilled down her cheeks. She swept a palm over her cheeks to quickly wipe them away.

"I couldn't watch the boys live like that." She hiked up her chin. "The truth is, I'm not their mother. I'm their aunt."

His expression didn't flicker. She rushed on, knowing she had to just get it all out.

"My brother has a hair-trigger temper and a reputation for cruelty, just like my father. Maybe even worse. He likes to pull his gun to scare people into giving him what he wants—even his family."

Isaac's jaw hardened.

The weight of it all settled on her shoulders like an iron yoke, cold and heavy. She shivered. Maybe she should just tell him everything. She was never going to outrun the Barlow name.

Blood will out.

Her father's words rang in her ears. She tried to believe Anne. That God would make a way. She met Isaac's intense scrutiny and sighed.

"I promised Anne, the boys' mother, on her deathbed that I'd keep the boys safe." She bit her lip, wondering just how much to tell him.

"And the mail-order bride ad?"

"Anne believed it was providential. She's the one who saw your ad. Prompted me to answer. She died, the boys' father went off to drink, and I . . . I needed to get away while the getting was good. I already had one train ticket, so I purchased two more, and here we are."

"You lied."

She grimaced.

"But I guess I can see why." He folded his arms across his chest. "You're not married?"

She shook her head, wished she could read him. "I need some time to get us on our feet. We can't go back to the farm. There's nothing there." Was he softening? The light in his eyes had changed somehow. "My brother is more dangerous than ever." She pressed her back against the rough clapboard wall, feeling the wood dig into her skin as she took a steadying breath. "I can't let Eli become like his father. I made a promise to Anne."

Isaac put his hands on his hips and looked her full in the face. "People in town are already talking about you and the fact that we didn't get married when you first arrived."

"I know."

His brows rose. She cocked a brow in return. Did he

think she hadn't heard the whispers or seen the knowing looks?

"If you stay on the ranch, they're gonna talk more."

Clare sucked in a breath. Held it as hope rose inside her.

Isaac looked away. A muscle in his jaw jumped. She waited, still not breathing.

"My brothers want to fix me."

She saw the flicker in his eyes, a long-buried hurt, and let out her breath.

"Do you need to be fixed?" she asked carefully.

A flash of fire lit his usually cool green eyes. "If I bring you back to the ranch, I don't want them to get the wrong idea," he said, his tone quiet and serious.

She bit her lip. "Maybe my being on the ranch could be a distraction. Maybe they'd leave you alone."

He stared at her. She caught a shadow of something moving across his face. He turned his face away momentarily. "Not likely," he sighed. "What do you have in mind?"

"We could pretend we're considering getting married. Like we already told—" She swallowed back the name Quade. "It might buy us both some time to figure out what to do."

He paused. A resigned sigh escaped him as he straightened his shoulders. "All right. I'll play my part. A man who is considering marriage to a mail-order bride. And you play yours, the prospective bride who hangs on my every word."

She blinked and choked on a broken laugh.

"I mean it, you'll do as I say." He sent her a serious look. "And no more secrets."

Six

ISAAC PULLED IN AT THE FRONT OF THE lean-to, the wagon full of supplies for Clare and the boys to move into Isaac's mountain cabin.

Eli coughed.

Ben whispered, "Is that it?"

What little solace Isaac usually found here was absent with the awareness of the three of them in his personal space.

The isolated cabin greeted him like a sickly old hermit. The golden rays from the setting sun illuminated the log-and-mud exterior of the cabin that had become worn, dull, and gray. Loose shingles hung at crooked angles on the roof. The faded boards had gaps that needed chinking. And the hitching post had fallen and lay at an angle.

Drew was right. The cabin was in bad shape. How had Isaac not noticed? He didn't want to look at Clare and see the horror in her eyes. The tips of his ears burned.

He cleared his throat. "Like I said, the cabin ain't much."

"It's fine," Clare said.

It wasn't and he knew it.

He pushed the repairs to the back of his mind, lowering himself from the wagon. She might be safer staying down at the main house, but there wasn't really room for her and the boys. His isolated cabin would keep her out of the sight of nosy neighbors who came to call on the ranch.

The river burbled where it widened into a shallow area here. He'd always thought it soothing, but now the noise roared in his ears. Would the boys be able to sleep tonight?

Clare climbed down from the wagon. She halted, her eyes moving from the cabin to the small clearing with the path that led to the river. She didn't look dismayed. In fact, she seemed almost giddy, pressing her fingers to her smiling lips as if to hold it in.

"I love the sound of the water."

Ben scrambled down from the wagon.

"Can we go down by the river?" Ben was halfway to the trail that led to the river before Clare could answer.

"Wait, Ben. Wait for Eli."

Isaac called them back. "The water can be deceptive," he said seriously. "It looks calm, but it flows faster than you think."

Eli frowned and crossed his arms.

Clare glanced toward the river, then back at them with a calm smile. "We can all go see the river together. Let's unload the wagon first."

The boys shared a look between them but didn't argue.

Kaitlyn had sent blankets and canned goods. Drew had

sent a couple of cots. Even David had brought up a straw tick from the bunkhouse.

Isaac pulled a heavy wooden crate from the back of the wagon and headed for the cabin. He set the crate on the floor, using it to prop the door open, then climbed the wooden ladder up to the loft and opened the dirty window. It might make the cabin chilly come nightfall, but the place smelled musty with a hint of river and soil. Isaac had been up here two weeks ago, and the rumpled blanket had never been tucked in. His ma would have been appalled at the unmade bed he'd left behind.

He surveyed the cabin from the loft. The place looked smaller, more cramped. A fieldstone fireplace dominated one wall, and a black wrought-iron frying pan and a couple of pots hung on hooks above the fireplace. He didn't have a stove. Hadn't minded when it was just him. But Clare would have to cook over the fire in the fireplace.

An ancient pie safe was jammed in one corner, and a narrow sideboard by the door stood bare, save for a solitary chipped water pitcher. Good thing Kaitlyn had sent some extra plates and utensils. Beneath a small rectangular table with turned legs, two chairs huddled, a creation by Ed, the best set of furniture in the room. But the once-gleaming oak top was suffocating under a thick coat of dust.

Clare climbed into the loft, brushing his shoulder as she skirted around him and placed a carpet bag on the floor and an extra blanket on the bed in the corner. She straightened the messy blankets and tucked them under the lumpy, worn hay mattress. Under the window, a small chest containing remnants from his days with the Marshals lay abandoned, collecting dust like everything else. He thought of the boys sleeping up here.

"I'll haul that chest down to the lean-to and bed down in there," he said to Clare.

"The boys want to know what's in the lean-to." She sounded far too happy about being stuck up here in this horrible cabin.

"Stall for my horse, some hay," he mumbled.

Suddenly, he was having doubts about this plan.

"We'll do our share. I promise." There were no curtains over the window, and she squinted in the sunlight as she took in the view.

"What a beautiful view."

He watched her face turn radiant. He couldn't help but agree with her sentiment. The view was beautiful from where he stood too.

He followed her down the ladder. She marched to the crate he'd left at the door and pulled out a small sack of flour. "I'll cook, and the boys can help with chores. We'll get along just fine here."

Turning, her eyes flicked around the room. Maybe she'd demand he take her back to town once she got a closer look at the rough shape of his cabin.

She brightened when her eyes settled on the fireplace and the cast-iron frying pan.

"It's just like the one I had at home. It's no trouble to cook over an open flame." She strode to the fireplace, reached for the pan on tiptoes. To his surprise, she was still too short to take it off the hook. Her courage and spirited nature made her seem bigger and the cabin feel smaller. He moved in behind her, reached up over her shoulder, and took it off the hook. His chest bumped her shoulder, and the cabin shrank more.

He handed her the frying pan.

She smiled gratefully at him. "Thank you."

He gave her a side-eye glance. She was giving him too much credit for the condition this place was in. He shoved his hands in his pockets, his embarrassment growing. Ever since the incident with the bear, when she'd taken the shot he couldn't, their lives had become tangled in a way he couldn't undo.

"Where's Eli?" Clare asked Ben as he pulled his boot and dirty sock off.

She glanced at the door, then at Isaac. They exchanged a knowing look. Eli had gone back to being sullen and insolent since Isaac had taken them to town. It'd become worse when they'd decided that Clare and the boys would spend some time with Isaac up at his cabin.

Isaac grunted. "I'll handle Eli if you can keep Ben occupied."

Ben was like the puppy he'd had as a boy. Lots of energy and cute as a bug's ear, but that little rascal could get into mischief.

"Ben and I are going to make supper." Clare turned and pulled an onion from one of the baskets on the sideboard. Isaac left her to cook and stepped outside.

Eli sat on the stoop, his bony shoulders sagging, elbows resting on his knees. Probably scowling.

"I need your help here. Let's get the rest of the stuff out of the wagon."

Eli slowly rose and trudged to the wagon without a word. Isaac followed him.

"Jump up there and push that barrel to the tailgate."

Eli did as he was told but with too much force—if not for Isaac's catching it, the barrel would have flown off the wagon. They eyed each other across the barrel's top. The challenge in Eli's expression reminded him of Ed when they were boys. The competition between them had been fierce at times, showing up in the little things—who could muck the stalls faster or who could round up the most cows in a single day. Isaac may have put a little more muscle behind pushing an empty barrel at Ed, but not a full one.

"Let this be a lesson to you. You can push things too far."

"I don't need you to teach me any lessons," Eli muttered back.

"If I hadn't been quick to react, the barrel could have slipped away and cracked open," Isaac said. "We need the grain inside. Worse, you could have taken a nasty fall and bloodied up your face or broken a bone."

Eli lowered his eyes. "Wouldn't be the first time," he said darkly.

Isaac's gut contorted. "Nothing bad is going to happen to you or Ben or your aunt. Not on my watch."

Eli shot him a venomous look. "You don't want us here. I heard you say it this morning."

Isaac's shoulders tensed, guilt gnawing at him as he met Eli's gaze. "You didn't hear the rest of what I said. It's too dangerous in town, so that's why we're here at my cabin, where I can keep a close eye on you, protect all of you. So do your aunt a favor and get those quilts into the cabin."

Isaac lifted the barrel down and rolled it over to the lean-to while Eli hauled the bundle of blankets from the wagon bed and into the cabin. Isaac took several steadying breaths. What had he gotten himself into? He didn't really know anything about this makeshift family. He tightened his grip on the last load—a box of mismatched plates, cups, and utensils Kaitlyn had sent—and reassured himself.

This was just a temporary fix. They wouldn't be here forever.

Clare moved onto the stoop to hold the door for them. Eli slipped inside.

Isaac nodded, walked into the cabin, and set the box on the table. He headed out again to unhitch Bullet from the wagon.

Ben met him by the lean-to. "Can I help you feed Bullet?"

"Sure. I'll open the sack of oats. You scoop some into the bucket."

Isaac tossed his bedroll to the ground and settled the horse next to the outer plank wall of the lean-to. The slanted roof was plenty tall for both him and Bullet to stand, but Isaac moved the chest containing remnants from his days with the Marshals near where his head would rest and stacked a couple of bales of hay between him and his horse. He didn't need his sleep interrupted by a horse hoof to his backside.

Through the wall, he could hear Clare humming a hymn.

Ben watched him rearranging, the kid's interest caught on the chest and its contents. Maybe he should put a lock on it since he stored his pistols inside.

"You sleepin' out here?" Ben eyed him.

Isaac nodded, a weariness settling over him. He motioned for Ben to give Bullet the bucket of oats he was carrying

"Why?" Ben wouldn't let it go. He stood hugging the bucket to his chest, waiting for an answer.

"Because it's the right thing to do," Isaac said.

"Why?" Ben persisted. The kid was full of questions.

With a heavy sigh Isaac said, "Because your aunt and I are not married. It's not appropriate for us to sleep in the same house." His face went hot. And got hotter when he remembered what it'd felt like back in town when he'd tucked her close to his side.

Ben set the bucket in front of Bullet and watched as the horse eagerly dug into his feed. The boy's gaze lifted again to meet Isaac's, his expression filled with the innocence and simple sincerity only a child could muster.

"You should marry Aunt Clare. Then you could sleep with us."

Isaac almost smiled at the boy's innocence. He wasn't going to marry Clare and didn't want to think about sharing a bed with . . . anyone. Clare wanted his protection not—

Beyond the wall, the humming stopped.

"Time to head in for supper," he said.

Clare had spread her cheerfulness to the cabin. She'd unpacked supplies and set things neatly on the shelves and pie safe. Steam rose from a boiling pot on the stove. The dark oak table gleamed, reflecting the jar of wildflowers sitting atop it.

The table was set. Ben took his place on an empty barrel, while Eli perched on a couple of stacked crates. Clare made a simple fare. Fried ham, boiled potatoes, and cornbread with honey. One of Isaac's favorites.

"I don't know about everyone else, but I'm hungrier than a coyote in a drought," Isaac said, blustering through the awkwardness.

His stomach growled. Clare and Ben laughed. Eli frowned.

A few minutes passed before Eli, who was downing his third piece of cornbread, asked, "Where are you sleepin'?"

Isaac studied Eli, then chewed and swallowed. "I'm in the lean-to," he said.

"Why would you do that?" Eli asked, not curious but disdainful.

"Because it's the right thing to do," Ben parroted and sent Isaac a crooked smile.

Isaac's stomach twisted. He hoped he was doing the right thing.

Clare couldn't seem to relax even though Eli had finally gone quiet, and Isaac was digging into his food as if he hadn't eaten all week. Isaac hadn't been easy on the ride back from town. But the glances he'd sent her had been different than before. She didn't know how to navigate this new . . . friendship? . . . between them.

"David says he's going exploring first thing tomorrow. Can I go with him?" Eli spoke up, breaking the silence.

A chill ran through Clare as she remembered the bear

and the rugged terrain with rocky outcrops she'd seen driving here. Wyoming was very different from the farmland they'd lived on in Missouri.

"We are going to help Isaac with chores first thing in the morning," Clare said.

She met Isaac's eyes across the table, a silent acknowledgment passing between them.

"I know. But I can get 'em done fast," Eli put in.

Clare's gaze flew back to Eli. He was chewing and calculating.

"I don't want you straying too far from the cabin." They could run into danger. Like a bear. *Remember the bear?* She certainly wouldn't forget it anytime soon.

"David has his own gun. He's had one since he was my age. Says in the West, ya gotta take a gun with you everywhere you go." He looked at Isaac. "You got any extra guns?"

Clare's voice rose. "Eli, you are not carrying a gun—"

"Pa let me shoot—"

Clare shot him a warning look that cut off his words. Victor had let him shoot his gun in the air after a robbery. Victor had used his own little boy as a lookout. Thinking about it made the cornbread turn to lead in her stomach.

"Eli, we will talk about this later."

"I can shoot a gun. Pa said I'm a sure hand," Eli grumbled, stabbing his ham with a fork.

Clare was the only one who had used the shotgun that had belonged to Anne's grandfather. They'd only had a limited supply of bullets. She had been the one to hunt to provide food when her brother and Pa were gone. Had

Victor taught the boy to shoot when they were outlawing? Her heart squeezed.

Isaac set his fork down with a rattle. He was such a big presence that he made the table feel small. "Doesn't matter if you are the fastest gun in the county. Out here, it's safer to always have someone who is looking out for you. Drew would have taught David that, just like he drilled it into our heads. Me. Ed. And Nick. Why do you think David didn't leave you the last time you boys wandered too far?" Isaac kept his voice even, steady patience woven through each word.

Eli crossed his arms and hardened his jaw. Isaac leaned back in his chair, glancing between her and Eli before he spoke again.

"When I was just a little older than Eli here, I was determined to be the best gun in the county. I started going out and finding things to use as target practice, sometimes killing for sport, not for eating or for protection." Isaac crossed his arms over his chest, his eyes going distant as if he was lost in his thoughts.

"Drew told me to stop. Said, 'One day your arrogant, cocksure attitude is going to catch up with you. And there won't be anyone around to help you.' I laughed at him. I had my pistols. I didn't need anyone. Until the day I was out past sunset, and a hungry wolf started trailing me. I'd used all my bullets save one. I wasn't too worried. If he got too close, I'd shoot him. No problem."

Clare rubbed her arms. She hated wolves. She'd never been pursued by one, but their howls at night always reminded her of the ravaging hunger and the desperation of her childhood. The time when Anne had taken sick and Pa and Victor had been gone for months. And she, barely a teen, had been left to provide.

"Then another wolf joined him, and another, and another. Until there was a whole pack growling and sniffing behind me."

Ben's eyes went wide. "What did you do?"

Clare gulped down some coffee, set her cup down carefully, and held her breath, waiting for Isaac's answer.

"I did the same thing Eli and David did. Found a tall tree and scrambled up it, pronto. Stayed up there almost all night with the sound of the howls running through me." He paused, letting the gravity of his situation hang in the air.

"It wasn't my fast gun that saved me. It was my brothers—took all three of them to chase the pack away. They'd been out all night lookin' for me."

A faint smile touched his lips but didn't quite reach his eyes. Clare saw the way his fingers tightened around the coffee cup. There was a fleeting look of pain in his eyes before he masked it with a distant stare. Clare felt that pain, a throbbing ache in her chest as if her heart were being gently squeezed by an invisible hand. She quickly changed the subject.

"We saw some trout in the river," she said a little too brightly. "Tomorrow we'll spend time fishing. There's nothing like fresh fried trout. Eli loves to fish."

"You ever shoot a man?" Eli ignored her shift in subject.

Isaac's face went white. Clare glared at Eli. A chair scraped against the wood floor. Before she could say another word, Isaac was out the door.

Clare and the boys did the supper dishes in silence. Eli's angry defiance still festered in his eyes as they prepared for bed. *Blood will tell.* Tears welled in her eyes. She blinked them away. Tears never solved anything. Another lesson her father had taught her well.

Clare skirted around the straw tick on the floor of the loft. The boys lay elbow to elbow on top of the quilt. She knelt beside Ben in the cramped space, keeping her voice to a whisper.

"I know this is confusing, but we have to keep up our charade. Everyone needs to believe that your father is—"

"But Isaac likes us," Ben piped up, his voice innocent. "He'll protect us from the bad guys. He was a marshal."

Eli sneered. "He doesn't want us here. I want to go back with Pa."

"You're lying, he likes us." Ben jostled Eli, who shoved him back.

Clare moved closer to Eli, seized his shoulders in a tight grip, and gave him a look designed to peel his hide. "Eli Ferguson Barlow. How can you forget what your father did to you? Worse, what he did to your mother." She swallowed hard. "He's a bad man. And the life they live on the run? How often do you think you'll have a warm bed like this? Or food in your stomach. Who's going to provide that for you? Victor? You know better. And what about Ben? Who's going to take care of him?"

Eli fought to keep his jaw tight, but he couldn't hide his tears.

"What do you think your father will do if he finds me?" She hadn't spoken the words aloud until that moment. Hadn't wanted to face the fear they brought.

He jerked himself out of her grip and turned his face to the wall.

She took in a shaky breath and let out an aching sigh. She had to get through to him. She hated to be so harsh.

She sat in silence until both boys were asleep. Climbing down the ladder, she sensed Isaac's presence before she glimpsed his tall form in the doorway. A new, fluttery feeling formed in her chest, and suddenly it was hard to get a full breath. She paused with one foot on the last rung of the ladder as the door closed softly behind him.

"Boys okay?" he asked.

She stepped down from the ladder, turned, and nodded, finding it hard to breathe through the sudden tension that settled between them.

"And you, Clare. You all right?"

"Of course" was all she could manage.

"It's a little nippy out there." Isaac's voice cracked slightly. He cleared his throat. "I could use a few more blankets."

"Let me get them for you." She scooted to the chest under the loft ladder.

He moved to the hearth, stoked the fire, and added a few more logs while she removed a couple of quilts, folding them over her forearm.

"Should last until early morning," Isaac said, leaning the poker against the stone wall. He turned and stepped toward her.

They'd be toasty in the cabin until the wee hours of the

morning. But he'd be in the lean-to with no fire. It'd been a long time since anyone, especially a man, had sacrificed his own comfort for her. She met him in front of the door.

"Thank you," she murmured, her voice barely audible. The firelight cast a warm glow on his face, emphasizing his chiseled jawline and the small dimple in his chin that she found so appealing. She handed the quilts to him. As he took them, their gazes caught for a breathless moment, and something else passed between them—an undeniable spark, an unspoken understanding that lingered in the charged air of the room. His lids dropped over his eyes, and he lowered his head. Without another word, he left the cabin.

As the fire softly popped and hissed in the hearth, Clare settled on the narrow cot, a quilt warmed by the fire tugged around her neck. The boys were safe. No one would find them here. Isaac hadn't sent them away. Instead, he'd brought them to his cabin.

Her thoughts drifted to the feelings she was developing for the man. Whatever his wounds were, something about the man resonated deeply with her. He'd offered her this uneasy truce. She needed to protect her heart from wanting more. But she was awake far too long into the night thinking about the way his eyes had looked in the shadowy firelight.

Seven

I GOT ONE!"

Eli hooted. "That's a big one! Swing it over here, and I'll take it off the hook for you."

Isaac heard the boys' voices before he could see them.

"It's the biggest one today. Bigger than yours." No mistaking Ben's enthusiasm.

"Might be."

Their innocent laughter reminded him of his nephew and nieces. David, Jo, and Tillie were as innocent as they came. But they were still caught up in this mess with Quade and the land.

Isaac dismounted Bullet and led him to the riverbank. The two boys came into view, both knee-deep in the river— Ben gripping a slightly bent rod, and Eli holding the thin line at eye level, inspecting the foot-long trout.

Isaac had spent the morning on Drew's homestead, patching and painting the big barn. It was a job that needed doing before winter set in, and it'd taken all the brothers, plus David, to accomplish it. Isaac had spent hours on the tallest rungs of the ladder, the only place he could keep his distance, but it hadn't kept him from overhearing Nick grumbling. Nick had met with the attorney in town, and the news wasn't good.

"It's legal," Nick had said. "At least in the way that slimy snake is going about it. He can move the dirt around on his land, reshaping it any way he sees fit. And if it just so happens the river is rerouted in the process, the legal precedent is that Quade isn't breaking any laws."

There'd been a heavy silence. In the process of dipping his paintbrush, Isaac had glimpsed Drew's devastated look before he'd blanked his expression.

"There's got to be some way to link that bandit who tried to kill Rebekah to Quade," Ed muttered, his paintbrush forgotten at his side.

Isaac knew that Marshal O'Grady would've found it if there'd been any evidence. It was too big a coincidence that the bandit had been found dead in his cell after being arrested. Quade claimed he'd been fired from the spread months ago, and with the bandit dead, there was no one to argue with him.

Ed's fingers tightened around his paintbrush until his knuckles turned white. "We have to do something." He spoke with angry conviction. "An eye for an eye. Isn't that in the Bible?"

Isaac knew better and so did Ed. But Ed hadn't gotten over nearly losing Rebekah.

"Remember what happened in Johnson County?" Nick

asked, the voice of reason. "Sheep herders and ranchers taking the law into their own hands. All that got them was bloody battles and lives lost."

Isaac kept his eyes on the patch of wall in front of him as images of other lives snuffed out vied for his attention. Then he realized the section was done. Painted. He needed to move the ladder. He was on the second rung, almost to the ground, when Drew spoke in a quiet, resigned voice. "We may have to fight. We can't lose the water."

Desperation was a dangerous thing. It drove men to do unspeakable things. The McGraws owned the land that the river flowed through. If Quade rerouted it, stole it . . . What would a desperate Drew do to protect and provide for his family?

"They can't use their shovels and picks if we fire on 'em," Ed said.

And Isaac lost his careful composure. "You want to put a rifle in David's hand?" he demanded, voice too loud, out of control. "Put a target on him for Quade's hired guns? Because it won't just be you three that become the target when Quade's men decide to shoot back. He's got a dozen hired guns—money to pay for more. Those men will come for you—and your families."

He'd stood there, red-faced and shaking, as seconds had ticked by. His brothers had stared at him, then he'd stormed off and spent a few minutes in the bunkhouse cooling off. When he'd returned and climbed the ladder again, they'd turned their quiet conversation to mundane things.

It hadn't kept his mind from spinning the whole ride back up to his cabin. His brothers resorting to more violence wasn't the answer. Quade's men outnumbered the McGraws four to one. If it came to a shoot-out, his family didn't stand a chance. Especially since Isaac couldn't draw on a man. And couldn't pull the trigger.

He couldn't see a way forward.

"He's a slippery one." Eli's words to Ben shook Isaac out of his dark thoughts. "I'll take it off the hook for you," Eli offered as the boys slogged back to the bank.

Ben spotted Isaac and waved to him excitedly. "Come see my fish. It's a big one."

Isaac dismounted, taking in the cutthroat trout and the pleased expressions of both boys. "That will be some good eating tonight. Either of you know how to fillet your catch?"

Ben's chest puffed out with pride while Eli wrinkled his nose.

They shook their heads.

"I'll show you when you're done fishing."

Ben whooped.

Over the past several days, Isaac had stepped into the unfamiliar role of teacher. Clare had come through on her promise that she and the boys would help with chores. This meant Isaac had needed to show them how he wanted things done. Just like his pa had shown him and his brothers.

Leading Bullet around a slight bend at the water's edge, he caught sight of Clare standing in the shallows. The hem of her practical work dress was soaked, her sleeves rolled up and revealing sun-kissed forearms. A soft breeze teased the strands of hair that had escaped from a low bun at the nape of her neck. When she saw him, a happy smile spread across her face.

"Isaac. You're back."

His heart kicked up at the warmth in her greeting. He should've greeted her back. But his tongue felt too thick to form words, so he just lifted a hand.

A basket of damp laundry sat on the creek bank. He'd caught her in the middle of hauling more water for the wash tub.

She pulled the half-submerged bucket from the river and stepped carefully over the rocky bottom, pausing to reach down and grab something out of the gurgling water. A familiar tube that made his heart drop to his boots—dynamite. He swung down from Bullet and surged toward her, his boots splashing in the shallows.

"Give me that!" he snapped.

His sharp tone must have startled her. She looked up but at the same moment lost her balance, teetering in the current. He was close enough to grasp her shoulder and steady her.

"Give it to me," he ordered softly.

Clare handed him the stick, brows creased. "There's no blasting cap. It's not dangerous. It was just floating downstream."

He thought her rambling was due to nerves until he saw her eyes flick to the right. Was she hiding something again?

When she glanced up at him again, he saw only genuine concern in her expression. "Who's blasting with dynamite?"

He didn't bother to hide his scowl. "The rancher whose

land is to the north of us, Heath Quade, is trying to reroute the river. Steal our water."

He saw the flare of recognition behind her eyes, the wheels turning. Clare was a smart woman. They'd had two run-ins with Quade since she'd arrived.

She tipped her head. "I suppose you've already tried to reason with him. Compromise."

He took the full bucket of water from her and gently gripped her arm with his other hand to steady her as they slogged toward the riverbank. "McGraws tried the neighborly approach years ago. That didn't work with Quade." He released her arm as they neared the laundry basket on the riverbank. He held the bucket of water and watched as her gaze flicked to the boys and a wrinkle of worry appeared just above her nose.

"Drew will think of something," he said. Not sure where the urge to comfort her had come from. He shifted his feet, disconcerted.

This is our legacy. Words his pa had said dozens of times beat inside him to the rhythm of his heart. It was true.

"We won't give up. You'll be safe here."

For now.

He waited for her to react with fear. Instead, those hazel eyes sparked.

She shoved her hands on her hips. "You McGraws are a formidable bunch," she said with a faint smile. "And you. I didn't know what to think when I learned you were a marshal."

Instinctively, he turned away from her.

You killed my boy.

The words of another woman echoed in his ears. A coldness slipped over him with the memory.

The boys came running up the bank, chattering about their catch. Eli carried a bucket and a string of fish. Ben's homespun shirt stuck to his ribs, and his rolled-up trousers dripped with river water.

"You're just in time to help me with the rest of the laundry."

Ben's face fell.

She stepped into the river, bent to cup some water in her hand, and splashed him. Ben shrieked.

"I need your shirt and pants—"

Splash.

She laughed. Had she distracted the boys on purpose? Seen Isaac's emotion?

"—completely wet"—she sent another wave of water Ben's way—"before I add the soap and start scrubbing."

Ben ran toward her. Eli, relishing the delighted shrieks, dropped the fish inside the bucket on the bank and sloshed into the river. He used both his hands to douse Clare. The water hit her full in the face. She let out a squeal of fake outrage.

"Oh, no fair. You guys can't gang up on me."

But they did, the water flying everywhere. She took a few steps toward Isaac, water dripping from her skirt.

"Better move back or you'll end up soaked," Clare warned him with a sassy grin. At that moment, the sunlight filtered through the trees and made her eyes sparkle. With her back to both boys, she couldn't see their next move, but Isaac did. A wave of water hit her from behind.

She shrieked, arms flailing, almost losing her balance again. Isaac laughed. The sound was rusty and surprised her as much as it did him, if her raised brows were any indication. Something hot lodged in his chest, and he couldn't pull his eyes from Clare—until a stream of icy water hit his cheek. With a playful growl, he took off after her, the boys' laughter ringing like a challenge behind him.

Perhaps it was time to be honest. To share the truth about Victor and her true self. In this fleeting moment, standing alone in the crisp autumn air with the water rippling nearby, Clare could admit it. She was drawn to Isaac McGraw. Yesterday, at the river, he'd laughed. A sound so unexpected that just thinking about it still made her heart flutter and her breath hitch.

She shook her head at the notion and reached to remove the clothespin from the line outside that stretched from the lean-to to a tall pine a few yards away. The stiff, dry garments bucked in the breeze. As she reached for a clothespin, she heard squabbling between Ben and Eli.

"I'm tellin' Aunt Clare." That was Ben.

"Shut your mouth, or I'll shut it for you," Eli snapped, the harshness in his voice sounding too much like their pa.

She dropped the folded trousers in the woven basket and moved around the side of the lean-to to check on them.

"You said you would feed him. You promised."

"I forgot. It'll be okay. We'll just give Bullet extra feed today."

Clare heard the scuffing sound of a metal cup hitting the

inside of the feed bag and the soft sifting of feed pouring into a metal pail. Ben's sniffle was cut off by Eli's angry command.

"Stop bawling like a baby!" Eli's irritated anger set Ben to crying louder. Alarmed, Clare raced to the lean-to. Eli had already poured a mountain of feed into Bullet's feed bucket.

"Stop!" She grabbed the cup from him and began furiously scooping feed back into the sack, hands shaking. "You cannot make up for not feeding Bullet by giving him double. That could make him very sick. If you didn't feed him last night, why did you tell Isaac that you did?"

"We didn't want him to get mad at us." Ben's face was streaked with tears and his voice wobbled. "Eli said he would sneak out after bedtime and do it."

She rolled her eyes. Like Eli could slip past a former U.S. marshal.

Eyeing the small but neat space, she noticed that only a few bales of hay separated Isaac's sleeping area from his horse. His bedroll with the extra folded blankets lay nearest the inner wall, and a chest occupied the other end,

She caught movement from the corner of her eye. The former marshal was suddenly in the doorway of the lean-to. Oh dear, had he heard their conversation? She looked at the cup in her hand and quickly shoved it back into the sack. Then she remembered this was Isaac. She didn't need to shield the boys. He would treat them fairly. Even when they'd been . . . what was that old saying? Caught red-handed.

But Isaac's attention went right to Ben.

"Hey, buddy. What's wrong?" His eyes shifted to Eli.

Her nephew folded his arms over his chest and tightened his jaw, biting down on his lips. He wasn't going to fess up.

Isaac's attention swung back to Ben, who dropped his eyes. "I was really tired last night." Ben paused, his voice breaking. "When you asked me if I fed Bullet . . . I lied." He sniffed, wiping his eyes. "I didn't want to get up and go out in the cold. So I said that I fed him, but I didn't."

"And this morning you guys were going to give him double the feed to make up for it, right?" Isaac locked eyes with Clare, silent understanding flowing between them.

Ben nodded, his chin wobbling. Clare braced. Isaac had a right to be angry. Victor would have slapped the boy silly. Isaac crouched before Ben, eye level. He placed a gentle hand on his shoulder, but Ben still flinched.

"Your aunt's right, that extra feed could be really bad for Bullet. He's kind of a pig. He'll eat all the food he's given, even if it bloats his stomach."

More tears slipped down Ben's cheeks as he wailed. "I'm sorry. I don't want Bullet to be sick."

"That's the thing about lying and covering up. Sometimes innocent people, or horses, get hurt." Isaac pulled a hankie from his back pocket and offered it to Ben. "Even if no one is hurt, lying is still wrong."

His eyes went to Eli.

Eli's expression remained stubborn. "My pa says sometimes a good lie is the only thing to keep you out of trouble."

"Eli!" Clare gasped. The words to reprimand him were on her lips.

Isaac stood. His gaze took in both boys. "If a thing is not true and right, even if it's spoken by your pa . . . or a brother"—his eyes went to Eli—"you can't heed the advice."

Clare saw the moment Isaac's own words registered on his face. Sure, he'd taken her and the boys up to his cabin so that they would be safe, but he'd been living this far away, isolated from his family, before she'd ever met him. What truth was he hiding? Their eyes tangled briefly. He frowned and turned his attention back to Eli and Ben.

"After the war, my pa left his past behind and moved here to Wind River Valley to make a new start. Told us boys that the Lord was good to us in giving us the land. And the McGraws should honor God by always living with honesty and integrity. Seems to me, your aunt is doing the same thing for you boys."

Joy mixed with guilt. He'd bought her lies.

"My pa taught us boys that you make a reputation by your actions," Isaac said.

Clare detected a fleeting trace of sadness on his face. An agony so intense it left her feeling heartbroken.

Isaac continued speaking, his calm composure back in place. He gently ran his hand down Bullet's neck. The horse nuzzled up against Isaac's shoulder.

"Bullet and I were on the trail of a man who lied about stealing items from people on a train—money, pocket watches, jewelry. He turned himself over to me in Beaver Creek. Said he knew he'd done wrong and wanted to make amends. He turned in everything." Isaac gestured to the west, where the faint outline of the Wind River Range was visible. "He lives up there in the mountains, owns a little cabin where he traps, fishes, and hunts. He's got a wife now and a son about your age, Ben. I consider him a friend."

As Clare listened to Isaac's story, hope bloomed like the tall autumn goldenrods she'd found growing behind the cabin. Ben's face radiated admiration. Even Eli was listening, though he was pretending to stare at the chest on the wall.

This was what the boys needed. A strong man to lead them. A man of God. This was what Anne had wanted for them.

"A good man decides he's going to tell the truth, even if it gets him in trouble. Swear to your own hurt. That's what the Proverbs say."

The words cut. Swear to her own hurt? Was that what she should do? Tell Isaac the truth—that her family name was a curse, tied to lawlessness and bloodshed? That she'd kept this from him, lied to him by omission, afraid that if he knew, his sense of justice would leave him no choice but to send her away? Because he would. He had to protect his own family.

Another proverb surfaced in Clare's mind, one Anne's grandfather used to quote. *A good name is to be chosen rather than great riches, loving favor rather than silver and gold.* Anne had chosen to hitch herself to the Barlow name. And her grandfather had taken his grief and disappointment to his grave. That's what the Barlows brought, even to the people that loved them.

A good name is to be chosen. A good name is to be chosen. A good name is to be chosen. Around and around, those words circled in her brain. She'd come to Wyoming as a mail-order bride to give her nephews a good name. Her own conscience pricked.

You are a hypocrite, Clare Barlow.

Eight

H E WAS STALLING. MATCHING HIS STEPS to Clare's slower, even leisurely steps, when he could have arrived at the main house a quarter of an hour ago had he set the pace. Tonight was just another family dinner. He'd get through it. They'd sit and eat with his brother's boisterous kids while his brothers talked about cattle and preparations for the coming winter. Rebekah and Kaitlyn would pry a little. What would Clare say? Isaac didn't know how to explain what was happening between them. Friendship? But sometimes when she looked at him, he caught a flash of... uncertainty?

"I can't wait to see Tillie." Ben fairly skipped across a flat stretch of brown prairie grass ahead of the two adults. "She knows the best games to play."

He whirled around like a tumbleweed caught in the wind to ask, "Do you think the kittens are old enough to hold now?"

How long had it been since they'd been to the main house? A week?

Isaac's "not sure" came out a little gravely.

"Jo said we can pet the horses," Eli said. He was more interested in horses than dogs or cats. He wasn't the best rider. They'd have to work on that.

Isaac's gut pinched. He wouldn't be the one who taught Eli to ride. Maybe one of his brothers. Isaac might not be around that long. A restless feeling stirred inside him, and a voice in the back of his mind whispered it was time to move on. He'd thought about it more than once—going somewhere else, starting afresh where no one knew him or about his time with the U.S. Marshals. But he hadn't been able to face abandoning his family. Not while Quade was causing trouble.

"Just be careful of that little black-and-white mustang," Isaac warned them. "That one can be ornery. Might even try to take a bite out of you." No doubt his brothers held the same sentiment about Isaac after their last exchange.

"I'm used to ornery things," Eli muttered.

Clare turned her face away, hiding a smile. Isaac could well believe it. The kid could be more ornery than the mustang. A chuckle rose in his chest but he managed to keep it down, the corners of his mouth twitching despite himself. Isaac lengthened his stride, regretting that he had decided to walk to the main house today instead of taking the wagon. He tightened his grip on the basket of jam and cornbread, their addition to the family meal, as they climbed a small hill and the homestead came into view. Eli and Ben took off running, leaving Clare and Isaac to walk the rest of the way alone. His gut churned. His brothers would have plenty to say about him and Clare.

We want you to be happy.

He gritted his teeth. They still thought they could fix him. Repair him like the old barn. Pull off the rotted boards, nail some new ones in place, slap on a new coat of paint.

Some things were beyond repair.

Clare moved closer to him and bumped his shoulder. He caught the faint smell of lavender.

"What's wrong?"

The concern in her hazel eyes gave him pause. He should warn her about his brothers.

"My brothers will be watching us, wondering if I've fallen for you yet." His words tasted as bitter as they sounded in his ears. If she noticed, she didn't give any sign. Instead, she nodded and gave him a side glance as they passed the barn.

"It's nice that they love you so much. They just want you to be happy."

His shoulder muscles tightened. There it was again. *They just want you to be happy.* "They think it's just a matter of fixing what's been broken. Like a wheel or a fence. Some things in life are broken beyond fixing."

Her eyes went to the mountains in the distance. "The God I read about is mighty. He made those mountains out yonder and parted seas. I don't think fixing whatever you think is broken is beyond His ability."

He followed her gaze to the mountains, taking in the grandness of the range. Yeah, the Almighty could fix what was broken in him, but why should He after what Isaac had done?

His throat felt hot and raw.

Before they even reached the house, the door flew open. Jo greeted them with her usual exuberance.

"Hi, Uncle Isaac, hi, Clare."

Jo eyed the basket Isaac was holding. "What did you bring?"

"Cornbread," Clare said, giving Jo a smile and gentle pat on the shoulder as she passed over the threshold.

"Oo-ooh." Jo lengthened the single syllable in a teasing manner. Her lips formed a playful smirk while her brows rose in presumption. "Cornbread is Uncle Isaac's very favorite."

Isaac cast a swift glance at Clare. She turned back to smile at Jo, noncommittal. Had she made the cornbread for him? No matter. Jo, normally a tomboy, was behaving like a spinster matchmaker. Pure mischief sparked from her eyes. He scowled at her.

"Ma's feeling peaked again," Jo informed Isaac just above a whisper as they gathered in the small entrance hall outside the steamy kitchen. Roast beef, onion, and joy permeated the room.

"Jo, let them in the kitchen," Kaitlyn chided, but there was a smile in her words.

After a few hearty welcomes and slaps on the back between the men, everyone took a seat at the table. By the time Isaac, Clare, and the boys had washed up, only two chairs were left empty, side by side. He felt awkward standing behind the chairs and waiting for Clare. She carried a platter of roast beef, carrots, and onions from the sideboard and placed it on the table. He couldn't help but admire her helpfulness. She'd done the same for him too, at the roundup and at the cabin.

He allowed himself to appreciate her pretty face, flushed pink from the heat of the kitchen, but snapped out of his reverie when he caught Ed eyeing him with an amused expression. Ed could be annoying and competitive, but Clare was right. Ed wanted him to be happy. Especially now that he'd found marital bliss with Rebekah.

"Seen anymore bears up around you?" Nick turned his question to Eli, seated to his left.

Eli flushed and kept his eyes on his empty plate. "No."

Drew's posture shifted as he leaned forward slightly, his elbows resting on the table.

His eyes locked with Isaac's. "Can't hardly think about that incident without a powerful gratitude that Isaac had his gun with him and reacted so quickly."

The scene flashed before Isaac. A terror so intense that the memory of the event left him feeling unsteady. Truth was, it had been Clare's quick action that had saved his nephew's life.

When the silence lasted a beat too long, Clare eased in beside him. "No bears, thank the Lord," she said with a playful smile. "But there was a wily little squirrel who staked a claim in the lean-to. Poor Isaac had to chase him away before he could get any sleep one night."

Ed laughed. Drew looked at Isaac. He shrugged it off.

"He didn't kill him though," Ben said, making an awkward attempt at cutting into his roast beef. Jo took his fork and knife and skillfully cut the meat into pieces.

He smiled at her. "Thank you."

Jo returned his smile. "You're welcome."

With the whole family tucked around the big table, Isaac was seated closer to Clare than at his small table at the cabin. He was careful to keep his spine straight and his hands in his lap. But she had to lean into him a bit to receive a bowl of gravy from Nick. Her shoulder brushed his arm again. The hair on his arms and at his neck rose.

"Can you place this in the empty spot in front of you?" she asked.

Kaitlyn cleared her throat. "Drew, could you lead us in prayer?" At her request, everyone joined hands.

When Isaac hesitated, Clare slipped her soft, warm hand into his bigger calloused one. It fit just fine. And that was a problem. Maybe he liked the feel of it a little too much. She gave his hand a small squeeze. He sent her a sideways glance. Could she read his mind? Her pink lips slid into a smile before she lowered her chin and closed her eyes. His gaze lingered on her graceful profile, taking in the long eyelashes set against her flushed cheek, before closing his own eyes to her beauty and the growing attraction that thrummed beneath his skin. What was wrong with him? She wasn't for him. They'd agreed on that.

The prayer ended with a chorus of "Amen." He felt Clare squeeze his hand again and realized he'd held it too long. He released it and picked up his fork. Rebekah nudged his shoulder, passing along a bowl of mashed potatoes.

He fumbled his fork, grabbed the bowl, took a scoop, and passed the bowl to Clare, careful not to brush her hand.

"David tells me you're a real fine fisherman, Eli," Drew said as he passed the cornbread.

Eli's eyes flew to Drew, then to Clare. She gave him a slight nod with widened eyes, silently urging him to answer the question.

"Yes, sir," Eli replied respectfully, color high on his cheeks.

"He catches more than everyone, even Isaac," Ben informed Drew. He chewed and swallowed. "But even I catch more than Isaac."

Guffaws and giggles erupted around the table. Clare cast Isaac an apologetic smile.

"Isaac never was very good at catching fish," Nick said. "He never had the patience to sit still that long. That's the one thing I'm better at than him. Well . . ." His lips formed a mocking challenge. "Besides roping."

Nick threw the hook, waiting for Isaac to take the bait. To send a teasing barb back. Isaac stayed silent.

"Thank God he was good enough to fish your fool self out of the water that winter you'd just turned twelve." Drew spoke up, filling in the awkward silence.

All eyes pivoted to Isaac. His chest tightened and his mouth went dry. He didn't want to think about what had happened that day when Nick had broken through the ice, submerged in the freezing water. How foolish Nick had been to be out on the ice in the middle of the river so early in winter. If Isaac and Bullet had not been heading by at that exact moment . . .

And he certainly didn't want to think about the way

everyone seemed to look at him now, like he'd been a hero. He wasn't. Not anymore. He shifted in his seat and focused on swallowing the lump in his throat.

"What did he do?" Eli asked, sitting up in his chair.

"He threw a lasso. The most perfect one you ever saw, according to Nick. Then he and Bullet pulled Nick out." Drew made it sound easy, but all Isaac could remember was the fear and his shaking hands as he'd thrown the loop.

Nick met Isaac's silence with a rueful grin. "Then he proceeded to scourge me with words that would make a gambler blush."

Disbelief crossed Eli's face.

Nick went on. "It's true. But later that night, he gave me his warmest blanket and snuck me some hot chocolate. Best cup of hot chocolate I've ever had."

Isaac felt Nick's gaze on him, but he couldn't look at him.

Memories flooded back, a stark reminder of the self-assurance that used to define him. He recalled a time when he'd effortlessly embraced risks, convinced that every outcome would favor him simply because he was Isaac Mc-Graw.

He'd been a fool.

"I remember hearing about that in school," Rebekah said.

Clare turned to Rebekah. "You all grew up together. Were you sweet on Ed in school?"

Ed scowled, but Isaac saw the spark of amusement in his brother's eyes.

Rebekah put her hand on the crook of Ed's elbow and blushed. "Actually, I had a walloping crush on Isaac back when we were in school together." She sighed. "But Isaac always had his eyes set on leaving Calvin. He knew he wanted to be a marshal since he was a kid reading dime novels. And Ed . . ." She turned and gave Ed a peck on the cheek. "He turned out to be a better writer than any dime novelist." She looked adoringly at her husband.

"Won her heart with a pen and paper," Ed said with a sly wink. Like Isaac hadn't been the one to talk some sense into him.

As the table quieted, Jo piped up, her words muffled a bit by the cornbread she was chewing. "I bet Clare could win Isaac over with this cornbread. It's real good."

Her comment drew a smirk from Ed, but Kaitlyn quickly interjected. "Jo, honestly."

Jo blinked, unfazed, and reached for another piece. "What? It's true."

Another moment of awkwardness settled over the table, thickening the air as Isaac remained silent. This was what he'd warned Clare about—his family assuming a genuine courtship, envisioning a romance unfolding like the one between Ed and Rebekah. He stared blankly at his plate.

Amidst the discomfort, he detected a subtle shift beneath the table—a gentle nudge, the discreet slide of a boot—Clare's boot—against his.

The meal passed. He left Clare to help with the dishes while the men and boys went to do the evening chores outside. Chores completed, Isaac stepped up to the screen door and was stopped by Kaitlyn's words to Clare.

"Jo's right about your cornbread. It is the best I've ever tasted. You could start making it to sell or even package it as a mix. I know the general store in town would carry it." Kaitlyn's voice rose with excitement. "And the towns near the mines. I have a little money to invest in supplies."

"That's generous of you, Kaitlyn, but—"

Kaitlyn stopped Clare, putting a gentle hand on her shoulder and looking her in the face. "Oh, I'm a business-woman. I think of it as an investment, not charity."

"Thank you," Clare said, bowing her head.

A sudden coldness hit him at his core. He had no doubt Clare could make a go of any business she set her mind to. Guess he'd grown accustomed to having Clare and the boys around, the shared moments and the routine. He should be breathing easier knowing she wasn't going to be trapped with him at the cabin for long. So why was he feeling so agitated about her finding a way to support herself and the boys? Wasn't that what he'd wanted all along—to be rid of them?

Clare listened to the murmur of Ben's and Eli's voices as she sipped a cup of coffee after supper. The parlor, dimly lit by the soft glow of an oil lamp, had the warmth of a room well lived in. The walls, lined with wood planks, displayed a few framed photographs along with a painting of the same mountain range that Clare glimpsed every day. The boys were sprawled on a braided rug that lay across the wooden floor, playing checkers with David. Ed and Nick sat on the sofa, Tillie between them. As Clare watched from her place standing near the window, Nick nudged Eli's boot, perhaps hinting at a move. She couldn't see his face, but

Eli's hand hovered over the board for a second before he jumped several of David's checkers and crowed happily.

Jo, coming down the stairs, cheered. Ben beamed when David said something she couldn't hear. Clare's heart was full to bursting.

This. Family.

These moments, right now and at supper, encompassed everything she'd dreamed about since she'd been a child herself. She'd never found it. But she desperately wanted to give it to Eli and Ben.

Isaac moved into the room to stand beside her. She couldn't help the flash of remembrance—his strong hand enfolding hers during the prayer. She shivered.

"We'd better get going," he said quietly.

She wanted to protest, even though she knew they still faced a long walk back to Isaac's cabin. She wanted more time with his family.

"Before you go, I'd like to read from the scriptures," Drew said from the doorway. "I was remembering one of Pa's favorite passages. Thought it might be good to remind us that Quade has been fighting us since Pa laid down roots here. And we're still here."

"'The Lord bless thee, and keep thee: The Lord make his face shine upon thee, and be gracious to thee: The Lord lift up his countenance upon thee, and give thee peace.'"

At the words, Clare felt Isaac tense beside her.

She chanced a peek at Isaac. He stood, his head lifted to the ceiling, his eyes closed, mouth set in a grim line. This man needed peace if anyone did. She prayed that he would find it.

For a few brief moments at supper, she'd seen a glimpse of the man he'd once been. A little freer with his smiles. Loyal, dedicated to his family.

Drew ended his reading with a prayer. Clare threw her shawl around her shoulders, tucked her empty basket in the crook of her arm, and began to herd the boys outside. Isaac joined them, his steps deliberate, almost mechanical. He lifted a hand at the goodbyes called from the porch. The boys ran ahead, Eli carrying a small lantern that flitted like a giant firefly in front of them.

This late in September, the moon was almost full and the night was clear. The lingering scent of wood smoke mingled with the crisp mountain air. Silence stretched between them as the words she longed to say bubbled inside her. Couldn't she have a few more moments of warmth?

"I didn't know brothers could be like that, get along," she said.

She sensed Isaac turn his head, the brush of his glance. Hadn't meant for the moment of vulnerability to leak out. She couldn't remember her brothers showing even one moment of kindness. Or a time when they'd been in the same room without quarreling.

"We argued plenty." Isaac's statement surprised her. "Especially when we'd catch Nick with his nose in a book when he should have been doing ranch work." There was quiet affection in Isaac's voice now.

"Did your pa let him get away with it?"

"Sometimes. But Ed and me didn't."

"You didn't what?"

"Let Nick get away with it." He released a quick sigh. "Ed and me fought all the time. I never gave him an inch."

She looked at his shadowy profile and couldn't reconcile this guarded man with the arrogant man he'd described. He'd helped Ed win Rebekah's heart, hadn't he? "I didn't get along with my brothers at all. I was never so happy than when my brother married Anne. For a while, even Victor seemed a changed man. He was happy and charming, determined to win Anne's favor. Anne fell for him like a summer storm, quick and hard, before she even saw what was coming."

For all the heartache it'd brought Anne to hitch up with her brother, Clare was forever glad she had. Clare had been fifteen, confused about life, and in need of a friend. God had brought her a sister.

A bolt of unease struck her. She'd let her guard down, and her brother's name had slipped out. She hurried to cover her mistake.

"I still can't believe she's gone. She and her grandpa taught me about God and how to live off the land."

"Now you're doing the same for Eli and Ben." The faint hint of admiration in his voice made her stomach twist.

"I would be happy if they grew up like you and your brothers."

A moment of tense silence fell between them. The glow of the lantern bounced ahead of them.

"I haven't been happy in a long time," Isaac admitted.

Clare was shocked by the quiet admission. Her mind whirled. What could she say to keep him talking, opening up to her?

"Would you tell me why? Sometimes it helps for someone to just listen."

She waited, not daring to breathe. He let out a long sigh.

"My last case as a U.S. marshal—" He measured his words and took a few steps. She stepped with him. "I was on the trail of a gang of outlaws tearing through several states, robbing stagecoaches and banks in small towns."

Foreboding crawled along her spine. Had Isaac lost a partner?

"I spent day after day belly up to the counter of the local café, waiting for the outlaws led by a snake named Judd Pickins and scouting the people around town. One of the waitresses had a son. Cody—" He choked on the boy's name, sucked in a breath, and forced himself to go on.

"The kid followed me everywhere, stuck to me like a tick. He was—" His voice turned rough, like a hand had closed around his windpipe. Clare heard the words die in his throat. A ragged cough escaped him, and she could hear the struggle to steady his voice.

"I let my guard down. I should have sent him away. Should have told him to leave me be. But I didn't. When Pickins showed, I thought it was all falling into place. I was ready to take him. But then Cody . . ." He stopped, his throat working as he struggled to go on. "He'd been following me that day. Pickins saw him first."

Isaac exhaled sharply, a sound steeped with bitterness. "He grabbed Cody. Dragged him into the street, used him as a shield. Held a gun to his head." He paused, and his jaw tightened. "I ordered Pickins to let him go. Even holstered my gun, tried to talk him down. But the town marshal . . ."

His voice cracked, and he closed his eyes briefly. "He came running in with his gun drawn. That's when Pickins turned. I had the shot. A perfect shot. Easy."

Clare saw the fingers on his right hand twitch. Her own hands tingled with a cold kind of tension. "I took it." His voice was quieter, rougher. "But Pickins moved. He pulled Cody right into the line of fire."

"Oh, Isaac," she breathed out, her voice cracking under the weight of his confession. It felt like the sound of her own heart breaking, torn between wanting to comfort him and the helplessness of knowing she couldn't fix this.

"I shot him!" The confession burst out, as harsh and fatal as the bullet that had killed Cody.

She stopped walking, unable to take another step. Isaac halted too, though he angled his shoulders and face away from her. He ran a hand down his face. The boys' voices grew fainter and the lamplight smaller in the distance.

Everything came into focus—she could see it clearly now. Isaac's wound, his tragedy. He was an honorable man. No wonder he had broken under the weight of it.

She reached out and took his hand. Couldn't stop herself, not when he was in so much pain.

"I'm sorry, so sorry, that you carry that kind of pain," she whispered.

He blinked down at her.

This close, in the moonlight, she saw the agony cut across his face, then faint surprise.

"I deserve to carry it. I can't ever forget."

"No one deserves endless grief."

The desolate look in his eyes as he shook his head tore at her. He turned his head away.

"It's not grief. It's guilt. I'm guilty of murder, but they won't lock me away because I'm . . . I was a U.S. marshal." His voice was gruff and full of self-loathing.

"No. Judd Pickins killed that boy."

Isaac shook his head, his gaze drifting to Eli and Ben as they moved farther into the night. The lantern in Ben's hand bobbed with his steps, its glow flickering like a firefly—there one moment, gone the next.

What could she say? Her own guilt weighed on her chest like consumption. She thought of Anne and the hollow ache she carried since Anne's death. What would Anne have said?

"No one deserves that kind of pain and grief," she repeated. *Especially not you, Isaac McGraw.* "We can't change what happened in the past. We can only live one day at a time. But we can depend on the God who promises steadfast love and mercy that is new, greeting us like the sunrise, every morning."

But as the words left her lips, something twisted inside her. She knew them by heart, had heard Anne say them so many times. And she believed them, in this moment, for Isaac. She wanted to truly believe them all the way through, deep inside, for herself.

As time passed, his grip loosened, and in that quiet moment, she smiled to herself, her insides relaxing. In step, they walked hand in hand under the moonlight, taking in the stars twinkling above. The same stars she'd prayed to God under at the farm in Missouri. The same God who would make the sun rise in the morning. *Oh God, we both need Your love and mercy.*

As they walked, his hand securely in hers, Isaac gazed into the night sky. Then their gazes met, her breath catching at the warmth in his eyes that hadn't been there before. Their conversation had changed something between them.

"What's taking you so long?" Eli traipsed up to them. Ben tagged behind, the lantern dangling from his hand.

Isaac released Clare's hand, and cool air rushed over her skin.

Ben yawned. "I'm tired."

Isaac reached for the lantern. "Let me carry that. It's not too far now."

It's not too far now.

Isaac had taken a few tenuous steps toward letting Clare in. She longed to do the same, but she knew she couldn't. The omission of her Barlow name had grown into an unspoken barrier between them. If she revealed it now, she would lose his trust—something she couldn't afford. The fragile yet precious connection growing between them could be severed, and she wasn't ready to risk that.

<h1 style="text-align:center">Nine</h1>

ISAAC HAD BROUGHT HER FLOWERS.

Clare dawdled over the jar of flowers in the window-sill, the rag she'd used to wipe down the table after a late lunch still clutched in her hand while her thoughts meandered. The bouquet of mountain poppies, with their papery white petals and sunny yellow centers seemed to smile at her. She shook herself out of her woolgathering, grabbed a shirt in need of mending, and went to sit on the porch step. A cool breeze rattled the curling yellow leaves in the trees as she sewed the frayed edges of a sleeve cuff with tiny stitches.

Boys being boys, Eli and Ben had collected sticks to use as swords. She heard the click, click of their jousting and a few "Ha, I gotchas" in the clearing a few yards away.

It had been a week since the family supper. A week since Isaac had opened up to her. Things between them were changing, slowly but surely. He'd stayed at the table after supper last night, lingering over coffee. Listening to her chatter about the boys.

And then this morning, he'd left after a quick breakfast and a warning to stick close to the cabin. When she'd gone out to fetch water, she'd found two full pails on the stoop. And the pretty poppies. She didn't want to read too much into the gesture. Isaac remained quiet and guarded.

"Bang!"

She glanced up to see Ben had turned his sword into a gun and was pointing it at Eli.

"You missed," Eli crowed from behind a tree.

Clare tucked the last bit of ragged shirt sleeve into the cuff and sewed it together.

On the surface, things were going smoothly, but guilt ate at her insides when she thought about the secrets she was keeping. *Blood will out.* Her father's words rang in her ears and thickened her throat. If she wanted to stay, wanted to deepen this . . . friendship with Isaac, she needed to find a way to tell him. Or she needed to figure out a way forward for herself and the boys.

"Come out, Victor Barlow. You're a bad man, and you're gonna meet your maker!" Ben shouted.

Eli stepped from behind a tree into the open, his face growing red with outrage.

Clare's pulse kicked up at the name Barlow. "Eli!" she shouted.

Her warning came too late. She threw aside her mending and sprang to her feet. Out of the corner of her eye, she saw Isaac approaching from the river.

"You can't kill Pa!" Eli cried. "And don't you say he's a bad man."

He hurled his stick aside and charged at his little brother, knocking him off his feet so that he hit the ground with a hollow thud. Her mind raced as she ran to stop Eli from pummeling Ben. Isaac reached the fighting boys first and swiftly yanked Eli off Ben. His arms formed a tight band around Eli's torso, but the boy kicked his arms and legs like a beetle turned on its back.

"Stop!" Isaac ordered as he strode a few yards to the cabin stoop and set Eli down. "Stay here. Don't move a muscle from this step." He paused for a moment, his mouth grim, waiting to see if Eli obeyed.

He moved back to Ben and picked him up. The boy threw his arms around Isaac's neck, sobbing and sniveling.

She took a few steps toward the two of them, arms extended. Her breath hitched. "I can take him."

He ignored her, avoiding her eyes and setting Ben on his feet again in the clearing a few yards from the stoop. He straightened Ben's torn shirt. Like a loving father would do. Clare blinked away tears—saw it then, a gold star pinned to Ben's dirty shirt. And the gun belt that lay in the dirt and pine needles near Isaac's feet. How had she not noticed they'd gotten into Isaac's things?

She maneuvered between Isaac and Ben. "I'm so sorry— they should know better. Stealing is not—"

"Enough, Clare," Isaac said, quietly resigned.

Eli, mulish, snarled from the step, "We didn't steal nuthin.'"

Ben wiped at his eyes, leaving dirty streaks. "I didn't steal.

It's right here. I can give it back." He fumbled with the star on his shirt, and it tumbled to the ground.

Isaac swept it up and shoved it into his pocket.

When Ben tried to throw his arms around Isaac's leg, the marshal held him in place with a hand on his shoulder.

"Go sit on the step next to your brother."

Ben did as he was told, lowering himself next to his brother. Eli gave Ben an evil side-eye, his left eye swelling from Ben's kick.

Clare's stomach knotted. What could she say? How could she fix this?

She moved to hover near the stoop.

Isaac reined in his anger, didn't lash out at the boys, but it was there, simmering under the surface.

He didn't crouch or kneel, didn't put himself on the boys' level like he had when he'd caught Eli brawling in town. This was Isaac, the marshal, with arms crossed and a stormy frown.

"I've never met your pa, but from what I just heard, you boys have some disagreement about the kind of man he is. One thing I do know, from what your aunt has told me— your ma was a good woman who raised you according to the Good Book, just like my ma raised me. So you know right from wrong. Doing right or doing wrong is like a path that you choose to take. Paths lead to somewhere." Isaac jerked his chin toward the path that led to the river. "Like that path to the river."

"The one that leads to a good life is narrow, and not many men choose it. Know why? Because it's hard to do what is right. The path that leads to destruction—it's wide. When I was a marshal, the men on this path were the ones I had to catch and arrest. Lying, cheating, stealing may seem easier at times. But men who take that path meet a bad end."

Ben, so much like his tenderhearted mother, broke the silence with a small and earnest cry. "I want to take the good path, Isaac."

Clare's heart squeezed.

Ben wore his adoration for Isaac like the star he'd pinned to his shirt.

Eli scowled at his brother, but it was Isaac's impassive expression and silent fury that twisted the knot in her belly tighter.

"Go on and start your chores. Clean the ashes from the fireplace and sweep the floors."

Eli looked like he might protest, until Isaac clapped his hands, the sound like a clap of thunder in the quiet clearing. Both boys scattered like startled birds.

"Isaac—"

He cut her off with a quelling glare. Pulled off his hat, swept his hand through his hair, and shoved it back on again. A gesture he made whenever he had finished talking and wanted to move on. A muscle in his cheek jumped as he jerked his chin toward the far side of the clearing. She followed him away from the cabin and the boys' listening ears.

"Victor Barlow is the boys' father?" His words were ice cold and hard, his eyes the same.

Everything she wanted to say—her apology, her plea for him to understand—was lodged in her throat, choking her.

He stared at her, waiting for an answer.

"You're a Barlow?" he demanded.

Blood will tell.

Blood will out.

"You're a Barlow?"

The question hung in the air.

Isaac saw the answer in her face before she spoke. Clare was related to a notorious outlaw. One who'd robbed and murdered in cold blood. She wrapped her arms around her middle, fingers grasping her elbows like she was holding herself together. At the same time, her chin hitched up stubbornly. All contradictions. That was Clare.

"I'm not my brother," she said.

"You're a Barlow," he repeated.

He saw the glimmer of tears in her eyes before she blinked them away. Part of him wanted to comfort her, and that just increased his fury. She'd lied to him, keeping this from him.

"You took those boys from their pa? Barlow?" She had to know Victor would search far and wide for his sons. And exact retribution on her. "You know what he'll do if he finds you."

He saw the answer to that, too, on her expressive face—a flash of fear, then a fierce frown.

"He won't find us!"

A bitter-sounding laugh escaped him. He looked down at his boots and took a calming breath. It didn't work. He shoved his hands on his hips and confronted her again. "A dozen people saw you get off the train in Calvin with the boys in tow."

Including Quade. His gaze instinctively went to the river. Quade would love nothing more than to stir up trouble, even murderous trouble, for the McGraws.

"All it will take is a few questions to find out who you left the train station with." Fear blasted through him. This was worse than imagining David going up against one of Quade's men. If Victor Barlow tracked Clare here, he'd shoot anyone who tried to get in his way.

"I couldn't stay." She took a few steps toward him, shaking her head. "You can't imagine what it was like . . ."

He could. He'd tracked plenty of men like Victor. Met the wives, children, and saloon girls who were the victims of their violence. Imagining Clare with the kind of bruises he'd seen made him feel sick. His eyes went to the scar on her wrist.

"I couldn't stay any longer. I told you the truth about Anne and my promise to her. I wanted to get the boys out before—"

"And now you've laid a trail right to our door. Right to Kaitlyn and Jo and Tillie."

"Stop!" she demanded. This time the tears spilled down her cheeks. She swiped at them. "Victor has no idea where we are. We took two different trains to cover our tracks."

"You can't run away from who you are." He saw the words hit, saw her shoulders fold in. He turned away, berating himself. He'd known, hadn't he? That she was keeping secrets. He'd gone soft. Let down his guard. He should never have spoken a word to her.

He swung back around to confront her one last time. "This changes everything—keeping this secret from me."

She closed her eyes against this last assault. The wind loosened some of her golden-brown hair and swept it across her face.

He jammed his hands in his pockets. His fingers met metal. His mind flashed to the star half buried in the dirt. And then to another scene—Cody, his lifeless body set in a pine coffin and lowered into the ground. He couldn't let that happen to David. Couldn't bear for Drew to know that grief. His first duty was to protect his family.

The points of the star stabbed his palm where he gripped it in his pocket. "We're done playacting, Clare."

Her face went pale.

"I'll take you back to town in the morning and turn you over to Marshal O'Grady. She'll help you find a safe place, but it can't be here."

He turned his back to her and stalked up the path to the lean-to. Halfway up the narrow path, he glanced back. Clare stood, eyes fixed upriver, bleak, her fingers tracing the scar on her arm.

Ten

IT WAS FULLY DARK WHEN ISAAC STORMED into the bunkhouse back at the main house. He couldn't stay at the cabin, not with the anger and frustration gnawing at him over Clare keeping secrets. So he'd saddled up Bullet and ridden home. Someone—Nick—stirred in the bottom bunk on the right side of the sparsely furnished room. Isaac stomped into the room and promptly banged his knee on the corner of a chest. He bit down on the howl that threatened to escape, then stalked to the empty bunk across from his brother and tossed his bedroll onto the bare mattress. He lowered himself onto the bunk across from Nick, his agitation coming out in steamy breaths. He yanked a boot off. It slipped out of his hand and clunked to the floor.

Nick propped himself on his elbows and squinted in his direction. "Wha . . ." His voice was slow and sleepy in the darkness. Isaac heard a chalky scrape and saw a match flare as his brother lit the lantern on the bedside table. "Land sakes, Isaac! What are you doing here, stomping around like a bear at a barn dance?"

"Nothing." Isaac untied his bedroll, batted at the thing so it rolled off the end of the bunk. He jerked it up a few feet and lay down on it.

He wished Nick hadn't lit the lantern. He felt the weight of his brother's stare. Isaac kept his eyes on the crisscrossed ropes that held the top straw tick mattress in place. He just wanted to sleep. And forget.

He felt ache of betrayal and a weariness that had nothing to do with the lateness of the night.

"What's the matter?" came his brother's sleep-laden voice.

"I don't want to talk about it."

Nick ignored the coldness in his voice. "Clare and the boys all right?"

Were they all right? He closed his eyes, but a picture flashed across his mind. Clare, standing on the clearing near the path to the river, her eyes filled with tears she was too proud to shed. He should have never trusted her.

Nick let out a resigned breath. "What'd you do?"

"I said I don't want to talk about it."

There was a rustling from Nick's bunk. Isaac opened his eyes to find his brother sitting on the edge of his bunk, hands clamped on the mattress at his sides, staring at him. "Last time I saw you, you were actually smiling."

Isaac recalled the boisterous family dinner. Clare's compassion when he'd told her about Cody. He punched those thoughts down. "I smile."

Lie. He couldn't produce a smile if he tried.

Nick scoffed. "How'd you mess things up with Clare?"

"Leave it alone," he ground out as he rolled so his feet hit the floor while he reached for his bedroll. He shouldn't have come in here. Maybe he could find some peace in the barn.

But by the time Isaac stood, Nick was already on his feet, facing him like a banty rooster spoiling for a fight, his expression grim. "Tell me," Nick challenged.

When had his brother gotten so tall? Matched him for height. Nick had grown into a man while he'd been away.

"I said. Leave. It. Alone."

Nick braced himself for a punch.

The action jarred Isaac, and he edged back so his calves hit the bunk. What was he doing? "I'm not going to hit you."

"You want to hit something."

He was right. Isaac turned his back, grabbed the rail of the top bunk, and leaned his face into his bent arms. He had to control his boiling emotions or risk doing something he'd regret.

Nick hovered behind him. "Isaac—"

"Clare lied," he blurted, the words muffled against his forearm. "About her name. Her identity."

He closed his eyes, but the image of Clare at the moment he'd told her he was done with her kept replaying. He clenched his fist. Couldn't take it anymore. Turning to face Nick, Isaac ran a hand through his hair and stared at the wide-plank floor, his throat constricting as the weight of betrayal settled in.

"I knew she was running from something, but—her

father and brother are notorious outlaws. Bank thefts, stagecoach robberies, and they've left plenty of dead bodies along the way."

Nick paused, letting the information settle. "How did she manage to escape? It takes more than luck to survive over two decades as outlaws. And she managed to outfox them. Downright courageous if you ask me."

Isaac was caught off guard by that thought. He'd been focused on Clare's betrayal, her lies and who might be following her. His own hurt feelings. He hadn't given a passing thought to what she had survived. Or the courage it had taken to leave the life she'd known.

She and her sister-in-law had planned her escape. But it was Clare who'd had the courage to act. To risk being caught or even killed by Victor.

Nick moved to the window, his back to Isaac, and let the silence of the moonlit night seep into the room. "Guess I can understand why she did it," he said finally, turning from the window, his expression pointed.

Isaac only grunted.

Nick bristled. "Maybe she's not the only one running scared."

"What's that supposed to mean?" Isaac jerked his eyes to meet Nick's level stare, tension bunching the shoulders that had barely started to relax.

"You've been keeping some secrets too. Distancing yourself from me, Drew, and Ed, keeping us in the dark. Haven't breathed a word in—what's it been now?—two years? About why you quit the Marshals."

Isaac tensed. This again? "You can't fix me," he bit out.

"I'm never gonna end up like Drew and Ed, with a wife and stars in my eyes."

Nick watched him, his gaze filled with a compassion that Isaac couldn't bear. His brothers still saw him as a hero. He'd never had the courage to tell them otherwise.

He did now. All of it flowed out of him like a rushing current. Everything. How he'd become friends with the boy and his mother and opened himself up to the thought of a family, had planned to court her once he'd finished that last assignment. And the shoot-out that'd ended in tragedy.

"I got Cody killed."

The words came out differently than when he'd told Clare. Somehow, telling her had shifted something inside of him and the way he saw the past. Didn't absolve him though. It was still his fault Cody had been close enough to grab.

He fell silent. In the stillness, his heartbeat pounded out the seconds in his ears. A heartbeat that reminded him that he was still alive . . . but Cody was dead.

He moved back to the bunk and sat down. Nick lowered to the bunk across from him, his hands clasped between his knees and his gaze pinned on Isaac's face.

Nick didn't look shocked or judgmental or even surprised.

"You knew."

Nick nodded. "Read about it in the paper. Ed and Drew don't know the details. I didn't talk to them about it. They know the Marshals determined it was an accident though."

Accident. A word that couldn't encompass the enormity of what he had done.

"They didn't fire you, did they?"

Nick already knew the answer, but Isaac told him anyway. "I couldn't do the job anymore. I can't fire on another person. Couldn't even pull the trigger on the bear when David was in danger."

Now Nick's face showed surprise. His quick assessment showed on his face. "Clare," he concluded.

Isaac nodded. Shame made him duck his head. He was broken. Now Nick knew the extent of it.

Nick sighed, the sound more like a shout in the silence. "I can't help feeling that you and Clare, you both deserve a second chance. But I'm not the one who needs to give it."

Long after Nick blew out the lantern and his steady breaths signaled he'd fallen asleep, Isaac lay in the dark, words spinning round in his head.

Accident.

Grief.

Forgive yourself.

Second chance.

Everything Nick and Clare had told him warred with what he knew to be true, or what he thought he'd known to be true all this time.

When the sun's rays shone through the small window in the bunkhouse the next morning, he still didn't have any answers.

"Boys! Time to get up." Clare straightened the blankets on her cot, then moved to the fireplace and stirred the coals, placing a split log on the embers.

The floor in the loft creaked, and Eli climbed down the ladder, yawning and sleepy-eyed.

"Where's Ben?" Her gaze lifted to the loft, waiting for the boy to appear.

"Dunno."

"He's not in bed up there?"

Eli stilled, his eyes widening, the sleepiness draining from his face when he saw her worry. "No."

Clare's stomach turned, dread knotting tight. Something was wrong. Where was Ben? "Let's look around. He can't have gone far."

They checked the lean-to, the area all around the cabin and along the river. Their calls for Ben echoed over the water, but no answer returned.

Clare was back on the front stoop, preparing to widen her search, when she spotted a familiar figure on horseback. Isaac. The choking panic loosened slightly. No matter what was between them, Isaac would help find Ben.

"Ben is missing!" she called out. By the time she'd scrambled off the stoop, he'd already swung out of the saddle.

He moved in closer, his eyebrows drawing together as he studied her face.

"When I woke up this morning, he was gone. Eli and I checked everywhere—the lean-to and down by the river. We can't find him."

Her nervous rambling was stopped by the tightness in her chest that choked off her breath. Why had Ben run off?

Why wouldn't he? She made for a horrible parent.

The cabin door banged. Eli jumped off the stoop, his boots sliding on the gravel. He looked as worried as she felt.

"Do you know where he went?" Isaac directed his question to Eli.

"He knocked into me in the middle of the night. Said he was cold and was gonna sleep by the fire. I didn't hear him go out. I woulda stopped him." Eli's chin wobbled a bit before he jerked his head aside and hardened his jaw, hiding his emotion from Isaac. He turned back, blasting Isaac with a glare, arms crossed. "He didn't wanna leave."

Clare saw the words hit their mark, causing a minute tightening around Isaac's eyes. She knew Ben had been upset last night after she'd told them they would need to pack up their stuff in the morning.

Isaac's eyes met hers briefly, and for a fraction of a second, the hard edge in his expression softened. "He can't have gone far in the dark. We'll find him."

The quiet strength in his voice and his use of *we* were her undoing. The tears she'd been holding at bay all morning broke free. Embarrassed, she bowed her head. Isaac's hand closed over her elbow. The comforting touch only lasted a moment, but it bolstered her.

He turned to Eli. "Can you find your way to the main homestead?"

"I think so."

"I know you can. You love your brother, and he needs your help. Find Drew or Nick. Tell them to head up here and help us search. Clare and I will search to the north."

Eli ran off on foot, while Isaac led Clare up the small rise near the river.

"How far up this way did you search?" Isaac asked. He was setting a fast pace, and she panted as she tried to keep up with him. Clare scanned the brush and rocky hills. The sun was up now, but the day was gray. Dark, angry clouds were moving in from the west.

"Ben!" she called out.

Isaac pointed out a partial boot print. Expression determined, he pushed them onward. The tree line began to thin and gave way to rocky terrain as they headed upland through a deep ravine.

Clare's boots skidded on some loose gravel, and a few pebbles rolled down the ravine. Her mind wound round and round like the trail Isaac was trekking up the rocky face.

The silence between them became unbearable.

"I couldn't sleep last night," she blurted.

Isaac pulled a branch aside for her, not looking back to see if she was through.

"You were right," she went on stubbornly.

He didn't have to look at her to listen.

"I should have told you the whole truth from the beginning." She panted through the words. Her chest hurt, not only from the pace.

"I was desperate. To escape." New tears welled in her eyes. She blinked them away and kept looking for Ben.

Isaac's longer strides put him several feet ahead of her. She drew in a breath, picked up her pace.

"I'm sorry that I put your family in danger." When he still didn't acknowledge her, desperation made her shout, "I had no choice. I had to get us out this time."

Now he swung around, eyes searching her face. "You've tried to get out before?"

Here is your moment of truth, Clare Barlow. You can play

it two ways. Tell the truth, and Isaac will know that you were a charlatan. Or . . . keep it from him and hope he never finds out.

Blood will out.

No, she would out herself. Just reveal the whole ugly truth about the woman she used to be.

"After my oldest brother died, my father needed someone to scout ahead. Get the lay of the land, meet people, and sniff out any vulnerabilities. When the bank might be left unlocked. Who had the keys or knew the safe combination."

Clare watched Isaac's jaw harden and his eyes go cold.

"I told myself I wasn't hurting anyone. Only gathering information."

But she'd known it was wrong. She cleared her throat, the guilt and shame rising to choke her again. She swallowed it back, determined to get it all out.

"Sometimes Pa and Vic would come home with wads of cash, and for a while, things would be good. They'd spend it all on fine saddles or whatever they could think of—anything but providing for the family." She shook her head, the words coming faster now. "And they'd be gone for months at a time, leaving us to fend for ourselves."

She paused, remembering the days when there had been no food to go around, the silence hanging heavy as Anne grew more ill with the children to care for and no one there to help. "Anne was growing weaker by the day. I could get us food and supplies while in town."

She sucked in a breath. Her heart beat faster with the memory of her pa and his demands. "And you don't say no to Pa Barlow." She didn't realize she was touching the scar at her wrist until she caught him watching her. She dropped her hands to her sides.

Surely he couldn't think any less of her than he already did, but she couldn't bear any more of his censure, so she ducked her eyes, turning to pick her way up the gully, leaving him to follow this time.

"I was seventeen when I met a young man in this tiny town in southern Missouri. A banker's son. I'd never known anyone so kindhearted."

Theo had been a complete surprise to her after Pa, Billy, and Victor. At times his gentleness hadn't felt real. She'd imagined herself in love with him before she'd known what love really meant.

"I thought I could outsmart Pa and Victor. Hatched a grand plan to run away with Theo."

When she glanced over her shoulder, Isaac paused his searching for Ben to meet her gaze. She saw the resignation in his expression. He'd guessed.

"Pa caught us and laughed in my face. He knocked me to the ground and quoted one of his favorite phrases—one he'd been repeating to me ever since I was Ben's age: 'Blood will out.' He told Theo that I was pulling a con. And Theo, the man who'd declared his undying love for me?" She released a derisive laugh and shook her head. "He believed Pa—that I was still in cahoots with them. I saw the doubt and distaste in his eyes."

She lifted her scarred arm. "My father left me with a little reminder of what happens when you cross him."

Isaac's lips flattened, then he motioned her on, taking

the lead again. Surely Ben couldn't have climbed this far. His tone deepened when he asked, "What happened to the banker's son?"

"Pa and Victor beat him to within an inch of his life."

She'd ignored the warning signs—the little voice inside that had told her she was putting them all in danger. She'd kept telling herself it would be fine. But then Isaac had said it out loud, and now she couldn't stop thinking about it. He was right. She was a Barlow, and trouble always found her.

Isaac was stepping over a fallen tree trunk when he froze, eyes focused on the ground. In the moist dirt near the log, a small divot was pressed into the dark soil. A boy's boot heel.

"Ben!" Isaac shouted.

They waited. No response. Just the twitter of a few birds and the sound of rushing water in the distance. Isaac kept climbing. Her heart pumped double time, but she could only manage shallow breaths. Were they close? She tripped over a half-buried root and lurched forward.

Isaac turned in time to break her fall. She clutched his shoulders when he would have let her go, couldn't tear her eyes away from the face that had somehow become so dear to her. She couldn't let Victor get anywhere near Isaac or his family. It would be Theo all over again.

"You're right. We can't say here. If Victor finds us, he'll bring violence against your family. As soon as we find Ben, we'll leave. I couldn't . . . I couldn't stand it if something happened to Drew or Kaitlyn or the kids."

Or you.

His fingers tightened around her upper arms. A steely

glint sparked in his eyes. "I'm not going to let anything happen to you."

"It's not your problem. I can't let you—"

He dipped his face closer. "I'm making it my problem." His voice came out low and raspy.

"What about your family?" She tried one last time, but he was immovable.

"They'd say the same thing. We may not be blood, but McGraws don't run from outlaws."

Eleven

A FAINT CRY BROKE THROUGH THE stillness, severing the connection between them. Isaac let go of Clare and turned his head, one direction, then another. Where had the sound come from?

"Ben!" he yelled, his voice growing rougher with each call.

From this higher vantage point, they could see the steep, rocky drops on each side of the river. Over the roar of the water came another faint cry. He stopped short and held out his arm to keep Clare from going too near the cliff's edge. He could see Quade's work across the river. His men had dug a wide swath, inching closer to diverting the water. But this was not the time to think about that.

They walked farther, and Isaac couldn't keep his mind from swinging between the current problem of locating Ben and everything Clare had revealed in the past hour as they'd searched for the boy. It was clear that Nick had guessed right. She'd left behind a life of violence and criminal activity. It had taken a strong will to see through the lies her pa and brothers had told her about what was right and wrong. She'd made her choice and run away.

But the compassion he felt for what she'd been through didn't explain his conflicted feelings about whether he should follow through with his decision from last night— whether he should send her away.

No, it was the twist in his gut when she'd explained about the young man she'd fallen in love with that left Isaac unsettled.

Clare had snuck under his walls. He'd started to care about her. And those boys. That's why her deception had stung so badly.

If he opened his heart fully to them and he couldn't keep them safe . . .

Isaac scanned the area ahead, taking in the dark clouds, churning and forming fast. Clare leaned over the cliff's edge and gasped.

Isaac peered down the precipice. His heart twisted. Ben lay on a narrow ledge, unmoving. His leg was turned at an ugly angle. Earlier, they'd heard his cries, but now there was only the sound of the wind picking up, whistling sharply through the canyon. Had he fallen unconscious?

The shallow rise and fall of Ben's chest shot relief through Isaac. He dropped to his belly, his head and shoulders hanging over the edge. Clare followed his lead, lowering herself beside him.

"He's breathing," Clare said.

"Isaac?" Ben whimpered. His eyes opened.

Clare rolled to her elbows. "I've got to get down there."

"Not a chance. It's a challenging climb in any circumstances. But in skirts? Go back to the homestead. You can lead my brothers here faster. We need a horse, and bring some rope and bandages."

She shook her head. "I can't leave him." She pinned her lips in a firm line.

"Then see if you can find some sticks for a splint. Sturdy ones."

She frowned but did as he asked, leaving Isaac to assess the cliffside and the distance between him and Ben.

Ben groaned. His tiny perch was barely wider than a water trough. If he rolled one way, he'd fall into a crevice. But if he rolled the other way? Well, it was a steep drop for a kid with a broken leg.

"Ben, just stay real still. All right?"

Clare reappeared at Isaac's elbow, two near-straight sticks in one hand. She pressed them and a white handkerchief into Isaac's hold.

"It hurts. My leg hurts," Ben cried. His small movement sent pebbles skittering down the side of the cliff. "I want to go home."

Isaac forced himself to look at Clare, not Ben. "I'm going to climb down. You keep talking to him. It'll help to keep him calm."

Clare's eyes locked with his. "Be careful."

Her bossy demand brought on a half smile.

He swung around, allowing his legs to dangle off the edge of the cliff. His work-hardened hands gripped the rough crags as his scuffed boots found footholds within the jagged outcrops below. One boot slipped, sending a small shower of rocks down to the ledge. He hung six feet above the narrow ledge. There were no more foot holds. He'd have to drop and keep his weight from going backward but not scrape his nose off his face.

"It hurts . . ." Ben's voice was growing weaker.

"Isaac is almost there. He's going to help you." Clare's confidence in him rang in her words.

He's going to help you. He was, right now.

But what about after this crisis was over?

Could Isaac really turn the three of them loose, knowing exactly who was hunting them?

These were the times he wished he'd kept a tighter hold on his faith. He wanted to pray, lean on a power greater than his own. Maybe that made him a hypocrite. He didn't care.

Lord, I guess I'm in Your hands now.

He let go.

His feet landed solidly on the ledge, just missing Ben. And his mug had avoided critical damage, just a stinging scrape on his right cheekbone. A powerful wave of gratefulness rushed through him.

Isaac crouched next to Ben, his back to the drop and the rushing waters below.

Tears dripped from Ben's wild, fear-filled eyes.

"You came back."

Isaac felt Ben's words, a vice gripping his heart. He massaged Ben's arms and neck. The leg seemed to be the only injury. He carefully pulled up Ben's pant leg and worked to keep his face from showing his shock. Ben's knee was swollen. Ugly purplish bruises were spreading fast. Blood seeped from a gash along his shin where the bone threatened to break through the skin.

"Yeah. Imagine my surprise to find my good friend had deserted."

Isaac lowered himself to a sitting position, his back resting against the rock wall. He pulled Ben into his lap and wrapped his arms around the boy's trembling body. Or was that him trembling? Scratches, dried blood, and tears covered Ben's face. No time to clean him up now. Not when the wind was picking up, carrying the scent of rain.

"Clare," he called. "I'm gonna splint his leg now."

It was worrisome that Ben was so weak he didn't protest.

Isaac pulled the sticks Clare had retrieved and her bandanna from his back pocket. He quickly untied his own bandanna from around his neck. He glanced up to see Clare's worried face peeking over the cliff. A memory of her stricken expression last night, when the truth had been revealed, flickered in his mind.

It was too late to keep his distance.

He cared.

He blinked the memory away, focused on Ben and figuring how to get the kid to stay calm.

"Why don't you give your aunt a wave, Ben?" he said gently. "She's been watching us like a mother hen."

While Ben was briefly distracted, Isaac pulled Ben's leg into position.

Ben screamed. His face blanched white.

With shaking hands, Isaac splinted the leg firmly. He had to get the kid off the cliff. How was he supposed to do that with a drop-off and no rope? There wasn't time to think about another plan, not with Ben going quiet and almost limp.

He tapped his fingers on his shoulders to signal Ben should put his arms around there. "My part is to do the climbing," he said. "Your part is to hold on tight."

Isaac maneuvered the boy into a piggyback hold, taking as much care as possible with Ben's leg.

"I got lost." Ben's words were barely audible, more breath than sound, but they hit Isaac like a fist gripping his heart.

"Yeah," Isaac said, his voice rough. "Easy to do in the dark."

Isaac clung to the rock face. The extra weight hindered his balance. Each step felt excruciatingly slow.

His mind shouted. *Hurry. Hurry.*

The rocks cut into his hands. He remembered this from his days as a teen when he and Ed had challenged each other.

"Gonna have to do some scouting together come spring. Won't be long before you know the lay of the land." And the cliffs. No answer from Ben.

"My pa used to say Ed and me could find our way home with our eyes closed and our boots on backward." One side of his mouth kicked up at the memory.

The wind gusted again. His arms were starting to feel like lead weights. He looked up—caught Clare's face looking down at him. The trust in her eyes . . .

It hit him hard on the side of that cliff.

It couldn't have been easy for her to accept his help. Isaac was a marshal, and he'd never met a criminal that trusted the law. Her family was probably the same.

She'd kept Isaac's secrets from the beginning. And he knew it wasn't because she wanted to use them as leverage or hold them over his head.

Clare had a good heart.

He knew it like he knew the land under his feet.

He kept his focus locked on her and scaled the last few feet. Near the top, he flattened himself against the rock wall while Clare gripped Ben under the shoulders and pulled him up over the cliff edge.

The weight lifted, Isaac pulled himself up over the ledge and rolled to his back on the flat ground, heart pounding. He sucked in a few breaths, then shakily raised himself to a sitting position alongside Clare. She held Ben nestled in her lap, his injured leg carefully extended, her hands gently patting Ben for other injuries.

The grit and pebbles embedded in Isaac's palms smarted, and his shoulders still quivered. He closed his eyes as he breathed deeply. Clare's gentle fingers grazed the scrape on his cheek.

"You hurt yourself."

His muscles, tense from the climb, relaxed at her touch, and he lost himself in her eyes. An expression he hadn't seen there before made him long for more. He had a crazy notion to reach up and brush a stray tendril of hair behind her ear.

"Thank you," she murmured, her voice quiet but earnest. Her wide, full lips pressed into a faint smile. The ground began to tremble with the beat of horse hooves, and the moment was broken. Drew, Ed, and Eli appeared on the bluff.

"Clare, hold his shoulder. Marshal, take the other side please. Hattie will cut away his boot." Doc Powell directed with a calm authority. Clare felt as shaky as her nephew, who lay pale and small in the examination bed in the doctor's office.

Isaac stepped up to the bed, like a soldier obeying his commander's order.

"Aunt Clare, is she gonna cut my boot?" Ben's face scrunched, tears flooding his eyes again. "I won't have a pair of boots then. I'll only have one. I can't just have one boot!" His cry escalated, his body tensing.

Isaac put a hand on Ben's shoulder. "We'll get you new boots."

"But, but . . . my ma got me these boots," Ben cried, overwrought.

Hattie, Doc's teenage daughter who was acting as his nurse, shifted her attention to Clare while the doc bustled away. Clare tensed, needing to comfort Ben without unraveling the delicate topic of his parentage. At least Eli wasn't here to chime in. He'd stayed on the homestead with Drew and Kaitlyn. She opened her mouth, but before she could speak, Isaac interjected.

"We'll hold on to those boots. It's not every day a man gets injured and has his boot cut off. We'll keep them as a souvenir."

"All right," Ben sniffled. "Can we put them in your special chest?"

A muscle in Isaac's jaw twitched. Clare dropped her eyes. Nothing was resolved between them. He'd returned from the main homestead this morning to a crisis. And risked his life to save Ben. But Isaac didn't want a wife or a family.

"We'll see," Isaac said softly.

Clare tried to focus on Ben, but the scent of disinfectant was so cloying she found it hard to breathe. When they'd arrived, the doctor had said he'd never seen a break so bad.

The tinkling sound of glass bottles startled her. She jumped.

Clare watched as Hattie dosed Ben with something on a rag and he slipped off to sleep. Apprehension tightened her chest. How would she pay the doctor? She closed her eyes and willed herself not to think about it now. Ben was safe, and he would heal.

Doc Powell motioned for Isaac to join him near the doorway. They were still close enough for her to hear every word.

"Your wife is agitated. I think it might be best if she left the room. We need to keep the patient calm."

A fiery blush burned across her cheeks. She stared at her threaded fingers and waited for Isaac to tell the doctor that she was not his wife.

When the silence went on for a moment too long, she braved a glance and found Isaac watching her. He arched one brow. The movement drew her attention to the bruise forming beneath the scrape on his cheek. Blond stubble shadowed his handsome jaw, but it was that mesmerizing dimple that truly stood out—especially when he flashed her a reassuring almost smile.

"She's a strong woman. She'll want to stay."

Something in his manner and words unlocked the tension in her chest, and she breathed deeply for the first time since they'd found Ben on the cliffside.

Isaac strode back to her side, his focus on Ben. Why hadn't he told the doctor she wasn't his wife? Just yesterday he'd been livid, ready to send her and the boys away. She didn't come up with any answers as the doc and Hattie worked. After what seemed like hours, Doc pulled her and Isaac aside.

"We'd like to keep Ben here overnight. We'll want to observe him as the laudanum wears off. I'll check for broken ribs, new bruising, and signs of internal bleeding."

Clare's eyes went to Ben, still out, pale as the bleached sheets on the bed.

"He'll sleep for a bit longer. Why don't you go stretch your legs and get something to eat?"

She knew she should eat. But her stomach was still knotted so tightly that she wasn't sure she could force anything down. "I can't leave him," she murmured with a look over her shoulder at the pale sleeping boy in the bed.

"Won't do him any good if you faint away from hunger," Isaac said.

"He's right." The doctor was already moving away. She could only imagine how busy he was, and he'd spent hours helping Ben this afternoon.

She shook her head. She felt sick at the thought that Ben had been hurt because of her negligence. She'd been sleeping so deeply she hadn't heard him rustling around in bed or climbing down the ladder. Had she heard the snick of the door closing in the deep of night?

"I don't like being away from the boys," she whispered to Isaac, aware of him standing just behind her shoulder and Hattie across the room, cleaning up the supplies on the counter behind the bed where Ben rested.

She knew Eli was safe on the ranch, knew that Drew and Kaitlyn would watch over him, but there was a part of her that wished he'd come along too, wished she could watch over him every moment of the day. Especially now.

"This wasn't your fault." Somehow Isaac had followed the trail of her thoughts.

She sniffled, then widened her nostrils to keep the tears burning behind her nose at bay. "Of course it was. I'm their aunt. I'm supposed to watch over them."

"He shouldn't have snuck out. He's old enough to know better."

That was the marshal talking, the same man who'd given Ben a gentle lecture about what'd happened in the night as they'd ridden toward town in the wagon. Clare had spent the time staring daggers at Isaac, but Ben had tearfully hung on to every word.

But when she sent a sharp glance over her shoulder, Isaac was watching Ben with a soft expression on his face. When Isaac caught her looking, his face hardened, turning distant.

"Ed wandered off once," he said now. "He was eleven, if memory serves. The horses had gotten out of the corral, and he went after them too close to dark. Got lost. He was out all night before I found him the next morning, shaking and sniveling and crying."

She wasn't sure the affable Ed would appreciate his brother telling this story. She couldn't imagine the calm, strong McGraw brother looking the way Ben had when they'd found him.

Isaac cocked one eyebrow as if he knew she didn't quite believe his story. "Ma was beside herself for a week," he murmured. His hand rested at her waist, and the touch shocked Clare so that her feet moved toward the door at his urging. "Until the terror of that night had time to wear off. And she remembered that us boys were good at getting ourselves out of scrapes."

Clare hung back at the threshold, a blip of fear stalling her feet. Isaac hadn't realized her intention and nearly bumped into her. The warmth of his shoulder brushed hers, and she caught the flash of consternation in his expression.

"You and your brothers must've been good at getting *into* scrapes too," she said, raising her chin.

She saw the slight crinkle at the corner of his eyes, though he didn't crack a smile. Her stomach did a funny flip.

She cut her eyes away and was opening her mouth to tell him she wouldn't leave when he pressed his hand to her lower back again. "C'mon, Clare. Let's get something to eat while he's sleeping. And then if you want to sit at his side all night, you can."

She couldn't. But somehow, she let Isaac lead her out of the office and onto the boardwalk.

Outside, the sun had fallen low behind the buildings lining the street. The moon was making a showing in the dusty-pink sky. Clare could just make out the subtle twinkle of the first star. Her stomach grumbled, but she didn't think she could eat. A couple of men moseyed down the street, and a staccato of raucous noises intruded into their silent stroll. Clare, no longer able to hide her confusion, blurted, "Why did you lie?"

He narrowed his eyes, his focus down the street.

"In the doctor's office, he called me your wife, and you didn't—" She cut off her nervous babble.

"Doc's a busy man. He doesn't keep up with folks. Besides, I thought that's what you wanted." His eyes took on a gleam she couldn't read when he looked at her again. Her face heated, but she didn't look away.

"I thought you wanted us to leave. Isaac, I don't want to put you or your family in any more danger."

"You won't. You were right too, Clare. Those boys deserve a real pa, not an outlaw. Wasn't that the point of all of this?"

Yes, that had been the plan. Before she'd come to know the McGraws. To know Isaac McGraw, the man who still wrestled with his past. Clare let her eyes caress his face: the strong, handsome jaw, the beautiful, discerning green eyes, and the expressive mouth that could light up her world if he learned to smile again.

"I can't pretend anymore," she whispered.

No more secrets.

No more pretense.

Isaac took her hands in his. He looked down at her, his expression serious. "No more pretending. We should get married. Make it real."

Isaac's words landed between them. Clare blinked up at him, her chest tightening. She drew in a shaky breath. "You mean it?"

His jaw flexed as he gave her a curt nod. "I'll share my name with you. But that's all it can be." His voice was low, steady, and brutally honest.

The words knocked the air out of her. *That's all it can be.* Even as the finality settled in, Clare understood the magnitude of what he was offering. A man like Isaac McGraw didn't give anything lightly, especially not his name. He wasn't offering love. He was offering safety—hers and Ben's and Eli's—and that was more than she'd dared to hope for after he'd found out the truth about her.

She swallowed hard.

Her voice wavered as she answered, "Yes."

His hands tightened around hers. Relief flickered in his eyes before his usual guarded expression returned.

"Good," he said, stepping back and releasing her. The cold night air swept between them.

Clare turned her face away, trying to rein in the storm of emotions churning inside her. She didn't love him—not yet. But she was falling, little by little, and she didn't know how to catch herself.

Twelve

A RE YOU SURE ABOUT THIS?" ED STOOD beside Isaac in the modest parlor the next morning, self-assured and at ease as if this was just another ordinary day—not the day he'd been called without warning to witness his brother's wedding vows. The preacher's wife had welcomed the wedding party into the parlor to wait for the preacher to return. He'd been called away to visit Mr. Slotkin, another parishioner, and would return any minute now, and Isaac's wedding would commence.

Isaac stuffed his sweaty hands in his pockets. Of their own accord, his eyes went back to Clare, perched on the narrow sofa across the room. His cousin Merritt talked animatedly, but Clare's attention was focused on him. He looked away, noting Ed's white shirt and starched collar.

"I'm sure," Isaac murmured, his voice barely audible. He wasn't sure about anything, but he wasn't going to tell Ed that. He'd stayed the night at Ed and Rebekah's tiny apartment above the newspaper office and hadn't slept a wink.

"Because just a few days ago, you were pretty adamant about sending her away," Ed challenged softly.

"Things change." His eyes fixed on Clare again of their own volition, some invisible line pulling his gaze to her whenever she was nearby.

Things change.

An echo of their words last night. Things had changed. She was in more trouble than he'd thought. Especially now that Ben was injured. Victor Barlow's sister. He kept reminding himself that his time as a marshal was over, but when he married Clare, there was a good chance he'd be pulled back into the violent world he'd left behind. His gut twisted. Clare, however, was quiet, her expression unreadable. She'd been reserved when they'd checked on Ben at the doc's office last night. He'd thought she was simply worried about Ben. When he'd picked her up this morning, he had witnessed a myriad of emotions pass across her lovely face as they'd walked side by side to the parsonage.

Ed continued his inquisition, his voice buzzing and biting like an annoying gnat. "I know you like her. We all do—"

"I don't like her," he snarled, keeping his voice low.

Ed's mouth snapped shut.

"This isn't about me," Isaac ground out. "It's about her nephews. Those boys need a pa."

Ed's eyes widened. Was he surprised? Or questioning Isaac's ability to be a father to the two boys? The previous night, on the boardwalk, in the wake of Ben's rescue, Isaac had felt some of his old self-confidence return. He had a chance to redeem himself, and he was going to take it. But in the black of night, sleep had evaded him, and the voices in his head had tormented him with doubts. What did he know about being a father?

The ropes in his gut tightened. He wasn't fit for the role of a pa. He'd gotten Cody caught in his deadly crossfire. Opening himself up like that again was like opening his chest and exposing his heart. The sudden urge to escape, to walk away, was so strong that he shifted his feet.

Ed stepped closer, turning in so that his back was to Clare and Merritt. Isaac met his brother's sober gaze. Ed, his biggest competitor when they were in their teens, the brother most likely to ruffle his feathers, had mellowed with Rebekah's influence. His brother's expression radiated a powerful concern.

"If you do this, it's forever. There's no going back. Are you sure?"

Panic swept through his chest and settled at the base of his throat.

"I said I was," he muttered. He swallowed hard. Was he?

The front door squeaked open and shut behind the preacher. Isaac turned to go and greet him. Ed's hand clasped Isaac's arm, a steel band around his bicep, his stare intent. He wouldn't let it go.

"I care," Isaac said. "I care about her. And the boys. Happy?"

Ed studied him, then nodded, giving Isaac's shoulder a squeeze. "I'll stand by you."

Isaac gave a tight nod in return. The weight of everything

unsaid pressed on him. He could keep Clare and the boys out of the public eye and isolated at the ranch until Ben healed up. He'd have time to figure things out, to tell his brothers about Clare and the Barlow Gang. But not today. Not until they'd had time to breathe. Clare was already stretched thin with worry for Ben, and he didn't want to add to it.

Moments later, Isaac found himself beside Clare in front of the preacher. Her small hands were clasped together in front of her, prisoner-like. At least she wasn't rubbing that scar. She gave him a tremulous smile. All he could think was—beautiful. Prettier than all the sunsets he'd ever seen in his twenty-six years. And she was going to be his wife.

"We are gathered together here in the sight of God, and in the face of these witnesses . . ."

The preacher looked to Ed, then Merritt.

". . . to join this man and this woman in holy matrimony, which is an honorable estate instituted by God . . . mystical union that is betwixt Christ and his church, which holy estate . . ."

The admission Ed had wrenched out of him reared through his mind. This was supposed to be a marriage in name only. A marriage to protect Clare and the boys. But somehow it was more.

Something was squeezing at his heart again, making it burn. He wanted to smile, reassure her, but he couldn't make his lips obey. The gravity of what they were about to do was closing off his throat.

"If any man can show any just cause why they may not

lawfully be joined together, let him speak now or else hereafter forever hold his peace."

Isaac didn't dare look at his brother, but he had a sharp awareness of him at his side. Today, his childhood rival was his fiercest ally.

The preacher instructed Isaac to take Clare's right hand in his.

Over the drumming in his ears, Isaac heard himself say, "I take thee, Clare, to be my wedded wife, to have and to hold from this day forward, for better and for worse, for richer or poorer, and in sickness, and in health, to love and to cherish, till death do us part."

The band around his chest cinched tighter when he registered the sheen of tears in her eyes, she quickly blinked away. The preacher led her through reciting her vows.

"I take thee, Isaac, to be my wedded husband, to have and to hold . . ." Her voice trembled slightly, and she searched his eyes. He wished he knew what she was looking for and that he could give it to her. His hand jumped with a slight tremor. Her fingers tightened around his, steadying him. ". . . from this day forward, for better or for worse . . . to love and to cherish, and to obey . . ." She swallowed hard on that word. ". . . till death do us part."

The preacher closed his worn black leather Bible and pronounced them man and wife.

"You may kiss your bride."

Clare had started to look down, but now surprised eyes flew to meet Isaac's. She had to have known that was how weddings ended.

Isaac let one hand settle on the curve of her cheek. He

leaned in, aware of his brother watching and the preacher. Right. There. His lips met hers in a soft, tender kiss.

He intended only a quick brush of his lips against hers, but the moment they touched, he felt a jolt like lightning buzz through him and heard her quick intake of breath—like she'd felt it too. The unexpected sensation had him stepping back. He released her, their hands dropping awkwardly between them.

Merritt and Ed were there along with the preacher's wife, offering congratulations. But he felt off-kilter, relieved when Clare said they should get back to Ben.

He'd married Clare.

Now he could only hope he hadn't made things worse.

Clare raised a hand in a parting wave to Merritt and Ed after leaving the parson's house. Her other hand rested in the crook of Isaac's elbow as he drew her down the boardwalk toward Doc Powell's office. All around her, the day awakened like any other, but Clare felt out of sorts. The sun spilled over the small town of Calvin, warming the wooden buildings that lined the main street. The scent of freshly brewed coffee wafted from a nearby café, mingling with the earthy aroma of horses and hay. The chatter of townsfolk blended with the rhythmic clapping of hooves on the dirt road. But part of her was still back at the preacher's parlor.

She'd felt the tension in Isaac as he recited his vows, right through their linked hands. She'd been waiting for him to call the whole thing off, even as she'd wrestled with her own conflicting emotions. Was this a mistake? Tying herself to a man who didn't really want to be married? Should she run farther from Victor's grasp? She hadn't come up with an answer to her whirling thoughts before the preacher had pronounced them "man and wife."

And then . . .

Isaac had kissed her.

The thought of his kiss made her misstep. Isaac steadied her with his hand beneath her arm and sent her a questioning glance. She smoothed her skirt and tried to smile, hoping he would ignore the blush she knew was scorching her cheeks.

Perhaps he was as discomposed as she was, because he kept his silence. Which left her to stew as they continued walking.

She hadn't realized how deep her feelings for Isaac had grown until the moment his lips had touched hers.

She wanted more than a marriage in name only. She'd come to care for the man who protected everyone else but couldn't protect his own heart. He'd given up his own comforts so she and the boys had a place to live. His honor and loyalty to his family ran deep. If she could win his heart, that would be her greatest treasure.

She sighed. It was out of the question. She knew it. The marriage was for the boys' sake. That was the deal they'd struck. She wouldn't, didn't dare, ask for more.

Maybe she didn't deserve more.

Lost in her thoughts, Clare failed to see that a woman and her boy were passing too close. Isaac instinctively drew her into his side.

"How about we have the café pack a breakfast basket

before we head over to the doc's?" Isaac said. "Ben will be hungry."

Oh, she hoped so.

A short time later, Clare had a wicker basket packed with food over her arm as Isaac ushered her back onto the boardwalk.

She hadn't missed the surprised and then curious looks they'd garnered during the short time they'd been inside the café.

A dozen people saw you get off the train in Calvin with the boys in tow. All it will take is a few questions to find out who you left the train station with.

Isaac had warned her about tongues wagging in town. It wouldn't be long before everyone knew they'd married, even though neither of them had breathed a word.

Her stomach knotted. Was she putting the McGraw family in danger? Putting them right in the crosshairs of Victor's sights? She knew he would come looking for the boys. Had prayed the change of trains would throw him off the scent.

Had she done enough?

It wasn't only Clare and the boys in danger now. It was Tillie, Jo, Kaitlyn, all of them.

She'd thought there would be a relief in taking Isaac's name. In having someone other than herself to rely on.

But as the preacher's words had rolled over her, she'd felt a fierce protectiveness for Isaac rise up inside her.

Had she made the right choice?

"We should see about those boots," Isaac said as they passed the general store.

She started to protest, but he raised one eyebrow in challenge. "He'll be up and around before you know it. And winter's coming on. He'll need them."

He was right.

But she wasn't exactly flush with money. "I can't pay you back," she murmured, ducking her head when a plump woman passed by them on her way out of the store.

For one moment, a flash of what looked like frustration lit his eyes, but then he nodded toward the door. "Get the boots. Ben's my responsibility now."

His words were clipped and brooked no argument.

But she still prickled with the urge to fight as he trailed her into the store. She didn't want to be a burden to him. A responsibility. How could she ever make him see her differently after all the subterfuge and this difficult start?

He didn't even want a wife. He'd said so himself.

Her head was ducked as she fingered a fine pair of boots on a counter against the far wall. Isaac was yards away, lingering over the jars of candy on display.

The boots were too fancy. Ben wouldn't be able to stand on that foot for weeks. Maybe they could wait for this purchase . . .

When she raised her head, she realized there was a teen boy behind the counter, talking to Isaac.

Rather, talking *at* Isaac.

". . . exciting to be a marshal. Goin' after real bad guys. Shoot-outs."

Isaac had shut himself off. She saw it in the set of his jaw, the long-distance stare, and the way he didn't meet the kid's eye.

She picked up the boots and made for the counter, sidling up beside her new husband. "Would you wrap these for us?" she asked.

She could feel the tension radiating off Isaac. Had a flash of memory of the way he'd shaken when he'd been faced with that bear attacking the boys.

The shop clerk had taken the boots and turned to the back counter, where brown paper lay ready to wrap items. But he was craning to look over his shoulder, his curious gaze still intent on Isaac.

"This store is so neat and tidy," she blurted. "I can tell you're a well-organized young man."

She felt more than saw the cut of Isaac's surprised, disbelieving look.

The young man puffed up with pride.

"How long have you worked here?" she asked.

The teen's hands flew over his wrapping now. "It's my pa's store," he said. "I've been working here as long as I can remember."

"You've a fine work ethic." She smiled widely as he passed the package over the counter. "Look how perfectly the wrapping is folded." She tilted the package in Isaac's direction.

He grunted.

She narrowed her eyes at him, but it was to no avail as he quickly paid for the boots and ushered her out of the store.

At least he'd lost some of the tension he'd carried.

He didn't comment on the way she'd distracted the boy as they made their way down the boardwalk toward the doctor's. But she caught several thoughtful glances sent in her direction.

Maybe she couldn't bring a large dowry to this marriage. Maybe there was the possibility of danger trailing her. But this was something she could do for Isaac. Smooth the way when someone brought up his former job. Distract his family from worrying over him too much, smothering him.

She caught another glance. Brushed a strand of hair behind her ear and hoped he wouldn't notice the way her cheeks were warming.

This time he asked, "Are you going to tell Ben about the wedding?"

She pressed her lips together. "Not yet. I think it's best to talk to Eli first when we get back to the homestead."

His jaw tightened and his lips pulled into a frown. He steered her past a barrel of brooms displayed outside a store, then down a side street.

"Do you think Eli's gonna be upset?" he said.

It wasn't really a question. Eli had acted out in front of Isaac numerous times. Isaac knew what he was getting in to. But she couldn't help herself from trying to smooth things over.

"He'll come around," she said hesitantly. "He misses his home. His pa."

She was opening her mouth to say more when she caught sight of a man exiting a general store across from the café. His frame and gait seemed eerily familiar. Her eyes locked on the man. That hat . . .

It couldn't be.

Alarm pulsed through her. She swiftly turned her head

away from the intruder, her grip on Isaac's arm tightening. Isaac pulled her closer, instantly alert.

"What's the matter?" he demanded. He tracked her gaze, his other hand moving instinctively to his side. Finding no gun, his fingers pulled into a tight fist.

She pressed her face into Isaac's shoulder and felt the tension coil in him. After a few terrifying moments, she backed away from Isaac, watching the man round the corner and stride out of sight.

"Who is he?" he asked, his voice low with a dangerous edge.

She had to get off the street. Hide. But Isaac gripped her elbow in his strong hand.

"Clare. Who is that man?"

"That's one of the Barlow Gang," she whispered. "If he's here"—anguish lodged in her throat—"that means Victor is here too."

Thirteen

ISAAC WATCHED CLARE PRESS HER FIN-
gers to her lips and slowly shake her head. She turned her
back to Ben, moving to the window.

"I don't like this," she said, her voice a watery whisper.

"I know." Isaac moved to stand at Clare's shoulder, a few
feet from Ben back in the exam room.

A few minutes had passed since the sighting of Lyle
Mueller, one of Barlow's men. Clare had insisted on rushing
back to the doc's, fearing that Ben might have been taken
by Victor or one of his men.

Isaac glanced over his shoulder at Ben, sitting up in bed
now. Clare had been overwhelmed by relief and burst into
messy tears.

Ben had stirred, coming awake. "What's wrong, Aunt
Clare? I ain't dead, ya know."

Isaac returned his attention to Clare, watching for danger out the window while Ben devoured the warm bowl of porridge on his lap.

"I want to go back to the cabin," Clare said. She yanked her sleeve down over her scar and knotted her fingers in front of her, her knuckles white.

He'd prefer to hole up at the main homestead. His brothers could help him defend Clare and the boys if need be. And with Ben's broken leg and low fever, they needed help.

He pulled the curtains back a few inches and peered out the window. A few townsfolk dotted the boardwalk. A man entered the saloon across the street. He checked to the west—no sign of the marshal yet. He'd asked Doc Powell to track down Marshal O'Grady and send her over.

He let the curtain drop and turned back toward Clare. "We can't take Ben out of town on horseback." She knew it. Jarring his leg might worsen the injury. They would need to take the wagon, which would be slow. Visible. He couldn't get Clare and Ben out safely until the Barlow Gang was out of the picture. But he'd been out of commission for a good long time. He needed help.

The bell on the other office door jingled. Clare startled. Marshal O'Grady appeared at the exam room entrance.

"Doc said to come quick," Danna said, concern etched on her face. From beneath her worn hat, the marshal's eyes darted from Isaac to Clare, caught his hand at Clare's back. With a subtle tilt of her head, she signaled for them to follow her into the outer office. Isaac dipped his chin and herded both women into the hall, where Ben couldn't hear their conversation.

"Got trouble," he said. "Clare spotted one of the Barlow Gang out on the boardwalk. They're wanted in three states." He swallowed back the words to explain what a threat they were to Clare and the boys.

The marshal studied Clare. "How are you acquainted with the Barlows?"

Clare's back tensed under his hand. He moved it, slipping his hand over her smaller one. Danna's gaze caught the move. If she was surprised, she kept it hidden.

"Clare's had some run-ins with the Barlow Gang."

Danna knew there was more to it. It was there in her pause before she said, "We'd better get a move on, then. Clare, can you identify him?"

"I saw him," Isaac blurted. "I'll go with you. Clare needs to stay with Ben."

Danna's raised brows were almost hidden under her hat brim. He knew why. He'd turned her down flat when he'd returned to town and she'd asked for his help. Now he was volunteering.

Danna glanced over his shoulder, through the doorway to where Ben was chattering to Hattie. He seemed just fine. But there was no way Isaac was letting one of Victor's gang near Clare. Not a chance.

"Fine," Danna said. "If you're sure that's the way you want to do this."

He wasn't sure, but he moved to follow the marshal to the door.

Clare snagged his hand and tugged him to a halt. "Please, be careful," she said, her eyes pleading.

"Doc keeps a hunting rifle in the back storage room," he told her. "Just in case."

Clare looked like she wanted to say more, but there wasn't time. He squeezed her hand and followed Danna down the hall and out the door.

Standing in the marshal's office a few minutes later, listening to Danna brief two deputies and her husband Chas, Isaac felt the panic rising to choke off his air supply. What was he doing?

"McGraw—Isaac."

His eyes flashed to Danna. The door was open, and the deputies had already moved onto the boardwalk after digging up an old Wanted poster for Lyle. It was a decent likeness, close enough to help the lawmen spot the outlaw in a crowd.

"I need you in your right mind for this. I don't want to lead my men into an ambush."

The door banged shut. Isaac tensed. Danna handed Isaac a gun belt strapped with a revolver.

It felt like a thousand-ton weight in his hands.

"Strap it on, McGraw. If you spotted one of the Barlow Gang, there are probably more on the way. I need all the help I can get."

He stood frozen, staring at the stupid gun belt as if it were a rattler.

In his mind, he saw his hands shaking on the rifle stock, unable to shoot the man who'd almost killed Rebekah. Unable to shoot the bear when the boys had needed him to.

He laid the gun belt on the desk.

"I can't shoot," Isaac said, swallowing back the shame. It was the first time he'd admitted it out loud, though

Clare knew. "I can identify the Barlow man, but I won't go armed."

Danna studied his face for a long time. Humiliation burned inside him, but he clenched his jaw and kept it at bay.

She gave a quick nod. "Let's go."

His pulse rushed in his ears as he followed Danna onto the boardwalk.

Chas O'Grady and another man Isaac didn't know strode down the boardwalk, away from them.

Danna waited, brows raised, until Isaac fell in step with her.

She led the way across the street and turned in the same direction as Chas, walking parallel. "We'll check each establishment," she said. "If we spot him, we'll signal the others."

It was a sound plan. Lyle wouldn't know that he'd been spotted, that the law was aware of his presence here. Danna would want to catch him unawares, keep any store proprietors or shoppers out of the line of fire.

Children's laughter floated on the brisk breeze, and Isaac realized it was a school day. It must be recess time. Kids playing.

But his mind used the sound and took him right back to the dusty street on the day Cody had died.

A tall form rounded the nearest building, and Isaac startled badly enough that Danna whirled to look at him.

It was Jack. Merritt's husband. He sent a concerned look between Danna and Isaac. "I was just coming back from lunch at home. You look like you're working. How can I help?"

Danna quickly filled him in, and Isaac didn't miss the narrow-eyed look Jack sent him.

Jack's right hand had gone to the revolver strapped at his waist. His intentional glance at Isaac's lack of belt and weapon was enough to make Isaac flinch.

Jack and Merritt had only been married for six months, but the man had been folded into their family. Knew Isaac's history but not why he'd left the Marshals.

Isaac felt a beat of trepidation. Was he leading the love of Merritt's life into a situation he wouldn't survive?

But it was too late to protest as Danna tipped her head and indicated they should keep on.

The leatherworks was empty save for a young woman behind the counter. She glanced up curiously as Danna and Isaac entered for only a moment and then ducked back outside to the boardwalk where Jack kept watch.

Chas waited at the corner of the next street up. When he caught sight of them, he tipped his hat at his wife.

"That's the signal," Danna murmured.

Chas motioned to the saloon. The other deputy must be inside.

"Think it's him," Chas said as they joined him out of sight of the swinging doors. "But you'll want to take a look to be sure."

"We can go through the back," Danna said.

Chas pulled a face, muttering about how the owner wouldn't be happy.

Isaac found himself sandwiched between Danna and her deputy husband as they moved through the small kitchen area and a hallway that led to the front bar.

Every instinct was on high alert as Isaac put his back to the wall, ready to peer through the door when Danna cracked it.

He was attuned to every sound. Soft footsteps from upstairs. Hadn't been able to keep himself from clocking all the exits.

He almost felt like he was on the job again.

But it was the bolt of pure terror that hit when Danna reached for the door that brought reality crashing back in.

He couldn't be the reason someone else got killed.

By the time the sun cast long shadows through the doc's front-room windows, Ben had gone back to sleep, and Clare had wound herself up tighter than a coiled spring. She'd never been in the middle of one of Victor's heists, but he'd often read aloud the newspaper accounts of his crimes. His voice had filled with a maniacal glee as he'd recalled the bankers they'd beaten and locked inside bank safes to suffocate. The dry-goods stores looted and ransacked while the owner sat tied to a chair at gunpoint, their livelihood destroyed. Victor's men were cruel and degenerate.

Isaac . . . Her mind flashed to him carrying Ben up the cliff. What if he was out there right now, bleeding from a bullet Lyle would delight in putting in him?

What was taking so long?

As if in answer, the door eased open with a soft creak, and Isaac's tall form stood on the threshold. Tall, strong, and alive. Her immediate urge was to run to him and throw her arms around him. Instead, she hugged her waist. Everything was so off-kilter since the wedding.

"Are you all right?" She scanned him from head to toe.

He nodded, his eyes pinned to her face.

She breathed in deeply. "And the marshal? Her deputies?"

"Everyone's fine, Clare. But Danna needs you to come down to the jail and identify Victor's man."

Hattie slipped into the room.

"Hattie will sit with Ben."

She couldn't refuse, no matter how much she wanted to. She was enveloped in numbness as she trailed Isaac outside, down the boardwalk, and to the marshal's office, which was apparently also the jail.

Isaac followed her into the marshal's office. She hesitated in the doorway, not wanting to look past the desk to the three jail cells beyond. The single room with a wide desk and a few chairs seemed even tinier knowing that an outlaw from her past was in one of those cells.

"We need to know if anyone else is in town," Isaac whispered from behind.

Lyle Mueller sat on a metal cot behind bars, his hands that were tied with a rope balanced on his knees, his expression tight-lipped and mulish.

"Is this him?" Danna asked.

Clare didn't have time to answer before recognition dawned on the man's face. His wiry brows shot up, and his lips turned down in an angry sneer.

"What are you doing here?" he spat.

The man seemed smaller, almost impotent, absent the

shotgun and pistol he always carried. Lyle's sinister glare settled on Clare. The air in the room thickened. All eyes shifted to Lyle. An uneasy silence followed, then Clare took a step forward and raised her chin defiantly.

"Did Victor send you after me?" Inwardly, she winced at the uncertain note in her voice.

Lyle clamped his mouth shut, eyes glittering. But he couldn't hide the genuine shock that played on his face. His eyes darted around the room, bouncing from the marshal, back to Clare, and onto Isaac. Clare crossed her arms, staring at him.

One of the deputies spoke up. "Could be scouting for some kind of robbery?"

The thought of Victor and his gang here, in Calvin, for nefarious purposes made her feel sick inside. Imagining the shop boy on the other end of Victor's gun was terrifying, and she blinked away the awful thought.

Danna mulled this over. "Found him loitering near the train station. Go ask the business owners nearby if he came inside."

Isaac's silent presence behind Clare's shoulder reminded her of the information they needed from Lyle. She had to push to get the words past the knot in her throat.

"Who else is here?"

Lyle smirked. "No one else here but yours truly. Victor wants his boys back—that's all he cares about." His tone held the annoying singsong tone that meant he was lying. "He's gonna kill you when he finds you," he taunted, a malevolent gleam in his eyes.

She turned away quickly, heart hammering like a fist

against her ribs. Isaac was right there, escorting her outside onto the boardwalk, a comforting hand at her elbow.

She couldn't breathe.

He took her hand in his.

"I want to go home," she whispered, her throat closing around the word *home*. For the first time in her life, she had a home where she truly felt safe.

But if Victor's men had tracked her to Calvin, they could find her on the homestead.

He squeezed her fingers. "You're not alone, Clare. Not anymore."

Fourteen

ALMOST THERE," ISAAC CALLED OVER his shoulder to Clare and Ben. His hat was pulled low over his brow, shadows obscuring his eyes and accenting the tension in his shoulders.

The wagon crested the top of the hill, and the homestead came into view. But the once comforting sight of the house, barn, and squatty bunkhouse didn't bring a sense of peace and safety. Instead, as the last light faded, the shadows deepened, turning the familiar buildings into looming shapes, and a sense of dread clung to her.

Sitting with Ben in the back of the wagon bed, on a pile of blankets to cushion their ride, Clare had struggled to keep Ben's leg from being jostled about while scanning the landscape for any sign of Victor or one of his men.

Ed had ridden Bullet alongside the wagon for most of the trip, leaving Rebekah with their cousin Merritt in town. They'd been about an hour into the journey when Clare had overheard Isaac disclose her true identity in hushed tones to Ed.

"She's a Barlow, then?"

Clare had felt Ed's penetrating glance but hadn't been able to look up, afraid of the censure she would see in his face.

"She's a McGraw now." Isaac's gruff reply reminded her of the promises he'd made at the parsonage.

The fresh start she'd hoped to find with a new name was a pipe dream.

Isaac had sent Ed on ahead when they'd been a few miles from McGraw land. Would Ed tell everyone the news about their marriage before they arrived?

A deep, unsettled pit formed in her stomach as she realized that everyone in the family would learn about her past. Would they be angry? They had a right to be. Clare had piled more trouble onto an already teetering stack. Tears threatened.

The wagon rolled up to the barn. Jo and Tillie leaped off the porch and began to whoop and holler as they sprinted to the wagon. Ben perked up. He used his arms to lift himself so he could peer over the wagon side rails.

"Look who's glad to see you, Ben," Clare said, a little surprised by their joy.

A wide smile spread across Ben's wan face, and Clare let out a breath of relief. He had been close-mouthed all day—a sure sign something was off.

Drew ambled out of the barn, offering her a hand down, then wrapped her in a warm embrace. "Welcome to the family," he said before shooting Isaac a look that said *We'll talk later.*

Kaitlyn pulled Clare close. "So good to have you back."

Nick and Eli lagged behind Kaitlyn. Nick embraced Clare gently for a few brief seconds but kept his expression guarded.

Eli climbed into the wagon, positioning himself beside Ben. Leaning into his brother, he whispered in his ear while glaring at Clare. Her hope for an easy evening wilted. She bit her lip and narrowed her eyes at him. She needed to speak with him about his father. Eli was as capricious as the wind, and he would be conflicted. He idolized his pa.

Without missing a beat, Isaac stepped closer, his voice low as he addressed the two brothers. Clare couldn't hear the words, but the look on Eli's face suggested a kind of reluctant acknowledgment.

The girls circled round Clare. Jo gave her a quick hug.

Tillie threw her arms around Clare's waist, pressed her cheek against Clare's ribs and squeezed. "Pa said you got married. We didn't even get to see the wedding." She pouted for a moment before her expression brightened.

Clare's gaze shot to Isaac. Their eyes met briefly. Her heart kicked up. What should she say? Had it only been this morning they'd recited their vows?

"We didn't get to wear our Sunday dresses and throw flower petals," Tillie added. She lifted her chin and kept her arms around Clare's waist. Clare smiled and brushed a loose chunk of hair back from Tillie's forehead.

"Yes, well, it only happened this morning."

"That means it's still your wedding day," Jo announced seriously.

"Can we bake a wedding cake? I love cake!" Tillie's voice amped up until she was fairly shouting "cake."

Isaac rounded the wagon.

"Whoa there, girls," he said, like he was settling wild horses. "It's late. Let's get Ben settled inside before we start baking."

Clare was surprised the girls were planning to bake a cake this late in the day. Kaitlyn stepped in.

"Girls, clear the way so Uncle Isaac can bring Ben into the house." Kaitlyn paused to let Tillie skip ahead while she and Jo strolled up to the porch and into the house.

Clare met Eli at the back of the wagon as he climbed down. As he stood waiting for Isaac to lift Ben, Clare reached out to hug him, but he pulled away and crossed his arms defensively. The rejection was a sharp pinch to her heart.

Eli was growing up. He was every bit like the dynamite they'd found. No telling what would set him off.

Isaac pulled on the blankets so that Ben was scooted to the tailgate. He carefully gathered him in his arms and carried him to the house, Clare and Eli trailing.

Kaitlyn met the group at the door and held it open to allow Isaac to pass.

"Ben here is going to need to stay in the main house." Isaac's gaze went to Ben's leg. "Obviously he won't be climbing the stairs anytime soon. Think we can put him in David's bedroom?"

Kaitlyn sent him a reassuring smile. "Of course. David

can bunk with Nick until Ben heals up enough to stay at the cabin."

Before Kaitlyn turned to lead them to a small bedroom off the kitchen, she flashed Clare a reassuring smile. Anxiety twisted in Clare's gut again. Kaitlyn didn't know about her past. This wasn't the joyous homecoming expected of a newlywed couple. Her marriage was hardly a real marriage at all. Isaac didn't love her, but he had offered her refuge and his family name, which to the McGraws, meant something.

Stop clinging to girlish dreams, Clare Barlow. No. She was Clare McGraw now.

She would play the hand she was dealt.

"I'll get Ben settled," Kaitlyn volunteered. "Go, take a moment to freshen up."

Exhaustion pulled at Clare's shoulders, her whole body weighted down with fatigue and stress. She drifted to the kitchen to pump water to wash with but paused outside the dining room, hidden from view. The brothers were hunched over the dining room table, sketches and notes, even legal papers, scattered across the tabletop. Clare's eyes lingered on one of Isaac's hand-drawn maps from his scouting work on the ridge. The river and the bridge were sketched from a bird's-eye view, long, dark vertical lines representing the rails, with shorter horizontal lines for the railroad ties. Icy dread seized her.

Nick said, "I rode out there yesterday to take a closer look at how far the digging has progressed. Those dunderheads are digging so close to the bridge that one major rainstorm might wash the bridge supports out."

Maybe that's what they want, Clare thought. But why?

"One thing's for sure, the bank will be ambushed with angry patrons if their shipment of cash gets delayed," Ed said.

Bank. As if the word was the missing piece, everything clicked into place. Victor was here for a robbery. He could use Quade's dispute with the ranchers to stage a train robbery, then walk away, no one the wiser.

She stepped into the dining room. Drew's shoulders tensed. Ed and Nick exchanged quick glances with each other, caution written on their faces. Isaac moved toward her, his brows furrowed, his green eyes concerned.

"Clare?" he asked. Placing a comforting hand at her elbow, he drew her farther into the room. Kaitlyn entered behind her. Sensing the tense atmosphere, she slipped quietly into Drew's side embrace.

Clare took a shaky breath. "Ever since we saw Lyle in town, I've been trying to figure out how Victor found me. I'm certain I didn't leave a trail." She sucked in a breath. "What if he didn't come to find me? What if he's here for another reason?"

"What do you mean?" Nick asked.

"The train … he likes to rob trains." Her voice trembled. "And he has a fondness for dynamite." Clare swallowed hard against the growing terror. "What if he's using Quade's dispute with the ranchers to stage a train robbery? Blow up the bridge. Help Quade divert the river. Rob the train. And ride away." She could see it so clearly—the whole thing unfolding—and it made her skin prickle with dread. His brand was stamped all over this.

Isaac's lips turned down in a grim frown. "We saw

Quade's men unloading crates at the train station the day I met Clare and the boys."

"You really think that's why he was in town?" Ed asked Clare.

"Yes, I do. Lyle, the man Marshal O'Grady is holding, was surprised to see me. He said he and the gang were coming for Eli and Ben, but he was lying. They're coming for the gold and money."

"Working with Quade," Nick added absently as he leaned over the table to riffle through some old newspapers on the sideboard. It was the only thing that made sense.

He blew out a long whistle as he lifted a newspaper and began scanning below the fold. "You may be onto something. The Union Pacific coming from Cheyenne passes through here in three days. There'll be passengers on that train along with the gold and bank notes in the safe."

"Victor isn't just a thief," she began, her voice wavering despite her best effort. "He does more than hold up banks or coaches or trains. Sometimes, for the right price, he takes on other jobs. Breaking someone out of prison, stealing a safe from your enemy—if the job's worth it, he'll do it."

Isaac's brow furrowed. "That's not common knowledge about the Barlow Gang."

Clare nodded, her throat tight. "Victor has a network of outlaws across the West. If Quade wanted him, all he had to do was talk to the right people."

Isaac's hand tightened on her elbow. He muttered under his breath, "Everything lines up—the crates, the timing. Quade's up to something more."

Kaitlyn stared at her across the room. Her hand went to

her belly in an unconscious protective gesture. "How do you know so much about this gang of outlaws?" she asked, her tone a mixture of curiosity and wariness.

A wave of nausea washed over her. Clare would have to tell the truth. She wanted to tell the truth. She blinked back tears.

"I'm not Clare Ferguson. I'm not a widow with two boys. I lied"—she looked around the room—"to everyone. I'm Clare Barlow. Sister to Victor Barlow."

Drew was taken aback but recovered quickly. Tears streamed down Clare's face as she watched Kaitlyn's expression turn from shock to hurt. Ed and Nick dropped their gazes to the table. They already knew the truth about her identity.

"I promised their mother before she died that I would not let the boys follow in their father's footsteps. Anne and I saw the mail-order bride advertisement, and I . . ."

"They all know about the letters," Isaac said. He stepped closer to Clare, his hand on her elbow both a support and a protective gesture. "If you'll excuse us, Clare and I have some things we need to talk about."

The serious discussions were interrupted by a late supper followed by the evening chores. Isaac heard Tillie and Jo tramp upstairs, Jo declaring she wasn't the least bit tired with every step. Drew had dispatched Eli and David to the bunkhouse. They had been bedding down there for several nights now. Isaac was glad for David's influence over Eli.

After everyone had scattered for evening chores and to

get the children in bed, Isaac stood at the corner of the dining table, looking down on a crudely drawn map that spread over several pages. A map of the corner where McGraw land met Quade land. The river and the bridge were sketched in.

When Nick had questioned Clare earlier, she'd revealed that sometimes the gang would meet at Anne's farmhouse. Clare had overheard enough of their planning to make a guess about what Victor was up to and how he would carry out his plan. They had put Xs on the map where Clare thought it was most likely for Barlow to place the dynamite to blow both the bridge and move tons of dirt to change the riverbed.

Isaac was at war with himself. He wanted to save the ranch, same as Drew. He knew how much it meant to all his brothers. He ran a hand through his hair, frustration and fear clawing at him. He hated this. He hated that they were caught up in some outlaw's scheme with Quade.

Clare's voice echoed in his mind. *I know how to disable the dynamite. My father taught me. He used to take me with him when he set charges . . . showed me all the ways to disarm it.* Her tone had been so matter-of-fact, but Isaac sensed something deeper. It was strange, a man like her father teaching his daughter to handle explosives. But he had, and even if she hadn't used it in years, the knowledge was there.

Isaac wondered if her father had realized, before it was too late, that Clare wasn't meant for that kind of life— not because she was weak but because of her strength. She wouldn't go through with it because she refused to let herself become like him. Isaac felt a quiet admiration stirring within him.

He stared at the maps until his eyes blurred. He couldn't see any way for this to end without bloodshed. And he was desperately afraid it would mean the grief of losing his nephew. Or one of his brothers.

"Isaac."

Clare's soft summons turned him away from the table.

She stood nearby, in the doorway of the small downstairs bedroom where David usually slept. One hand was braced against the jamb, and with the other, she waved him forward.

He was drawn to her, but he told himself it was the lines of exhaustion around her mouth that put his feet into motion.

She looked apologetic. "Ben asked for you."

He nodded and angled his shoulders to pass her in the doorway, aware of her watching him as he approached the bed. Ben looked so small, skin still pale from the long wagon ride he'd endured today. Isaac perched on the edge of the bed, careful not to jostle the boy's leg.

"You were brave today, riding in the wagon for so long when I know it hurt your leg."

Ben jutted his chin out. "Didn't hurt as much as on the way to town."

Isaac tousled his hair, still gentle.

"Wish I was in the bunkhouse with Eli 'n' David." Ben's gaze flicked to the window, where the shadowy outline of the bunkhouse was just visible across the yard. "Bet they're having fun."

"They'd better be asleep," Isaac said.

But he'd guess that Ben was right and the older boys were whispering, discussing the news that had unfolded today and how they might be a part of whatever the men planned tomorrow. Drew and Ed wanted to take immediate action, but they hadn't decided what to do. He and Nick would join them later to discuss their next steps.

Ben yawned widely.

"Clare said you needed to talk to me," Isaac prompted.

Ben fiddled with the quilt, bunching it in his fingers. "We're McGraws now, right?"

Isaac heard Clare's indrawn breath from the doorway.

But if he'd expected her to join in the conversation, he was disappointed. "That's right," he said.

Ben ducked his head so Isaac only had a view of his cheek and chin. "And McGraws take care of each other?"

Those were Drew's words. How many times had Isaac heard them after Pa had passed, when it'd seemed like they wouldn't have enough food to last through the winter? When he'd come home from the Marshals and hadn't even been able to look his brother in the eye when he asked whether he could stay on.

He hadn't realized he'd said them enough times to Ben that they'd stuck.

There was a knot in his throat that made his voice rough when he answered. "McGraws do."

"If—if some bad men are here"—Ben's voice was so quiet that Isaac had to lean in to hear—"what if they try to take me 'n' Eli away?"

Oh.

Ben had heard enough of the adult conversation to be afraid. To know his pa's gang was close.

Movement from the doorway drew Isaac's attention, and he glanced up to see Clare with one hand over her mouth and tears welling in her eyes.

Isaac put his hand on Ben's shoulder. "You don't need to worry about that. You're right about being a McGraw. No one is going to take you away from your aunt."

Ben watched Isaac's face carefully, then broke into a small smile. "I like it here. But not all the chores. Just the ones in the barn."

Isaac couldn't help but smile.

Ben settled further under the covers, and Isaac took that as his signal to leave.

Clare met him in the doorway, her eyes shadowed. "Sorry," she whispered.

He didn't understand why and was about to press when Drew, Ed, and Nick traipsed into the room and gathered at the table.

Clare retreated to stand by the window, her hand pressed against her mouth, her slim shoulders sagging as she stared into the darkness outside.

A heavy quiet settled over the house like a thick wool blanket. Darkness had fallen—it was too late to send for help. They'd have to wait till morning.

Drew, Ed, and Nick crowded around the table, their heads bowed over the map. Isaac should join them. But his eyes were drawn to Clare, alone by the window.

He shouldn't. But he went to her anyway.

As he stepped behind her and caught their reflection in

the windowpane, Clare's eyes met his in the shiny glass. He saw her misery and fear.

It's going to be all right.

The words to comfort her stuck in his throat. They both knew how dangerous Victor and his men were. If they had hitched their wagon to Quade and his henchmen, they made for a formidable group.

Isaac let both hands settle gently on Clare's shoulders and felt her tremble.

"We'll think of something," he said. He'd promised to protect her and the boys, but ever since she'd made the connection between the dynamite on Quade's land and her brother, Isaac had been spinning. Trying to figure out a way to keep her safe. To protect the McGraw land. And keep his family from getting themselves killed. He was failing at all of them.

"I'm afraid Victor's going to send another scout into town," Clare whispered. "Discover Lyle's in jail, and the trail will lead right to the boys and me."

Of course she would be worried about the boys. Ben couldn't be moved easily. He'd been pale and hurting by the time they'd arrived home. Clare was effectively trapped here.

"We won't let them get close," he promised. And watched the reflection of her face crumble. Her shoulders convulsed with the effort to hold back a sob. He went a little light-headed. What could he do? She didn't trust him to protect her. Why should she? She'd seen firsthand how broken he was.

"I can't stand the thought of your family—of you—being hurt—because of me."

Her halting words surprised the breath out of him. He went stone-still.

"I—care about y-your family."

Her show of emotion wasn't about not trusting him. It was about her. And her big, open heart. She loved with all of her being. For a moment, he let himself wish he wasn't so broken. That he had something more of himself to offer her.

He found himself squeezing her shoulders and pulling her back against his chest. His jaw brushed her temple and rested there for a scant second.

When his unfocused gaze rose, inched higher and sharpened, he caught Drew's reflection from where he stood across the room. Drew jerked his chin, summoning Isaac.

He pressed his jaw into Clare's hair, breathed in the scent of her, then let her go.

He crossed to join his brothers at the table. She stayed where she was but turned her back to the window and faced the room to listen.

"Quade's got at least a half dozen men working on re-routing the river," Drew said.

Isaac placed both hands on the table and flicked a glance to Clare. "How many in the Barlow Gang?"

"There have been as many as a dozen, but for the jobs that involve dynamite, Victor only takes the men that have been with him for a while and have experience. I would guess maybe four plus Victor."

"We should sneak over there. Scout out if Barlow's really

there," Nick said, drumming his fingers on the table. "So far, all we have is conjecture."

"No," Isaac said. "We get the marshal and her deputies involved. Three days is plenty of time. We need to let the law handle this."

"We've got the advantage of knowing the area," Ed said. "Maybe we could take them out one by one."

Drew's eyebrows rose as though he liked the idea.

"No," Isaac said again, his voice a little louder, urgent. "Tomorrow, we ride for the marshal. Get the help we need."

His eyes cut to Clare. She sent him a slight nod.

"Danna will help," he said. "She'll have a plan."

Hopefully one that didn't get his brothers killed.

Fifteen

THE FAMILIAR RUSH OF THE RIVER greeted Clare as the wagon pulled into the clearing in front of Isaac's cabin. The warm autumn sun filtered through the now bare branches, reminding her that winter was not far off. She'd once found the modest log cabin and lean-to comforting, but knowing Victor was in the area had destroyed her sense of peace and contentment even here. An unsettled feeling churned in her stomach.

Eli rode in the back of the wagon. When Isaac reined in, her nephew frowned at the cabin and the lean-to.

"Why'd you have to bring me here?" he complained.

"You know why we're here. To pick up some clothes and the supplies we have stored here and take them back to the main homestead." Isaac also wanted to make sure no one had been sniffing around his property.

And Clare needed to have a serious talk with Eli before they returned to the homestead and Ben. A part of Clare feared Eli had unintentionally been privy to too many conversations among the adults. He was thriving working with the men on the homestead, but occasionally, like now, his old attitude resurfaced.

"I should have stayed back," Eli muttered. "David will have to wrangle that stubborn calf by himself and muck the stalls and feed the horses without me to help."

He scrambled down from the wagon and headed to the stoop.

Isaac called to him. "Fetch some water from the river, and give the horse a drink, son."

Clare was stepping off the wagon when she saw Eli go still and whirl round. Red bloomed on his cheeks, and his dark eyes narrowed.

"You can't tell me what to do. You ain't my pa." He stomped to the step and sat down.

Tension strung tight through her shoulders as she looked over the wagon to Isaac, whose gaze was shuttered.

"I'll talk to him."

Isaac frowned but nodded. Exhaustion lined his handsome face. He had worked part of the day helping his brothers catch up on more preparations for the winter. The work had to be done. While they'd waited for Nick and the marshal to return to the homestead, he'd offered to take the late-night watch.

Clare met him at the threshold. "Thank you," she said. He nodded, grabbed a bucket, and headed down to the river.

The air was stale inside the cabin, but everything else was neat and tidy. She left the door cracked open to let some fresh air in, then motioned for Eli to sit on the stoop while she lit a fire inside. Once finished, she steeled herself and returned to sit beside Eli.

He dropped his gaze down, stubbornly avoiding her eyes.

"Isaac is not your father. I'm not your mother either. But this is the plan your mother made for you. She believed it was God's providence."

How could she reach the stubborn boy?

How did one explain a thought like that to a young boy? A boy who'd lost his mother and had been taken from the only life he'd known.

His frown twisted into a more hopeful expression. "Is Pa really here?" The hunger in his question made Clare's heart skip a beat.

"I don't know," she said. "Isaac and I saw Lyle Mueller in town earlier. But not your pa."

His eyes lit. "Do ya think Pa came for me?"

Clare stared at him. Her heart hurt for the boy who so desperately wanted his father's love.

"I want to go back to Pa," Eli pushed.

She wanted to scream. How could he want to go back to that?

She breathed in deeply, clenched her jaw, wrestled to keep her tone even. "Eli, have you forgotten what it was like back in Missouri? Remember how many times we didn't have enough food?"

She and Anne had tried to shield the boys from the worst of it, but she would never forget the terror of those bare cupboards. Or the panic of knowing there were only a handful of bullets left. She couldn't afford to miss her target when she hunted game.

"He was cruel to your mother when she burned some of the fish you spent all morning catching. We didn't eat that day, remember, because your pa brought his gang to the farm."

Clare moved her shoulder into his and looked down into his face. She could see her words had hit their mark, the way his thoughts raced behind his eyes.

His ma had also burned herself that day. The long red welt on Anne's arm had taken weeks to heal. She'd hidden her pain and kept cooking while Victor called her unspeakable names. Clare had never heard any of the McGraw men use such language.

"Pa wants me," Eli said stubbornly.

"What about Ben? It wasn't that long ago he beat him, left bruises on him, because he forgot to feed the chickens first thing one morning."

Eli's face crumpled at that. He was so protective of his little brother.

"Ben likes it here," she pressed.

"Ben's a baby," he scoffed, but she could tell he didn't mean it.

"Eli, you have to trust me on this. We need the McGraws."

He didn't answer, just got up and went inside the cabin. She heard him clamber up the ladder to the loft. The floor moaned when he threw himself on the mattress. Clare heard his stifled sniffles and a shuddering breath. She wanted to hug him like she had when he was little.

She took a shaky breath, then got to work packing. In no time, her baskets and crates were stacked near the door. Maybe Isaac could use some help gathering some things from the lean-to. She'd give Eli a little time alone in the cabin.

The door was propped open. She leaned a shoulder against the door frame. Isaac looked up from the chest on the wall and cast her a grim look.

"I suppose you heard all that?" She sighed and stepped into the small space. It smelled of hay and horse and earth. A rope hung by the door on a peg, and she fingered the tightly twisted strands of twine. Her heart was still tender from seeing Eli's hurt. "I wish my childhood had been more like yours must have been."

He turned questioning eyes on her, his wide stance blocking the chest and the gun belt lying on the quilt like some deadly snake poised to strike.

She hesitated, then took a deep breath. "My pa and Victor . . . and my oldest brother Billy, were gone for months at a time, leaving us at home without money or food. Have you ever been so hungry that the gnawing in your stomach never goes away?"

He shook his head. His eyes filled with compassion.

"I was a little older than Eli when Anne's grandpa began to teach me how to hunt, fish, and grow vegetables. He stayed on the farm with us after Victor and Anne were married. I think he knew his time on this earth was running out. He and Anne showed me there was another way to live." Clare coiled the rope in a circular motion, looping it snug against the peg.

"Grandpa Ferguson knew I would need those skills for survival after he passed. But it was hard for a young girl at first, you know, killing and dressing rabbits and such." Revulsion churned her stomach thinking about the other things she'd been forced to do.

Isaac's expression turned from compassion to anger. His fingers curled into a fist.

"I didn't actually like Anne at first." She lowered her voice, glancing at the wall that she knew was too thin for secrets.

Isaac looked surprised enough that she went on.

"She seemed like such a Goody Two-Shoes." The confession stung a little now, and she moved to the end of the cot, where an extra quilt was unfolded and had been thrown half off the bed. It was easier to remember if she had something to keep her hands busy. "All these rules. No lying. No stealing."

When Anne had caught Clare with a chicken she'd butchered after stealing it from a neighbor, there'd been no punishment or shouts. Only a disappointment that had somehow stung worse.

"Once I started to see her in a new light, I didn't think she'd want to know me if she knew the things I'd done for my pa and for Victor."

It had taken weeks of chores together, of Anne's gentle nature and patience, to break through the walls that Clare had built to protect herself.

"She taught me about true forgiveness. About real love."

Anne had had such a pure heart. Clare still couldn't understand how she'd fallen for Victor—cruel, heartless

Victor. But after Eli had come, Anne was trapped in the marriage, and they'd all known it.

"I think I would've liked her," he said quietly.

Clare was surprised to find a tear tracking down her cheek and quickly brushed it away. "You would have," she murmured. "Victor wasn't always like this, you know. There was a time when he tried to be better. He loved Anne. For a while, I thought maybe she could save him." Her voice faltered for a moment before she continued. "But my father wouldn't let him go. He called him weak. Kept dragging him into their schemes. And when Anne got pregnant, Victor got desperate. He tried . . . but honest work wasn't enough. That's when he gave in and decided to do a few jobs with the gang. A few jobs turned into a way of life, turned Victor into someone not even Anne could reach."

She took a breath and continued, hugging the folded quilt to her chest. "After Grandpa Ferguson died, Victor and my father began using the farm as their hideout. As the years passed, Anne and I . . . we were happier when they were gone—we were trying to do our best by the boys. We never meant—"

"I can see how much you love those boys, Clare," Isaac said. "They're fortunate to have you."

Clare loosened her grip on the quilt and let out a slow, trembling breath. "I wish I could believe that. But sometimes I think being a Barlow means I can't ever be . . . anything else. Anne married into the name, but I was born to it. It's in my blood."

Isaac's gaze was steady, the heat of his presence filling the small space between them. "Anne took Victor's name, sure, but she didn't take his legacy. You said yourself she was a child of God first and last. And that's what made her special—not the name, not the past. Don't you think the same could be true for you?"

Her throat burned as she swallowed back the knot rising there. "It's different for me, Isaac. I've done things—things Anne never would've even dreamed of."

"You know Jacob's story?" Isaac asked gently. "He was born clutching his brother's heel, and his name meant deceiver. He lied, cheated—did plenty of things he wasn't proud of. But when God got ahold of him, He gave him a new name: Israel. A name that meant he'd struggled with God and come out changed."

Clare blinked hard, her vision blurring. "You think that's true for me?"

Isaac's mouth curved in a faint smile. "I think you're more than the name you were born with, Clare. And I think God's got a way of making people new no matter where they came from or what they've done."

Clare set the quilt back on the cot. She faced Isaac, her fingers going to the scar on her wrist. "I just want Eli and Ben to have a chance at something better. Like the life you and your brothers had growing up here."

"We had a good childhood." Isaac stepped toward her and stilled her nervous movements with a hand over hers. "But it wasn't perfect. Pa lost his temper at times."

She liked having him close.

"You're good with them. So patient. I want that for Eli and Ben."

"They'll have it." As Isaac said the words, the air seemed to grow charged between them.

She couldn't keep herself from voicing her hope. "When this is over, will we . . ." She hesitated. She didn't deserve someone like him. But she wanted him. "Can we be a real family?"

Isaac felt the weight of Clare's question. He pulled his hand from hers and looked away. He forced out the words jammed in his tightening throat. "I don't know if I can—I honestly don't know." He knocked his hat off with one hand and ran the other through his hair. He had no idea if he could be what she needed or what the boys needed. His attention involuntarily shifted to the gun belt and the revolvers lying on the cot. How was he supposed to protect his own when he couldn't even make himself strap on his gun belt?

"I understand," she said softly, but he could clearly see the hurt on her face.

To hide it, she brushed past him and reached into the open chest by the cot. She pulled out one of his old dime novels. "What's this?" she asked as she let the pages flip through her fingertips.

He couldn't stop watching her. "Nothing," he said absently.

Reaching inside the chest again, she pulled out another one. "There must be nearly a dozen books here." A wry smile emerged on her lips. "Are you secretly an author? What's your pseudonym?"

He scowled as heat flushed up his neck. "Hardly. Rebekah is the author around here."

Clare's eyebrows rose in surprise.

He sighed. "I used to read these kinds of books," he said as she handed him the book with the cowboy on its cover. He scoffed. "They're all about some made-up hero who swoops in and saves the day, then rides off into the sunset." He laughed bitterly, tossing the book back into the chest.

"I knew a guy like that when I was a kid," he said. "A deputy from town named Sam Nerat. Thought he was a real dime-novel hero. Made such a big impression on me that I made it my aim to be just like him."

Clare's expression went soft.

Nerat had been the fastest gun in Converse County. Back then.

"I practiced all the time with my revolver and some cans. So much that Pa got onto me for wasting ammunition. I musta been about fifteen when I came to town with Pa to fetch some supplies. He was busy with the store owner, and I wandered off down the street. Saw a coupla drunk cowhands terrorizing a stray dog."

He shook his head at the memory of it. Imagining David doing something stupid like Isaac had made him realize how young he'd been. And that Drew had been right about what would come of Isaac's arrogance some day.

He sighed and pushed the words out. He'd started this conversation. Might as well tell her all of it. "I drew on them. Shot the barrel of one of their guns before they could draw it." He'd gotten lucky. The man had been drunk enough that his draw had been slow. "Scared them off."

"And rescued the dog." She finished the story for him.

He didn't deserve the soft, admiring light in her eyes. "Few minutes later, when I was walking back to meet my pa, one of 'em came out of nowhere—"

The drunk had skirted through the alleyway and emerged from behind a different shop. Back then, Isaac hadn't known to watch for danger lurking in every direction. "Knocked me off my feet. Roughed me up a little, but he didn't hit me."

Isaac had been terrified for those few moments.

The drunk had seemed to come to his senses, seemed to realize how young Isaac was. And stupid.

"He let me go, and I went back to Pa. Never said a word." He'd been ashamed at the time. Drew's warning words from two years before had echoed through Isaac over and over for the entire wagon ride home.

"I thought if I could work hard enough, prove myself"— he shrugged—"that I could be like Deputy Nerat. Better."

"Where is that deputy now?"

"I dunno. I saw him in action once." Reminiscing was easier than talking about his own mistakes. "Fella walked right up to the stagecoach to rob it. Nerat called him out— demanded he leave town. The robber pulled his weapon right there on the street." Isaac remembered being enthralled with the drama unfolding even as Ma had tried to drag him to safety. He'd watched over his shoulder as Nerat had drawn faster than the blink of an eye and shot the outlaw through the heart. "I wanted to be just like him." His voice turned to gravel. Breaking free of the memory, he realized Clare stood just behind his shoulder. Hovering close but not touching him.

"I was—for a while, until my arrogance got Cody killed." Just like Drew had predicted. "I can't let anything happen to Ben or Eli."

Or you.

He heard an unexpected noise. A sniffle. And turned to see her with a wrinkled nose and misty eyes. She dropped her gaze to stare at the belt on the bed. He did too.

"You don't have to do this," she whispered. "We can have the marriage annulled. The boys and I—we can just go."

Run. She meant run.

"No!" The instant rejection rang out. Inside him, it felt right. "Won't solve anything," he rasped. "Victor will still come looking. And I have to protect my family."

"It doesn't have to be you," she argued. "The marshal can round up a posse. It's not your job anymore."

It's not your job anymore.

Isaac felt that to his core. Another gutshot. Could he really leave this job? Or was it a calling, like Nick had said? Something that was a part of him, that he'd never be able to escape. He'd taken an oath when he'd joined the Marshals. One he'd vowed to keep to his grave. Same as the vows he'd said to her.

"I meant those vows I spoke," he said before he could stop himself.

He caught the hope in her eyes, another bullet ripping through him. After all she'd been through, she could still hope.

He reached for the belt and began to strap it on. She

grasped the brace of pistols lying on the cot and brought them to him, one in each hand. He cupped his hands over hers. They stood there, suspended in time.

"You are my hero, Isaac McGraw."

With their hands still connected, he leaned in and kissed her. Saw the sweep of lashes against her cheeks as her eyes closed. The press of her lips was heady and sweet. He kissed her tenderly. Outside, the horse whinnied. Eli's boots thudded in the dirt.

Isaac pulled back, touched his forehead to hers. He took a second to memorize her flushed face and the way her eyes shimmered with something he didn't dare name. Lifting a hand, he curled some loose hair behind her ear. "We'd better go."

She nodded and released the revolvers to him. He only hesitated a moment before slipping them into the holsters at his hip. His family needed him. Clare needed him.

Sixteen

MOMENTS AFTER THE KISS, ISAAC HAD gone down to the river to fetch the reed whistle he and Ben had made together. Passing through the propped-open cabin door, folded quilt on her arm, Clare played his words in her head.

I meant those vows I said.

Isaac's words, his kiss, had bolstered her hope for the future.

Eli wasn't waiting in the wagon like she'd asked.

"Eli?" she called out. A sudden rush of wings startled her. Three doves scattered from somewhere near the back of the cabin, and the sound made her skin prickle with an uneasy chill. Disoriented, she registered someone stepping out from behind the corner of the house. A blow to her shoulder sent her crashing to the ground. Victor loomed over her, and Clare was paralyzed with terror.

From nearby, a footfall sounded. Eli stood frozen, his

gaze ricocheting between his pa and Clare. Recognition and hope flashed across his young face, quickly replaced by horror as Clare tried to scramble to her feet and Victor's boot drove into her stomach. The vicious kick had Clare doubling over, one shoulder pressed to the ground

"Run, Eli," she cried. But her nephew stood frozen with shock and fear.

"He ain't gonna run." Victor stepped close enough to land his meaty hand on Eli's shoulder. Eli quivered, his eyes darting once again from Clare back to his pa.

When Eli didn't move, she pushed to her hands and knees. An ache pulled beneath her ribs.

Run! She willed him. *Race to the woods. Get Isaac!*

Victor's right hand hovered over his holstered gun. "Be still." His threat was obvious, and she had no choice but to obey.

"Where's that man you've been living with?"

Clare tried to hide her surprise. Victor's lips curled into a malicious smirk.

"Been here a few days. I seen him scoutin' from across the river."

Across the river. It was true. Victor was working with Quade. She didn't dare close her eyes, but she carefully drew in a breath through the pain in her ribs and tried to still her spinning thoughts. It was just like Victor to bide his time and strike when she and Eli were isolated from the others.

She needed to distract Victor. Isaac would come. He was wearing his guns. He would do something.

"Where is he?" Victor demanded.

"How did you find us?" she choked out.

Victor spat on the ground, uncaring when his spittle landed on her. "Lyle wasn't the only guy in town. Tom Crow saw you and ducked behind the depot." His tobacco-stained teeth flashed under a thick mustache. "You thought you could outsmart me?" He kicked her booted foot, and pain radiated through her ankle. "Crow tracked you from town all the way to the big house."

Her heart shrank in fear. Victor had already scouted the McGraws' homestead.

She saw Eli register his father's words. David was down at the big house. Tillie and the others. Shadows chased through her nephew's expression. He loved David. Loved the McGraws. Knew what his father was capable of.

Run. She mouthed the word to Eli.

But he remained frozen.

Victor's eyes darted from her to Eli. "Your brother in there?" He jutted his chin in the direction of the cabin.

Eli shook his head almost imperceptibly, and Victor frowned. "What, boy?"

"N-no, sir," Eli stammered.

"Down at the main house, then?"

Clare saw fear and panic cross Eli's features. They both knew that if Victor descended upon the main house, he might shoot the whole family without a second thought.

"Answer me!" Victor demanded.

Eli jumped. "I've been staying in the bunkhouse. Helpin' with the chores, the cattle and such. Been learnin' to rope, Pa." The words rushed out of Eli, each one filled with a hopeful pride.

Victor slapped Eli across the face. "You think you're a rancher, boy? Barlows ain't ranchers." He gave Eli a hard shove toward the cabin. "Git your brother."

Eli stumbled. "Ben's not here."

While Victor was distracted by Eli, Clare saw her chance. She hesitated, guilt twisting in her gut.

I will come for you, Eli.

She forced herself to her feet and ran for the woods.

One heartbeat passed. Two.

She heard Victor's grunt of surprise, the sound of a metal barrel clearing leather.

Clare braced for a bullet to rip into her back. A shot rang out as she sprinted around the trunk of an old elm tree. She pressed herself against the trunk, her fingers clutching at the smooth bark. Breathless and dizzy, she squeezed her eyes shut, wheezing as she sucked in air.

She needed Isaac. Where was he?

Victor fired another shot, this one causing the dirt to fly up only inches from her feet.

"That tree ain't gonna save you, Clare. I want my boys."

"I'm right here, Pa. We can go," Eli cried.

"We ain't goin nowhere without Ben."

Clare panted for breath, trying to calm her whirling thoughts. Could she run to the main house? Through the woods?

Victor had a horse. He'd catch up to her.

She heard his steps coming closer. Clare sprinted to another tree a few yards closer to the wagon. A third shot split the air. Branches snapped in the distance. Victor had missed. She leaned with her hand against the tree for support, her ribs aching with every breath, her ankle throbbing.

Bang!

A shot sounded from only a few feet away, rattling Clare's chest and leaving her ears ringing.

Isaac.

His powerful fingers encircled Clare's upper arm, pulling her farther into the woods.

"Eli's back there!" she cried.

She saw the grim set of his lips as he hauled her down to put their backs to a giant fallen tree.

"I know."

She pressed one hand to her middle to staunch the pain. It was only then she got a good look at his face. Isaac was shaking, and his complexion had leeched to the same shade of gray she'd seen when he'd faced the bear. The blood that had raced through her veins moments ago froze.

He was not going to be able to save them.

Isaac's whirling thoughts were a blend of the past and the present as he huddled behind a log next to Clare.

He'd had a split-second sighting—the fury-inducing moment when Barlow had viciously kicked Clare before Isaac had faded back into the woods, rounding the cabin.

The violence of it had thrown him back in time.

Fingers of hot sunlight licked the exposed back of Isaac's neck where his hat didn't fully shield his skin.

But if he moved at all from where he crouched, half hidden behind an unhitched wagon and a couple of barrels out in front of the grocer's, it might signal to Pickins that he was watching the bank.

Isaac figured Pickins would be striding down the street at any moment. He'd given a warning to the bank owner and manager, and they'd cleared everyone out from inside the bank, just in case.

Isaac was going to follow Pickins into the empty bank and arrest him. There'd be no casualties. It'd be cut and dry. Another win, though this one had been hard fought as he'd tracked Pickins across three states.

Isaac was poised on the balls of his feet when movement from behind him caught his attention.

A startled cry rang out. He knew that voice.

It had taken Isaac far too long to draw his weapon after seeing Victor towering over Clare. Far too long to pick his way silently through the woods. The gun trembled in his hand now as the memories surged.

Isaac twisted, still crouching in his hiding place, only to see Pickins drag Cody out from behind a jumbled stack of crates in the alleyway beside the saloon.

Pickins held Cody in front of him, one meaty arm around Cody's shoulders and across his neck.

Isaac only had a glimpse of Cody's terror-stricken face before Pickins passed out of sight. Isaac eased farther behind the wagon, mind whirling.

What was Cody doing out here?

It hit him like an unexpected punch. Cody had been sneaking around, following Isaac while he'd patrolled the streets and watched and waited for Pickins to arrive in town.

Somehow, Cody had figured that Isaac was aiming to take

down the bank robber today. He must've followed Isaac from the hotel and been hiding behind those crates.

As the realization dawned on him, Isaac edged back from the wagon and crept quickly around the corner of the grocer's, out of sight behind the building.

A shot fired and Isaac jumped. There was a muffled scream from nearby and sounds of other feet abandoning the board-walk nearby.

"That you, McGraw?" Victor called from somewhere distant.

The past echoed in Isaac's ears.

"That you, McGraw?" Pickins shouted.

Isaac's breath was locked in his chest as he leaned his back against the wall, trying to figure out what to do next.

Isaac had been careful to disguise his movements all morn-ing—but he hadn't counted on Cody. If Cody had been fol-lowing him up and down the streets, Pickins could've seen the boy. And then all of Isaac's careful planning and the strategic hiding place outside the bank didn't matter.

Pickins hadn't needed to know where Isaac was.

He'd grabbed Cody.

Isaac peered around the corner to see Pickins in the center of the street, approaching the bank slowly.

Cody was pale, struggling to dislodge Pickins's hold, toes barely dragging the ground. Pickins put the gun to the boy's head.

And Isaac holstered his gun and stepped out onto the board-walk in plain sight. "Let the boy go," he called out.

Pickins turned so he was facing Isaac, but with Cody be-

tween them, only Pickins's head and feet were in view, the only clear targets.

Too small to risk a shot, even if Isaac had his gun drawn.

Cody caught sight of Isaac, and his wide, terrified eyes locked onto his hero.

Isaac tried to silently convey that he would get the boy out of this mess. Somehow.

"Let the boy go, and I'll walk inside the bank with you and get your money." Isaac made his voice as reasonable as he could.

"Why should I believe you—"

It happened before Isaac could blink.

The town marshal ran out from his office a block down the street, revolver drawn.

Pickins turned, taking Cody with him. And Isaac had a perfect shot. Back or shoulder. Isaac drew and fired, but in that split second, Pickins whirled—and brought Cody right with him.

Isaac shouted something incomprehensible even as he saw Cody's body jerk with the bullet's impact. The bullet Isaac had fired.

He was running into the street as Pickins fell from two shots the marshal had taken.

By the time Isaac reached Cody's side, it was too late.

Cody was gone.

There was blood everywhere. But it was Cody's sightless eyes that knocked Isaac onto his knees as despair rushed over him like a wave.

"Isaac!" Clare's frantic hiss drove the memories away for the moment.

Victor fired off another round, this one rattling the branches of an elm a few feet to Isaac's left. The outlaw was getting closer.

Isaac shifted around so he could peer over the log. His movements jostled Clare. She inhaled sharply, and he remembered that her ribs were likely bruised. He tried to send an unspoken apology with his eyes, not wanting to alert Victor to their location.

Victor was a dozen yards away to the west, half hidden behind a sturdy oak. He had one hand clamped around Eli's neck in a punishing grip. Eli was out in the open, exposed.

"Barlow," Isaac shouted. "Let the boy go."

"Eli's my boy. He's stayin' with me," Victor barked. "Ranch foreman told me there was a U.S. marshal livin' up here. But you ain't shootin' like a marshal. You turn yeller?"

"He's using Eli for cover," Isaac whispered.

Clare, already pale, went white, the fear in her eyes raw. "Eli, run! Get away!" she shouted.

"Shut your mouth, Clare!" Victor bellowed and fired another shot, hitting their fallen log with a heavy thump.

"Did she charm you, McGraw? She's got a way with men. Can weave a tale better than a snake-oil salesman. Ain't that a hoot? My best inside man . . . is a woman."

Isaac's eyes tracked to Clare's face. His thoughts went back to the times she'd lied. Victor was lying. Isaac knew it. But part of him—just for the briefest second—wondered if Victor was telling the truth. He swallowed back the bile that burned in the back of his throat.

Clare tensed.

She read it on his face, that moment of doubt. He saw

the hurt etched across her face and the moisture in her eyes before she blinked and looked away.

"We have to get Eli away from Victor," she whispered urgently.

"How?" he ground out. "We can't risk hitting Eli."

She stared at him, both hands fisted in her lap. His mind raced through several options, but he couldn't figure a way out of this without bloodshed.

"We have to do something," she said.

He didn't like the stubborn jut of her chin. "Clare—"

Before he could react, she'd slipped the second revolver from its holster and leaped over the log.

"Don't!"

But it was too late. Clare fired a shot that went a few inches above Victor's head. Isaac watched in horror as Victor aimed his gun at her. She rushed toward him and Eli.

Isaac crawled over the log after her, feeling as if he was moving through molasses.

Everything seemed to happen in slow motion.

Before Victor could fire, a wail erupted from Eli, and he knocked his father's gun hand so that the shot went wild. Victor swatted Eli back, but Eli roared and threw himself against Victor's gun hand. The gun dropped to the ground.

Victor's face was red with rage.

Isaac scrambled over the log, running several paces behind Clare. Victor backhanded Eli, who nearly fell to the ground before his father grabbed him around the waist and hauled him onto his horse.

"Isaac!" Eli shouted. He struggled against his father's hold to no avail.

Clare took aim.

"No!" But Isaac's warning came too late. She fired. Victor jerked but spurred his horse into a gallop. Within seconds, Victor and Eli were gone.

Seventeen

ISAAC STOOD MOTIONLESS, HIS EYES locked on the far-off horizon where Victor had disappeared.

Isaac!

Eli's desperate plea echoed in his mind.

He turned at Clare's frustrated cry. Her hands shook as she desperately tugged at the leather straps, trying to unhitch the horse from the wagon. Bullet's massive frame shuddered, and the horse exhaled with an agitated snort. He should help her, but the adrenaline that had furiously pumped through his veins a moment ago had drained out, leaving him powerless. It had happened again. Played out a little differently, but the result was still the same. He'd failed Eli.

Clare whirled around to face him. "Why are you just standing there?" she demanded, tears streaming down her cheeks. "We have to get Eli back. We can't let him take Eli."

Isaac drew in a long breath, shoved his palms into his eye

sockets. Red and black spots danced before his eyes. He dropped his arms to his sides. She wasn't thinking straight.

"We can't go after him," he said. "Victor has at least four men with him. You said yourself, Quade's men are in on this too. There are too many."

She turned her back on him. But not before he saw the fire in her eyes and the resolute set of her jaw. This was the Clare who had fired on her own brother, who was angry and desperate to get Eli back.

He stepped toward her, needing to find a way to get through to her.

"Clare, if we go after Eli, Victor will try to kill us. Maybe his men will finish the job. Then who will be here for Ben?"

She ignored him, still fumbling with that strap. His eyes went to the gun she'd tucked in the back of her skirt waist. If only he could have taken the shot at Victor when he'd had it.

Suddenly her shoulders slumped. She let out a muffled sob that ripped his gut.

"Clare . . ."

Whirling, she rushed at him. "Stop standing there!" she railed. "Stop looking at me as if I'm out of my mind!" One fist beat against his chest. "I know you've lost trust in me. I don't care. Help me get Eli back."

"We need to go back to the main house," he said. Victor had meant that threat against the family. Isaac was sure of that much.

"Do something!"

She was shattering, and there was nothing he could do

to help her. He stood there, rigid and silent, and let her pound her fists against his heart.

She collapsed against him, forehead against his chest, sobs racking her slim body. He clasped her shoulders but couldn't bear to hold her closer.

"I can't. Clare . . . I can't save him," he choked out. He wasn't her hero. He closed his eyes against the scene that played in his head. The street, the blood. This time it was Eli who lay unmoving.

You killed him.

"I should have known Victor would come here," he said in a rough whisper.

And now his failure would put the whole family in danger. He should have stayed away—never come home. Never married Clare. He wasn't like Drew or Ed. He wasn't a man who could nurture and protect a family.

The sound of horses' hooves drummed in the crisp air, and Drew and Ed eased into the clearing.

"We heard the shots!" Drew said as he reined in. "What happened?"

Clare turned from Isaac, arms around her middle, holding herself together. "Victor was here. He snatched Eli."

Ed's eyes flew to Isaac. His mouth was tight, but his eyes held compassion. Isaac cut his gaze away. He didn't deserve it.

"Victor knows Ben's at the main house," Clare said.

Drew jerked. His horse sidestepped, reading his agitation.

"If we go after him now, we could catch him," Clare pressed.

Isaac's nerves stretched tighter with every word. She sent a beseeching look at Ed.

"We should make a stand from the house." Drew addressed the words to Ed. "Wait for Nick to bring the marshal." His worry centered on Kaitlyn and the kids.

"Clare's right," Ed said. "It will be dark soon. We know the land better than Victor does. We can catch him. The fewer men involved, the better."

"We could be riding into an ambush," Drew said.

Isaac listened while his brothers spoke as if he wasn't there. Clare stared into the woods, looking small and lost. He couldn't stand here and listen to their plans. Not when every plan was a bad one.

He strode to the wagon and finished unhitching Bullet, slipped on the bridle, and was in the saddle before his brothers realized what he was doing. Behind every movement were images of Cody's blood pouring out in the dusty streets.

"You riding with us?" Ed asked.

"I want no part of this," he said, his voice as icy as his heart felt.

He rode off into the growing darkness. He didn't know where he was going—only knew he couldn't stay. Clare was determined to go after Eli. And Isaac couldn't erase the scene that was playing over in his mind. This time it was Clare lying in the street, blood flowing from her chest, emptying the life from her.

He closed his eyes against the thought of a world without Clare.

He'd tried to keep his heart guarded, but she'd snuck inside anyway.

He'd lost Eli. And now he was going to lose Clare too.

Clare watched Ben's chest rise and fall under the quilt. He'd only just fallen asleep, and his eyelashes were clumped together from the tears he'd shed.

"What's Pa gonna do to Eli?" he'd asked tearfully.

She didn't have an answer.

Agitated, she rose from the side of his bed and slipped from his room, past the two brothers conferring over the map spread on the table, and into the kitchen.

Drew and Kaitlyn's children had been sent to bed. It seemed wrong somehow for the household to still be going on with routine tasks without Eli here.

Everything felt wrong.

She needed something to do with her hands while she figured out the next plan for herself and Ben.

Run.

She'd felt the word with every heartbeat since Isaac had ridden off alone earlier.

Victor knew where she was.

Victor wanted his son back.

Victor would cut down anyone who stood in his way.

And Isaac wasn't coming back.

Kaitlyn was at the counter, her back turned to the door. Rebekah stood at her side, neither of them paying a lick of attention to the detritus from the supper preparation that remained out on the counter and needed to be cleaned up.

Neither of them seemed to have registered that Clare had entered the room.

"—never seen Jo so frightened," Kaitlyn murmured. "She was crying."

Rebekah made a noise of reassurance.

Ben wasn't the only one upset to learn that Eli had been taken. Both girls and David had expressed their emotions in different ways when Clare had ridden back to the main house with Ed and Drew.

"We all are," Rebekah said now, voice low.

Clare must've made some movement, because both women glanced in her direction.

There was a beat of awkward silence.

"Can I—can I help clean up?" she asked.

Kaitlyn shook her head tightly, glancing away and out the window where it'd grown dark outside.

Rebekah's face was somehow less open than when she'd been comforting Kaitlyn. The distinction was so slight, but it was there. Clare was an expert at reading folks, every minor detail of their expressions.

"We'll get to it," Rebekah said.

There was no hint of unkindness in her manner. It was more a hesitation.

A momentary hesitation that told Clare all she needed to know.

The two women held her responsible for bringing danger to their family.

She couldn't blame them. Her breath locked in her chest as she remembered the moments when she'd been face-to-face with Isaac as Victor had threatened them. The moment she'd seen his doubt creep in.

After everything—every moment she'd tried to prove her trustworthiness, everything she'd told him that she'd never told anyone else, every tender moment they'd shared—when it had counted, he hadn't trusted her.

Blood will tell.

She felt that same despair wash over her now.

"All right," she said softly. "I—" She shrugged. She didn't know what she'd meant to say, only that her throat was choked with tears. If she'd thought to find the family camaraderie she'd experienced over the past few weeks, she was sorely disappointed.

She blinked back tears as she retreated to the living room.

"Isabella must know about this scheme," Ed argued as he stacked another rifle in the line of guns already on the dining room table.

Clare shivered as she passed by the brothers.

Ed and Drew barely glanced up, and when they did, their eyes were shadowed.

She took a seat on the sofa across the room, one where she could see the outline of Ben's head, where he slept in David's bed, through the cracked door.

Victor had taken Eli. Had hit him. Now she couldn't bear to take her eyes off Ben.

She needed to make a plan—but she was all alone.

"Isabella is as upright as they come." Drew sounded so reasonable, even as he counted bullets and put them into piles in one corner of the table. "She'd alert the marshal if she knew about this."

Ed blew out a breath. "And implicate her own pa?" Ed asked skeptically.

Clare tuned out their conversation, couldn't stop thinking about Victor. Boom. Tom. And the other men in the Barlow Gang, every one of them vicious and cruel.

"Keep Eli safe," she prayed desperately.

"Quade's been keeping a tight rope on her," Drew said, and Ed nodded.

"I guess that new foreman has his thumb on her too."

The dark beauty she and Isaac had met in town, Clare thought. The woman with the fear in her eyes.

"Right," Drew said. Clare watched him open the rotating cylinder of the revolver she had taken from Isaac. He slid a bullet in the chamber. "That leaves, what? A dozen or so men?"

"Quade lost a few when that foreman hired on." Ed threw the oil-soaked rag down on the table. "Telling, isn't it? There are some men that even Quade's long-standing hires aren't willing to tolerate."

Clare's vision blurred, and the brothers' voices faded. She inched her hand into her skirt pocket and fingered the blasting cap she'd found weeks ago. The stairs creaked with Kaitlyn's careful steps. She appeared at the landing, her face tight and drawn, worry lines around her eyes. Clare hadn't even realized she'd gone upstairs. Had she drifted off? She couldn't afford to sleep.

Drew pushed his chair back, rose, and met Kaitlyn at the landing. He took her hand and pulled her to the living room, but Clare heard their whispered conversation in the desperate quiet.

"Tillie is finally asleep again. The girl is terrified. I have to be honest. I am too."

Drew's arms engulfed Kaitlyn in a protective embrace. One that made Clare long for Isaac. She remembered how it felt to be held close by him, the safety she felt with his beating heart against hers. She wanted what Drew and Kaitlyn had.

She'd gone and fallen in love. Thought that she could overcome her past. But as soon as Victor had shown his face, Isaac had realized she was still a Barlow. That had to be the reason he'd left. There'd been no sign of him since.

Clare turned her gaze away from the loving couple, remembering the coldness that had come over Isaac when Victor had told his lies. Tears smarted her eyes.

"Don't worry." Ed glanced up from the table. "We'll get Eli back."

He looked confident and reassuring. She knew he thought she was afraid for Eli, for herself.

She cared deeply for this good, honest, and hard-working family. She didn't deserve their protection or care. She was a Barlow.

Blood will tell.

Clare pressed her palms into her eyes, then dragged her hands down her face. Isaac was right, they were going to get themselves killed. She hadn't wanted to admit it before, but watching Drew's tenderness toward Kaitlyn and Ed's careful counting and re-counting of their ammunition, she saw it clear as day. They were no match for Victor's gang.

And Isaac was already deeply wounded. He couldn't lose

one of his brothers. Clare would never forgive herself if she let that happen.

"I think I'll try and get some sleep." She stood, her legs trembling. "I'd like to bed down in the room with Ben, if you don't mind. I can be right there if he needs anything."

No one protested. A soft chorus of "goodnight" followed her into the bedroom.

Ben slept peacefully in the small room. She stepped close to the bed, watching his chest rise and fall. Long, thick lashes rested against pink cheeks. He'd been inconsolable earlier upon hearing Eli had been captured. Oh, how she loved him. She leaned over and brushed a light kiss on his forehead. She wouldn't let Victor steal his happiness. He was safe with the McGraws for now. She knew what she had to do. It was dangerous, even foolhardy, but it might work.

She lay on the pallet in the thick darkness, fully dressed, and waited an hour or so until she was sure everyone had turned in for the night.

Time to move.

Clare rose from the pallet on the floor, careful not to rouse Ben. Moving with the stealth ingrained in her, she slid the window open, climbed out, and closed it. She raced to the barn and quickly saddled one of the horses. She was already in the saddle when her eyes went to the tools hanging on the wall. There. A small pair of wire cutters, perfect for the job. She snagged them off the hook and rode out into the starry night.

She had one chance to save Eli.

Eighteen

J UST ONE MORE," CLARE WHISPERED. SHE worked by feel in the last moments of dark, racing against the dawn. Her fingers shook as she pulled the fuse and blasting cap from the top of the dynamite stick and cut the fuse in tiny pieces.

She guessed an hour had passed since she'd crossed the river onto Quade's land. Cold had seeped into her bones. She slipped a lone blasting cap into her pocket. Shivers racked her body as she buried the rest of the caps and the remaining powder in the crumbly soil near the bank. She hadn't thought to bring a shovel, and her nails were cracked and bleeding by the time she was finished.

She covered the spot with several large rocks to camouflage the work she'd done.

With dawn painting the horizon pink and orange, she could see that more digging had been done since Ben's accident. Quade's men had widened the river so that a long, flat pond had pooled. Water still flowed toward the Mc-Graws' homesteads, but when the last barrier was broken, it would send the water to a new man-made river carved out in Quade's land.

Her heart sank.

Clare pictured Isaac's cabin and heard the rushing of the cool water. She remembered splashing in the river and Isaac's laughter and his steady hand clasping hers. If Quade's and Victor's plans succeeded, the river near the cabin would become a trickling creek, eventually a dry bed.

She'd done all she knew to do to stop the dynamite blast. Now she needed to find Eli. That was the only thing that mattered.

As she approached Victor's camp on foot, her fingers began to tingle—whether from the cold early-morning air or the surge of blood through her veins, she couldn't tell. At one point, she dropped to crawl on her belly to stay out of sight as the sun rose. The brown autumn grasses were chilled and sliced into her palms like tiny knives.

A horse blew from nearby, startling her. She froze until she was certain no one was moving. Victor's cronies tended to sleep late, thanks to the drink they usually consumed into the night.

She crept around the perimeter of the camp, avoiding the half dozen horses roped near a stand of trees, and crouched behind a flatbed wagon.

A silhouette of a short, stocky man with a potbelly moved near the fire. Shorty Jenkins.

Four canvas tents had been pitched around a large cookfire and an aging chuck wagon. Eli had to be in one of those tents. But which one?

A snore emanated from the tent nearest her. Her heart was pounding in her ears, drowning out any other sound. If Victor's men were asleep, could she creep through the tents themselves? It would keep her out of sight—

Suddenly, she was yanked backward, an arm banded around her waist. She felt the tip of a cold blade against the skin on her neck.

"What have we here?" The familiar and despised voice of Tom Crow rasped in her ear. "Clare Barlow, out for a stroll? I don't think so."

She felt the sting of the blade tip cutting into her skin beneath her chin. Every muscle in her body tensed. She wanted to reach for the derringer in her skirt pocket but thought better of it. Tom would slit her throat in an instant.

"I need to see Victor. To make a deal." Clare made her voice strong even though she quaked inside.

"You ain't in any position to make deals." His arm cinched tighter, crushing her rib cage.

"I have something he needs," she gasped. "For that surprise you have waiting under the bridge."

He hesitated.

"Take me to Victor," she ordered, acting on her brief upper hand.

She'd hoped to avoid Victor completely. To find Eli and run before anyone knew she'd been there.

Too late for that.

Tom Crow kept her upper arm in a bruising grip as he marched her past the horses. Shorty gave them a narrow-eyed look before opening the back of the chuck wagon, the old hinges sending a grating screech into the morning. Men stirred in their tents.

Victor exited the middle tent, bare-chested, as they neared camp. He walked with a limp. She must've hit him. She hadn't seen him stagger when she'd fired, but ... A grim spark of satisfaction flared before dread smothered it. He pulled on his shirt, not paying a lick of attention to them until Tom cleared his throat. Victor scowled when he saw her, eyes lit with deadly anger.

"Where's Eli?" she asked quickly.

"You check her for weapons?" he demanded of Tom.

"Eli!" she shouted.

Tom backhanded her, the hit wrenching her head and making her see stars. "She ain't armed." Tom tossed the derringer on the ground at Victor's feet.

Clare strained her ears. Had that been a sniffle from one of the nearby tents?

"Where'd ya catch her?"

"I came here of my own accord," Clare said evenly. "I want to make a deal."

Shorty snorted as he stepped in and handed Victor a plate of cold beans and hardtack. He was gone a moment later, Tom following.

There was no point in her running. Victor was armed, and the open prairie offered nowhere to hide. Even so, her eyes moved to the horses near the flatbed wagon they'd passed.

Victor stood with plate in hand, scooped some beans into his mouth, and chewed slowly, watching her through slitted eyes. "Tell me what the McGraws are planning," he ordered as he bent and set his plate aside.

"I don't know."

He lunged toward her and slapped her so hard that her head was knocked to one side.

The blow stung, and tears spilled before she could stop them.

"Tell me!" he roared.

She blinked, trying to clear her vision. In a soft but firm voice that had Victor leaning in, she said, "I can't tell you what I don't know." It was true. She'd left the room.

His next blow sent her spinning to the ground.

She lay in the dirt as blood flowed from her nose. Felt the bruise blooming at her right cheek bone. She'd have a black eye soon—not the first he'd given her. But this wasn't the time to fight back. Not yet.

Victor loomed over her. "You bait? They coming for you?"

"No," she croaked. The denial hit hard with all its truth. Isaac was gone. The McGraws were mounting a defense— for their family and legacy. No one was coming for her.

She was more alone than she'd ever been.

She straightened her shoulders as best she could. She couldn't afford to let herself become distracted from her mission. Where was Eli? She couldn't do anything before she knew where he was.

Out of the corner of her eye, she caught movement from inside the nearest tent. A tent flap flicked, and Eli peeked out. Relief washed over Clare. She mouthed, *Run.*

The tent flap slipped back into place. Had he gotten her message?

Victor squatted at her shoulder and grabbed her braid, yanking her head up and back so that her scalp stung. "Anne filled your head with all that Bible nonsense, but I guess it didn't stick."

"Anne believed it was real. And Anne loved you. Her love was real, Victor. She was the only true thing you ever had in your life."

For a fleeting moment, something passed through his eyes—regret, or maybe just a memory—but it hardened just as quickly. "You stole my boys!" he shouted.

A cold and merciless look met her eyes.

"One verse I do like is 'An eye for an eye.'" He chuckled when an involuntary shiver racked her body.

"Where's your yellow-bellied marshal?" he demanded with contempt.

"I took his money and left," she lied. "He made for a terrible husband. Too many rules."

Uncertainty crossed his expression. He let her hair go, and her head flopped down, forehead resting on her arms.

Run, Eli. Please run.

Victor nudged her side with his boot. "You're a Barlow through and through. Like Pa said, 'Blood will out.'"

Victor's mocking of Anne brought the sting of tears. Anne had believed Clare could make a new life for herself, that she could rescue Eli and Ben from the future their father had dictated for them. But Clare wasn't strong enough.

I think you're more than the name you were born with, Clare.

Isaac's words echoed in her mind. She'd read the story of Jacob again, how God had given him a new name—Israel—and a promise that stirred something deep in her soul. *Fear not: for I have redeemed thee, I have called thee by name; thou art mine.*

Mine. She belonged to the Lord.

She was not Victor's sister.

Not a Barlow. Not anymore.

The realization rooted deep and brought a ridiculous sense of peace. She pushed to her hands and knees.

"I'm not a Barlow," she said, meeting Victor's eyes. "I'm a McGraw."

A subtle tremor crossed his hard face, revealing a loss of control. He kicked her in the side. "No, you ain't."

Pain and nausea overtook her. She curled into a ball. A long, breathy moan escaped her lips. Yet the truth settled inside her like a numbing anesthetic.

"Maybe I'll never really be a McGraw. But one thing I know for sure—I'm not a Barlow either." She placed her hand over her heart. "I'm a daughter of the living God. The One Anne believed in until her dying day. I'm His. And that's enough for me."

Victor's face contorted. He drew his gun so quickly she was looking down the short end of the barrel before she could blink.

A calm courage filled her. She would play this out till the end—come what may.

"You can shoot me," she said with quiet resolve, raising a defiant chin. "But then you'll never find out where I buried the blasting caps. And Victor? I took Every. Last. One."

Isaac's frustration mounted as he lay on his belly in the damp grass, trying to peer through the dark and make out Victor's camp. If only he had his field glasses. In the hazy glow of a dying central fire, he could make out the outlines of four tents. What he couldn't determine was the number of scouts prowling and men sleeping in the tents. Or which tent, if any, Eli was in.

Isaac crept forward carefully, drawing nearer to the cliffs and using the brush as cover.

He'd started to ride away from Converse County entirely. Leave his family behind. Leave Clare. He'd gotten as far as the foothills and turned back. He couldn't do it—couldn't just ride off into the sunset.

He wasn't the hero Clare needed, not the hero any of them needed. But he had to do something.

He was still trying to work out his next move when he heard a movement in the brush behind him. He swiftly rolled to his side and drew his gun.

His oldest brother's head and shoulders appeared through the underbrush.

"I never could sneak up on you." Drew smiled grimly. He glanced over at Bullet, standing with the pack horse Isaac had snuck out of the barn.

Isaac's eyes followed the trajectory of Drew's stare and caught sight of the soft brown shawl with its wispy fringe. He'd tied it around his saddle horn.

Clare's shawl.

Isaac wasn't proud of it, but he'd found the shawl in the barn and taken it. He couldn't even say why he'd done it—only that he'd wanted a piece of her with him, even if he didn't deserve her.

Drew's glance swept the rest of the empty clearing, and he moved toward Isaac, eventually crawling on his belly to lie shoulder to shoulder with him. Drew raised a pair of field glasses to peer out over the camp. He pulled the strap over his head and handed them to Isaac. A rush of gratitude swept through him.

"What are you doing here?" Isaac asked, eyes on the camp.

"Same thing as you. Getting Eli back. Capturing Barlow."

Isaac's stomach knotted. Drew wasn't finished, and his face was as serious as Isaac had ever seen it.

"Nick brought back Danna and reinforcements. Ed rode out and rounded up several neighbors. Got a baker's dozen riding with us."

Isaac let that settle on him. Thirteen riding with the Mc-Graws. For so long, he'd tried to keep himself isolated from his family. From friends. Had tried to punish himself. And still, they'd come.

"I'm a little surprised to find you out here," Drew said quietly. "Looked like you were leaving for good."

Isaac lowered the field glasses. "We both know the family would be better off without me."

"What?" Drew snapped.

"I'm not a hero." The words cost him. He turned his face so Drew wouldn't see the emotion he couldn't keep from his expression. "Not the man Clare needs. Not the brother I should be."

Drew shifted closer. "What exactly do you think a hero is?"

Isaac thought of Deputy Nerat. "A man who stands alone, protecting the innocent and leaving a town and its people better for him having been there."

Drew put a hand on Isaac's shoulder. "Look at me. I've got something to say to you. And I'm going to say it looking you straight in the eye. A hero isn't some dime-novel character with a shiny badge and a pistol. A hero is a man like Ed, working from sunup to sundown during calving season to help provide for the family. A woman like my Kaitlyn, who comforts Tillie when she wakes up from a nightmare. And it's you, Isaac, showing those Barlow boys what it means to be an honorable man." Drew's words felt like a relentless assault on everything Isaac believed. He wanted his brother to be right.

Isaac lowered his gaze and shook his head.

Drew squeezed his shoulder. He wasn't done talking. "You were working a mission with the Marshals when Amanda left me."

Isaac felt a beat of guilt. He should've written home more.

"Her leaving broke me. She walked away from me, from the kids . . . I kept asking myself why I hadn't been enough for her to stay." He shook his head, his eyes focused on the far distance and his thoughts in the past. "I was still in that same dark place you are now when Kaitlyn arrived. Ed, Merritt, Kaitlyn. All of them worked at setting me straight."

Was that what Drew was trying to do for Isaac now?

"I knew something had happened just before you came home for good," Drew admitted. "Thought I'd give you time to sort it out. But maybe that wasn't the right thing." He paused, his eyes searching Isaac's. "Nick told me what happened."

Isaac let that sink in. He wasn't angry with his younger brother. Maybe it was time to lay everything bare.

Drew wasn't finished. "You've held on to this grief and shame for far too long. It's like a wound you set festering till it's poisoned everything. You weren't to blame for the tragedy that happened."

Drew's blunt assertion hit like a hammer, battering against the self-blame Isaac had carried for so long.

"But even if you think in that cockeyed brain of yours that you're to blame, you have to know that you're forgiven. God has forgiven you. You know this as sure as the sun rises."

Drew's words hung in the air. A declaration that was too good to be true. One Isaac hadn't dared believe until now.

"You've got to come to the end of yourself and let God be the hero in you. Who do you think gave you that quick draw?"

Isaac couldn't speak. Emotion rolled through him.

Drew sighed. "It's time to let it go."

The words reminded Isaac of what Clare had said during that quiet, starry night. He wasn't to blame. He'd never be a dime-novel hero. But he could be a good man.

His eyes went to the mountain range in the distance, turned back to the river, and the camp beyond. He took in a cleansing breath, feeling steadier. Cody was dead, and Isaac couldn't bring him back. But Isaac was alive. Eli was still alive, as far as he knew. Isaac wasn't going to squander any more of the time he had left.

He looked at Drew. His brother seemed to read this new peace stealing over him. Drew smiled. "Let's go get Eli."

Isaac stood and they walked together toward the horses saddled and waiting. A new determination filled Isaac. After this was all over, he was going to beg Clare to give him a chance to make things right.

He had to know. "Is Clare all right?"

"Clare?" Drew's forehead creased. "She's not here?"

Isaac stiffened in alarm. "Why would she be here?"

"She snuck out and rode off during the night. Everyone assumed it was to meet up with you." Drew motioned to Isaac's saddle. To the shawl. "Isn't that hers? I figured she was somewhere close."

"She's not here." Isaac's heartbeat kicked up. Drew had made an assumption. It was a mistake, but one he could understand.

But if Clare wasn't here with Isaac, and she wasn't at the main house, that meant . . .

Clare wouldn't ride out in the middle of the night to meet up with him. She'd gone after Eli.

Isaac strode to his horse, a new urgency gripping him. "We need to get down there."

Nineteen

THE BREAKING DAWN CHASED AWAY the last of the shadows, like the truth Drew had told him had chased away the doubts that had haunted him for years. A quiet steadiness had settled in Isaac—a peace he hadn't felt since boyhood, or maybe ever. Fog hovered over the surface of the frigid water as Isaac swam alongside his horse up the center of the river. He was soaked and freezing, but every sense was razor sharp.

Drew was right behind him. They approached Victor's camp slowly, keeping low in the water and trusting that the tall banks would hide their approach. Nick and Ed, along with two neighbors, were supposed to make a wide circle and come at the camp from the opposite side. Danna, Jack, and another deputy planned to cross the train bridge on foot. Isaac caught sight of a shadow moving on the bridge. They were in place.

Drew paused as they edged to the end of the bluff. Any

farther and they'd be in plain sight of Victor's camp. For a moment, there was only the sound of water lapping around them as it rushed past.

Then a voice rang out. One that had become so dear he'd know it anywhere.

Clare.

Isaac couldn't help himself. He grabbed Bullet's halter and urged him out of the water and onto the riverbank. The camp came into sight—the smoke from the fire, the tents, and the chuck wagon.

Where—

Everything happened in an instant. Isaac saw Clare on the ground, Victor standing over her with a gun drawn. Someone shouted from the edge of the camp. Nick's whip-poorwill whistle trilled out.

Chaos unfolded.

Isaac vaulted into the saddle and spurred Bullet into a gallop toward the camp, Drew on his tail.

Gunshots rang out from the camp, answered by shots fired from the bridge.

A bullet whizzed by Isaac's ear. Realizing he was too easy a target on horseback, he slid off Bullet's back and hit the ground at a run, slapping the horse's flank. Bullet bolted for the trees.

Danna and Jack rushed toward the camp on horseback, hooves pounding as their rifles fired from the saddle. Drew wheeled off in another direction.

Isaac crouched low, still running. He'd lost sight of Clare. Closing in on the tents, he scanned the chaotic scene. Danna and Jack had taken control of the camp's far edge, their rifles cracking with precision. A few of Victor's men were fleeing toward the trees, their shouts fading into the night. Drew's gunfire echoed from the opposite direction, pinning down the stragglers.

Hope surged. They were winning.

Closing in on the tents, he saw a man's head and shoulders lean out of the nearest one, gun aimed. Isaac didn't think. He drew and fired, intentionally hitting the tent pole. The man ducked back inside, the pole toppled, and the tent folded in on him. Isaac looked beyond the collapsed tent, but the place where Clare and Victor had been was now empty.

Guns fired. Bullets flew. A howl of pain erupted from nearby. He turned on his heel, searching the area—

Another tent flap opened, and a shadow moved inside. Clare?

Isaac dove inside, gun at the ready.

And came face-to-face with Eli—pale, wide-eyed, and terror-stricken. A bruise darkened one cheek. The boy fought to keep his composure, but the moment Isaac whispered "Hey, kid," Eli's face crumpled.

Isaac held out his left hand, and Eli threw himself into Isaac's embrace, burying his face in Isaac's ribs. Isaac lowered his head to press his chin against the boy's hair, holding his shaking body tightly. Memories of Cody surfaced anew, this time without the sharpness of the guilt and grief Isaac had carried so long.

He'd always have a place in his heart for Cody. But right now, Eli needed him.

"I'm sorry," Eli choked out.

"Shhh," Isaac whispered. "I'm gonna get you out of here."

"Is Ben all right?"

Isaac was so focused on listening for noise outside the tent that he barely heard Eli's quiet murmur. Was that cry Clare's voice?

"Come out, McGraw!" Victor shouted.

Eli's body jerked.

They couldn't stay here. Isaac knew it. The canvas offered no protection. If Victor started shooting, he and Eli would both be easy enough to hit.

"I know you're in there!" Victor called.

The pop of gunshots had tapered off. What did that mean? Had Danna subdued most of the gang? Or perhaps not.

Not if Victor was still free.

Had Victor's men prevailed?

Boots scuffled in the dirt outside the tent. He had to get Eli out of here. Isaac's gaze swept around the small tent. The call of a whippoorwill broke the eerie quiet. Not a particularly good call—Nick was losing his touch. But he was out there somewhere, thank God.

Eli pulled away, lifting his hand to reveal the rusty knife in his tight grip. "Pa's a bad man." He blinked away tears. "I'll help you fight him."

Oh, Eli.

Isaac put his hand on Eli's shoulder. "You're a good boy. And you're gonna grow to be a good man. One I would be proud to call my son."

Eli pulled in a mighty sniff, fighting to hold back more tears.

"Your job now is to stay safe. Leave Victor to me." Isaac took the knife from Eli, moved to the back of the tent, and quickly slashed the canvas. He lifted a corner for Eli.

"Drew will be watching for you. Look for his horse, Solomon. Go!" he urged.

Eli scrambled out and fled.

As Isaac crawled out of the back of the tent, a volley of shots rang out, pitting the tops of the tents.

Must be Danna.

"Call them off, McGraw!" Victor shouted. Isaac peered around the tent to see Victor standing in the open, one arm around Clare's neck and shoulders, holding her like a shield. In his other hand, he held a gun pointed under her chin.

Nick and Drew sat on horseback a few yards away, rifles trained on Victor. Eli was in the saddle with Drew. The way Victor was holding Clare, jerking her close, neither brother had a clear shot.

Heart pounding in his ears, Isaac stood tall and stepped out into the open.

Clare was his wife. And this was his fight.

Clare's eyes locked onto Isaac's as he emerged from behind the tent. Her heart surged with a mixture of surprise and terror—he'd come for her! His face was set with grim determination, not pale and shaky like before. Her eyes darted to the gun, still in its holster at his side.

What did it mean? Was he bluffing?

He stepped forward, and Victor dragged her one step

back. The two men were in a standoff. Clare's mind shuffled through her limited options.

"I have the blasting caps," she said quickly, desperate to stall. "I can take you to them."

He jabbed the barrel deeper in her neck. She gasped for breath.

"What am I gonna do with them now?" he snarled in her ear. "You've ruined everything."

Clare skimmed the scene around her. Victor's heist was well and truly foiled. Two men were sprawled out, dead on the ground, their blood staining the hard dirt. Danna and Jack stood near the fourth tent with their guns on Shorty and Tom Crow, the outlaws' hands raised above their heads. Ed and a man she didn't know had given chase when the two others had ridden away from the camp.

"Run," she told Victor. "You can still get away."

His arm tightened around her neck. In addition to the McGraws and Danna and her deputies, two men on horseback were patrolling on opposite sides of what was left of the camp. Victor wouldn't escape. And he seemed to know it.

"Let her go, Victor," Isaac called.

She felt Victor's rising desperation in his jerky breaths and erratic movements. His arm tightened around her neck. Victor would never give up. He'd once said he'd never go to prison. He'd die first. He was in this to the death. His or hers.

Isaac's eyes were shadowed as his hand hovered over his holstered gun.

Anguish tore at her heart. She didn't want to give him another reason to punish himself.

Her mind flashed back to the first time they'd met, at the train station. What had she thought then? That he was dangerous and handsome? Now she knew his heart. She raised her chin, feeling the gun barrel jab into her neck.

Isaac's eyes narrowed. "It's no use, Barlow," he warned. "You're surrounded."

Victor's finger twitched on the trigger, and Isaac went very still, eyes locked on the movement.

I love you, Clare mouthed. She saw his eyes widen as the words registered.

Victor's hand slid to her throat and squeezed with choking force. She reacted instinctively, going limp, hoping the fall would loosen his hold.

She caught the flash of metal from Isaac's gun in the gleaming sun. His gunshot split the air. She flinched, waiting for the pain. Victor's hold loosened and his body fell away, hitting the ground with a heavy thud. Thrown off-balance, she dropped to her hands and knees. The acrid scent of gunpowder drifted on the air.

And then Isaac was there, drawing her away from Victor's unmoving body. Someone rushed in.

Nick.

She couldn't bear to look at Victor's fallen body, so she let Isaac turn her face into his chest and enfold her in his arms.

"It's over," he said into her hair.

She could barely believe it. Maybe she wouldn't if it weren't for her palms, taking in his warmth through the fabric of his shirt. Or her cheek, relishing each breath he took where she pressed close.

"I . . . I don't know how you did that," she whispered, her voice shaky as she looked up at him. "It all happened so fast. How did you make the shot?"

Isaac's gaze softened, his expression humble, his eyes shadowed with something deeper. "I didn't know if I could do it. I prayed that God would make my aim true. And I trusted."

Her heart felt impossibly full, as though it were expanding beyond its limits, leaving her breathless with gratitude—for him, and for God's faithfulness to rescue all of them. Especially Isaac. The haunted look in his eyes was gone, replaced by a quiet strength.

"Oh, Isaac." She slid her arms around his neck and hugged him tight.

"Danna's got her deputies tying up the last two. Eli's safe. Drew's got him. Taking him home," he said, his voice rumbling through his chest.

Somehow, he'd known how to calm the storm of fear inside her. But she couldn't quite calm the storm of tears that came on like a cloudburst. He didn't seem to mind that she clung to him.

"Ben will be wanting you," he murmured.

It almost felt as if he pressed a kiss into the crown of her head. But that couldn't be right.

He held her until the camp had gone quiet, until it was just the two of them. Until her tears were spent.

When she pushed away from his chest, she couldn't meet his eyes. She'd blurted out her feelings, albeit silently, but nothing between them was resolved. There were still doubts between them. She couldn't forget the look in Isaac's eyes when Victor had claimed she was still working for him.

He didn't let her get far, stepping forward to close the distance when she tried to step back. He gently tipped her chin up with a finger. His eyes held an unexpected warmth.

"What were you thinking, running off in the night? Coming here alone. And what was that about blasting caps?" he chided gently.

Chagrin turned down her lips. "I had to."

He shook his head. She didn't know this teasing Isaac, with one corner of his mouth drawn up in a partial smile. "McGraws don't ride alone. Trust me. I keep learning that the hard way."

She saw it again, that settled look, the peace in his eyes. He glanced over his shoulder to Ed, in the distance, sitting on horseback. Watching over them.

Her heart warmed for Isaac. He had his family back.

McGraws don't ride alone.

"I'm not really a McGraw," she murmured.

"Yes, you are." His reassurance came swift and fierce.

I meant those vows I said.

He'd told her once before. But she hadn't been able to believe it. Not totally. Not with how they'd started, with mistrust and lies and a bargain-struck marriage.

He'd come for her. Fought off the demons of his past to be able to draw against Victor.

She was shaking.

He wasn't finished. "And I'm sorry that I left. Sorry you felt you didn't have any other choice but to come for Eli alone. I'm not living in the past anymore. I want to be a real family, like you said."

New tears welled in her eyes. Joyous tears, for him. For what he was offering her.

Her heart was full to bursting. "You do?"

He nodded gravely. "I love you, Clare. You came and brought my heart back to life. Brought me back together with my family."

She reached a hand up to cup his cheek. "Oh, Isaac, I love you too."

Maybe he'd needed to hear the words spoken out loud, because the vulnerable light in his eyes faded, giving way to a deep, abiding joy.

He pulled her back into his arms, close to his heart, and kissed her. She met his kiss eagerly, pouring all her overflowing emotions into the moment. Isaac loved her. She'd found the place she belonged, right here in his arms.

She'd come searching for a new name, a way to protect herself. But at Isaac's side, she'd faced her own demons and found the home her heart truly craved.

Twenty

J UST CAST MY LINE ONE MORE TIME," BEN
begged. "I won't get it snagged this time."

Isaac looked over from where he was sprawled on
the blanket, one hand holding his head up on a propped
elbow. Clare was perched next to him, watching too. Ben
sat on the riverbank under a twisted lodgepole pine. He
inched forward so that he was as close to the edge of the
bank as possible without falling in.

Eli stood in the river, boots submerged in a few inches
of water.

"You said that about a hundred times before." Eli sighed.
"Give me the pole."

Ben's leg was healing well, but he'd taken to hopping
on one leg all over the ranch. Isaac had lost count of the
number of times Eli had had to step in and steady Ben as
he'd teetered precariously on one leg, ready to topple, after
he'd mislaid his crutches.

A few weeks had passed, and November had sent them a surprisingly warm and clear day—the kind of day perfect for fishing. Clare had decided it was a grand day for a picnic. Who was he to argue? In fact, he couldn't quite remember why he'd fought so hard against settling down.

"He's too close to the edge." Clare eyed Ben like the proverbial mother hen, her body tense, ready to fly into action.

Isaac clasped her hand, and her gaze turned to him. Ben chattered and Eli groused some more, but it was a good-natured response.

"Eli won't let him fall in," Isaac said. The oatmeal cookies could wait. He'd let his eyes feast on her pretty face. With the boys constantly underfoot, a moment alone with his wife was as rare as hen's teeth.

"Look, it's a frog! We ain't seen a frog since we were on the farm. Let's catch it." Ben started to get up.

"Haven't seen one. We haven't seen one," Eli corrected. "You can't chase a frog with your bum leg. Here, take the poles. I'll get 'im."

Something in Isaac's chest hitched.

Ever since the shoot-out and rescue on Quade's property, Eli had settled. There were still moments of stubbornness, but Eli had made his choice—to be a part of this new family.

"Hurry! Oh, you missed him."

Eli bent and tried to close two hands around the frog. It jumped just in time to evade his grasp. "He's a clever little critter," Eli said.

Ben laughed in response.

The laughter rippled across Isaac's soul.

His gaze moved back to Clare, who was watching him, not the boys.

She smiled. Her hazel eyes reflected her deep, heartfelt love for him. "They're just boys being boys," she said softly.

Isaac nodded. He knew she was grateful for the new life she and the boys had found here. She'd told him so, one of the nights they'd lingered over coffee after supper. She'd told him her worries and listened to Isaac's in return. They were on their way to becoming that real family she wanted.

"He jumped thataway!" Ben's shout echoed over the water.

"Got 'im!" Eli grunted and lifted the frog in his hands in front of him.

"It took a lot of courage for him to testify against Victor's gang and their past activities," Clare said. They both watched Eli hand the frog over to Ben.

"He's got courage to spare all right." Isaac turned to give Clare his full attention.

"Yes, but I worry—"

Isaac squeezed her hand. "We'll keep 'em both close. McGraws have a way of staying annoyingly cozy, even when you don't want them around."

His thoughts wandered as he watched the boys absently. His brothers and their posse had taken down most of the Barlow Gang. Victor and two of his men had been killed at the camp. Tom Crow had been captured by Jack. Crow had had his day in court and received a long prison sentence, thanks to Eli's testimony. Eli had heard his father lay out the whole plan. The Barlow Gang had hired on with the Diamond Q as a cover. They'd had an agreement with Quade's foreman. They'd blow up the bridge and help divert the water, but they would do it on the day the train came through so they could rob the safe.

Boom Dawkins had escaped.

And Quade had gotten off scot-free again. Quade and his high-paid lawyer, plus a couple of character witnesses, had been able to convince the circuit judge that Quade had had no knowledge of the plan to blow up the bridge and rob the train. Quade had blamed it all on his foreman.

The only good thing was that, because of the scrutiny, Quade had had to abandon his plan to divert the river and ruin the McGraws. There were some rumbles in town about the ethics of that plan. Maybe the tide would turn.

Isaac wouldn't hold his breath.

"When will you leave?" Clare asked quietly, her eyes on the boys.

Leave.

She meant go back to the Marshals. They'd talked about Isaac's work with the Marshals, whether he should return. He didn't want to leave Clare and the boys, but she had become his staunch advocate, going on about how it was the work he was called to do. She was right.

But not before Christmas. Those boys deserved a family Christmas.

"I'll be home before you know it. Can't stay away from you."

He wasn't going to think about that right now. The sun was shining, his boys were happy to play along the water's edge, and he had his beautiful wife all to himself. In a gun-fighter's lightning-fast move, he wrapped his arms around her and pulled her to him. She let out a startled squeal before his warm lips found hers in a searing kiss, one that lasted long enough for Ben's tattling, singsong voice to ring out over the gurgling water.

"Ew. They're kissing again."

Clare lifted her head and laughed. She got to her feet, straightening her skirt.

"I'm going to head up to the cabin and take the clothes off the line. Hand me the basket."

As Isaac handed her the basket, she teased him. "I made bread this morning. Maybe between the three of you, someone will snag a few fish for supper."

"You want me to multiply the fish while you make the loaves?"

She marched away, but he caught the smile that spread across her face.

"Finally! I thought she'd never leave," Ben said, hobbling toward Isaac using the crutch.

When he saw Isaac's brows lift, he hurriedly added, "She's a good aunt and all, but we've been waiting for days for you to show us how you learned to quick draw."

Eli leaned their poles against a tree nearby. "Nick says he doesn't remember a day when you didn't practice when you were young." Eli met his eyes. "You said you'd teach us." Eli remembered every one of Isaac's promises like they were scripture.

"We won't tell Aunt Clare. We promise," Ben cajoled, putting on his most innocent expression.

Isaac saw right through the manipulation. "Whoa. We're not keeping this from Clare. A man doesn't keep secrets from his wife. Since I aim to be an honorable man and a good husband, I don't keep secrets from Clare."

"None?" Ben's face was screwed up in a comical mask.

"Not one," Isaac said firmly. But he ruffled Ben's hair on his way to set up several cans on a thick branch between two stumps just a few feet apart. Returning to the spot they'd shoot from, Isaac put his hands on his hips and waited until both boys gave him their attention. "Secrets cause mistrust, make you distance yourself from the very people you think you're protecting. The hero may fight alone and ride off into the sunset in those dime novels Clare's been reading to you. But in real life, you're gonna need family and friends to ride with you if you're going to survive out there."

He let that settle while he went inside to get his belt and gun. Surprise and excitement flickered in Eli's eyes when Isaac held the belt out to him. Eli took it and strapped it on, his fingers fumbling with the buckle and missing the belt hole on the first attempt.

The three of them stood for a moment in silence, side by side, staring at the cans. A light breeze whispered through the pines. Isaac held the gun at his side.

Isaac needed to give Eli the words that had been running through his mind for days. He was afraid he would fumble, the same as Eli with his belt, but he needed to say them. He'd come full circle. God had sent his brothers and Clare at the right time to talk sense into him and save him from himself.

"I'll always have your back, Eli." He paused for a deep breath. "You ever need me, I'm there. No matter what. I'll ride for days, over mountains, through the prairie. I'll fight alongside you if need be. I'd take a bullet for you, son. You never have to ride alone. You're a McGraw now, if you want to be."

Their eyes locked. Eli nodded, a solemn understanding passing between them.

Isaac spent the next hour demonstrating the art of the quick draw. Ben was determined, but with his still-weak leg and the gun in his small hands, his aim was cockeyed, and most of his bullets flew past the cans and into the trees. Eli approached the lessons with silent resolve. Isaac was amazed that Eli managed to strike one of the three cans by the end of their session.

Maybe with practice, Isaac's aim to be a good father would hit the mark too, at least some of the time.

"You're looking so much better, Kaitlyn. Your face is fairly glowing," Rebekah said as she turned a crispy browned chicken leg in the cast-iron skillet.

Clare had to agree. Kaitlyn's color had returned along with her vigor, though she had to let out her dresses.

"I'm looking forward to eating your fried chicken again," Kaitlyn said as she set a bowl of corn on the table.

Clare filled a basket with slices of bread. Isaac and the boys had returned to the cabin without a single fish but full of smiles and the smell of gunpowder. Fortunately for them, David had arrived from the main house, sweaty and breathless, with an invitation to supper.

Ed and Rebekah had made a surprise appearance from

town, so the whole family was present. Pans shuffled and plates rattled in the kitchen as extra chairs were brought in and pushed around the table. While Rebekah arranged the chicken on a platter, Clare placed the breadbasket on the table, then turned from the table and skirted around Tillie. Serving meals at the McGraws was like falling into the steps of a familiar dance. One that Clare got to be a part of now.

Tillie slid into the seat, and the boys rushed in, taking their places on the bench on one side of the table. Ed, Isaac, and Drew pulled out chairs for their wives to sit on before settling themselves into their own chairs. Nick was the last man to mosey into the kitchen. A lone chair sat empty next to Jo at the table.

"Looks like you're the last man standing," Ed commented, the double entendre causing smiles, smirks, and a few giggles from around the table as Nick took his seat.

"None of our mail-order bride ads went as expected," Rebekah said, her mouth pulled up in a one-sided smile for Ed in the chair next to her.

Ed leaned over and kissed her cheek. "No, but they did end up bringing us love."

Clare's breath hitched. It still surprised her the way these McGraw men said the loveliest things.

Rebekah cast a cheeky glance at Nick. "When are you going to place an ad? I can help you write it. Maybe even get you a discount," she teased.

Isaac grinned at Clare. She returned his smile as warmth filled her chest. He flashed his green eyes at Jo. "Maybe you should have Jo and David write it."

David's head jerked up. "No way. I'm not getting talked into writing those stupid letters again. Just look at what happened last time." He ducked his head, as red-faced as he'd been when he'd run to their cabin.

But the look in Isaac's eyes caused Clare's own face to burn. His satisfied expression said he was more than pleased with the outcome of their mail-order marriage.

It's God's providence.

She heard Anne's whisper in her mind and smiled, knowing that somehow, Anne could see her now.

Nick cleared his throat and unfurled a napkin with a flourish, like a fancy waiter, before setting it on his lap. All eyes turned to him. Except for Ben's. His attention remained on the platter of chicken in front of him.

"Thank you for your offer, but I've already got it handled."

"You do?" Jo and Kaitlyn asked at the same time. They looked at each other with surprised grins.

"No, he doesn't. He's just trying to put us off," Rebekah protested.

"He's a cunning one all right." Isaac studied him through narrowed eyes. "However, he never says anything he doesn't mean. What's your plan, Nick?"

Nick lifted his chin and steepled his long fingers. But he kept his lips sealed tight.

"He's not going to tell us," Clare said. He liked to tease and provoke a bit. But she was thankful he hadn't given up on Isaac. Or her. She caught the twinkle in Nick's eyes when he looked at her. She smiled at him, warmed by their special bond.

"Of course he's going to tell us, or I'll pull out one of the letters we still have," Rebekah threatened with an impish grin.

Ed and Isaac groaned, while Jo shouted, "Good idea!"

Nick set his fork down and pressed his shoulders back. He let out an exaggerated sigh. "No need to dig into the archives, Rebekah. I've already asked Merritt to help me meet someone. She's got solid connections and will use her considerable social prowess to introduce me to the perfect future bride."

Clare caught the brothers looking at each other with wide eyes and raised brows. Both Ed and Isaac lowered their chins to hide their grins.

After supper, Tillie slipped out of her chair and danced over to Drew. "It's almost Thanksgiving, and then it will be Christmas. How many more weeks till Christmas, Pa?"

"Five more weeks, sweetheart," Drew said, tugging lightly on one of her braids. The discussion moved to Christmas preparations and winter chores. Clare watched Nick stare out the window. A solemn expression crossed his face.

He's lonely. Her gaze traveled around the table. Lonely amid this boisterous, doting family. *Good for him for taking matters into his own hands.*

"Uncle Isaac, Ben said you've been giving him and Eli shooting lessons," Jo whined, breaking into Clare's musing. "That's not fair. Can I have lessons too?"

Clare met Kaitlyn's exasperated expression across the table before Kaitlyn quickly hid it from Jo's eyes.

"That's a question for your pa first . . ." Kaitlyn cut in.

Clare took it all in. The men who loved their families and this land.

The women and children who made the family complete.

She glanced at the man by her side, her husband. Isaac leaned over to speak to Ed. Love swelled in her heart.

Isaac folded her hand in his under the table and gave it a squeeze.

She closed her eyes in a silent prayer.

Thank You, Lord. I was desperate for protection for the boys, just looking for a safe place. But You gave me more than I could hope for. You brought us into a family. You gave me a husband, a fierce protector, and lasting love.

She lifted her head and turned to see Isaac looking down at her. His face softened, and he squeezed her hand again. He'd given her a new name: Mrs. Isaac McGraw. She'd given him her heart. He'd keep it safe.

Bonus Epilogue

Are you are a member of our new releases newsletter? You can receive a special gift, available only to newsletters subscribers.

This Bonus Epilogue to *A Dangerous Heart* will not be released on any retailer platform—it's only available to newsletter subscribers.

Find out what happens next with Isaac and Clare. Scan this QR code to subscribe and get your free gift. You acknowledge you are becoming a Sunrise Publishing, Wendy Galinetti and Lacy Williams subscriber. Unsubscribe from any newsletter at any time.

Thank You

Thank you again for reading *A Dangerous Heart*. We hope you enjoyed the story. If you did, would you be willing to do us a favor and leave a review? It doesn't have to be long—just a few words to help other readers know what they're getting. (But no spoilers! We don't want to wreck the fun!) Thank you again for reading!

We'd love to hear from you—not only about this story, but about any characters or stories you'd like to read in the future.

Contact us at www.sunrisepublishing.com/contact.

Journey once more with our mail-order brides with our final romantic Wind River Mail-Order Brides story, *A Forgotten Heart* by Lacy Williams and Traci Summeril.

Rancher Nick McGraw had his dreams of teaching shattered and lost his chance for true love in one fell swoop. Years later, he's finally moved on. The best Christmas gift he can give himself is a chance for a new start—with a mail-order bride of his own choosing.

After he broke her heart, schoolmarm Elsie Atchinson hoped she would never see Nick again. But moments after they come face to face, Nick is attacked and left for dead in the midst of a white-out blizzard. Elsie can't abandon him in his time of need.

There's just one problem. The Nick who wakes up with his head wrapped in bandages doesn't remember leaving Elsie. This Nick only remembers falling in love with her. But Elsie knows that once Nick regains his memory, their fragile reunion will be shattered, leaving her heart broken once more.

And when Nick's attackers threaten the family ranch, things only get more complicated between them. It may just take a Christmas miracle for them to find their way back to the love they once shared and work together to save everything they hold dear.

One

"HEY, MCGRAW!"

Nick McGraw glanced up at the shout as he guided his horse down the muddy, icy track that was Main Street in the tiny town of Calvin, Wyoming. His dog, Patch, circled the horse, careful to stay clear of its hooves.

Nick's old school chum Ames Lancaster was on the boardwalk outside the leather-goods store, bundled in a coat and red scarf, his black wool derby tucked low over his head.

"What're you doing in town? Don't you know there's a storm brewing?" Ames's eyes drifted to the heavy clouds sinking closer to the tops of the buildings.

Not so different from the heaviness weighing on Nick's chest.

"Business." Nick patted his satchel, the strap looped across his chest, with a gloved hand.

An icy gust sliced through Nick's coat, minuscule snow-flakes stinging his cheeks beneath his hat.

Ames scoffed. "It couldn't wait until this storm clears?"

Not when his family depended on him. "It didn't look so bad when I left."

Nick's oldest brother, Drew, had insisted that the sale contract be finalized at the land office as soon as possible. With Christmas only a little more than a couple weeks away, Nick imagined Drew didn't want to worry about anything—or anyone—causing trouble with the simple transaction. Drew was big on legacy, on protecting and expanding the land their pa had left them.

Nick blinked away the snowflakes gathering on his lashes.

Another arctic blast blew over them, making him shiver. He urged Surrey on.

"Don't get caught out in it!" Ames called out after him.

Ames wasn't joking. Dense moisture thickened the air, promising a dump of snow. Nick would need to finish his errands and seek shelter. Soon.

Normally he looked forward to his trips to town. Seeing friends. Catching up on their lives. But today was different.

How long would it be before he saw town again?

After his business at the land office, he'd be stuck in a winter cabin on the side of a mountain for months. Isolated. With only cows for company.

Children's laughter wafted from the schoolhouse as a few stragglers scurried home. Probably released early on account of the coming storm.

He tried not to look. He really did. But when he passed

the white clapboard schoolhouse, his eyes devoured the snug little building.

He hadn't been inside the new schoolhouse, built after the first had been destroyed by fire almost a year ago. That had been just before his cousin Merritt, the longtime schoolmarm, had gotten married and stepped down.

He'd heard the town had hired a new schoolteacher this past September, but he didn't know who or whether they were filling the position well. All he knew was that the new teacher wasn't him.

For so long he'd dreamed of being the one standing at the front of that classroom—

Nick slammed the lid on those pointless thoughts and nudged his horse faster.

Piano music filtered out into the quiet street from the saloon. A familiar horse hitched outside snagged Nick's attention.

He slowed to a stop.

There was no mistaking the blood bay Thoroughbred standing out like a king among its subjects. It belonged to Heath Quade, a neighbor to the McGraws and a constant thorn in their side. The man had poisoned their family's well months ago, and weeks later, had attempted to reroute the river that flowed onto McGraw land, their only source of water.

Why was the man at the saloon instead of at his ranch with his daughter?

Nick's stomach dropped. It didn't bode well.

He nudged his horse forward, but his gaze stayed on the horse as he rode by.

The man had been a menace ever since Nick's pa had refused to sell his homestead to the greedy rancher decades ago. The man was still targeting the McGraw family, like a wolf hunting its prey.

Maybe it was telling that Quade was at the saloon. Two months ago, he'd suffered a hit to his reputation after his foreman and cowhands had been caught working with outlaws.

All of them had been arrested.

All except for Quade.

It unnerved Nick that Quade had kept his nose clean during that debacle—somehow. Still, whispers in town had finally turned against him. Some of the more prominent ranchers in their county had pulled support from Quade in his position as president of the Cattlemen's Association.

Something like that could make a man furious.

If Nick's gut was right, more than one storm lay on the horizon.

Nick puzzled over the rancher's business in town until he reached his cousin Merritt's house. He reined in his horse and dismounted, shaking snow from his shoulders and arms.

Patch faced the snow-splattered street with a whine. Nick reached down and scratched behind Patch's right ear. "It'll be fine, pup. We'll hunker down at the newspaper office with Ed."

With the snow threatening like this, the half-day's ride back home to the ranch would be treacherous. It would be safer for Nick to stay with his brother Ed and Ed's wife,

Rebekah. They were newlyweds, so it would be awkward, but safer than being caught out in the storm.

Merritt swung open the door at Nick's knock. Both eyebrows flicked up, concern etching her forehead. "Nick? I didn't expect to see you. Everything okay?"

She opened the door wide enough for him to slip inside, but Nick hesitated, pinching his lips together.

He saw the quick flash of what he imagined was disappointment before she smiled.

He'd never told her why he'd returned to Calvin before completing his teaching certificate. She'd never asked.

Nick inhaled and removed his hat. He stepped past Merritt into the warmth of her entryway. "I can't stay. I gotta rush over to the land office but wanted to find out . . ."

Merritt tucked her shawl closer around her and tilted her head.

She was going to make him say it.

". . . whether you'd had an answer to one of your letters." Nick's words tapered off as his attention drifted behind Merritt, toward the parlor and the decorations saturating the house.

"Jack decorated," she explained in a murmur. Her husband was new to celebrating Christmas.

Pine garland swagged along the ceiling and over the fireplace mantel. Perfectly tied bows of red velvet accented the boughs. A large fir tree stood in the corner, draped in strings of popcorn with ornaments of dried apples and starched yarn.

All of it screamed of a joyous season. Joy Nick could not share. Not anymore.

Outside, a gust pelted snow against the window. Merritt's expression softened. "I didn't realize you were in such a hurry to find a wife. It's only been a couple of weeks."

Nick rubbed the back of his neck, his face going hot. She was right. It'd only been a couple of weeks since he'd asked her to write some letters on his behalf, hoping that one or two of her long-distance acquaintances might be interested in corresponding with him.

But in those intervening weeks, he'd had plenty of time to observe his oldest brother, Drew, doting on his pregnant wife, Kaitlyn, and his next oldest brother, Isaac, teaching his adopted sons to carve a whistle. His other brother Ed had been holding Rebekah's hand in church last Sunday, their clasped hands almost hidden in the folds of Rebekah's skirts.

Nick had still seen it.

He didn't begrudge his brothers their happiness. Quite the opposite. But he wanted someone to look at him the way Kaitlyn looked at Drew.

After what'd happened five years ago, Nick had given up on the idea of finding himself a perfect match. But watching his brothers find love had reminded him that man wasn't meant to be alone.

He sighed. He'd figured it'd been a long shot. "I'll be wintering up on the mountain with the cattle. After everything that's happened with my brothers and their wives, I'd prefer it if they didn't have a chance to interfere in this."

Her lips twitched. She knew all of it. Kaitlyn's unexpected appearance, answering a letter from Drew that had been addressed to someone else. Ed's failed attempt at securing Isaac a mail-order bride—romancing Rebekah himself. And then David and Jo's misguided attempt at matchmaking that had resulted in a wife for Isaac.

Nick didn't want a surprise bride.

"You want me to hold your letters?" Merritt asked.

"Better you holding on to them than any of my brothers getting hold of one. That is, if there are any."

Merritt stifled a smile. "Of course there will be letters. You're a good catch, Nick McGraw."

He wasn't so sure.

Footsteps sounded on the front porch, followed by someone stomping the snow off their boots.

Nick quirked an eyebrow. "Expecting someone?"

Merritt shook her head. "No. Since I know you need to leave, do you mind seeing who it is outside while I get something from the kitchen for Kaitlyn? It's a new book for Jo that I'd like to send home with you."

She didn't give him a chance to answer as she disappeared into the kitchen.

He reached for the door just as it swung open. Nick stumbled backward to keep it from knocking into him.

"Sorry, Merritt!" But the woman with snow dousing her black coat and blonde hair peeking out from beneath a lopsided hat didn't sound sorry.

She turned away and closed the door before he could get a look at her face. He felt a beat of recognition, even as she said, "Brrr, the temperature is dropping fast."

She patted away the clumps of snow from her coat, the motion somehow familiar, then peeled off her gloves and shoved them into her coat pocket. "I sent the kids home early today with the snow settling in. It's the last day before break anyway. I hope it was early enough for them to get home."

She turned while unbuttoning her coat. "I really need to talk to you."

Her head tilted up and their gazes collided.

Nick's breath seized in his lungs. He couldn't move, his heart frozen mid-beat.

The overdone Christmas decorations faded away as he looked at the only woman who had ever noticed the real Nick McGraw.

Elsie.

Even thinking her name released a rush of memories from the place where he'd barricaded them. They rubbed against something so tender, so raw within him, that all his nerves fired at once.

Her face paled as she gave a heavy blink—as if she, too, wanted to make sure her eyes weren't playing tricks on her.

A drip of melted snow slipped from her hat. Her hand trembled as she brushed away the drop from her cheek.

His hand twitched, as if it remembered the softness of her skin, her hair, and longed for the connection. He clenched his hands until his nails cut into his palms.

Her jaw slackened before she said, "Nick?"

What was she doing here? In Calvin, Wyoming. At Merritt's house.

The door—his means of escaping this torturous moment—was behind her. He couldn't hear Merritt in the kitchen, but she was only steps away. He didn't want to wait for a book or for anything.

He just wanted out of here.

Elsie fiddled with the pleat of her skirt, the same way she always had when nervous. "What are you doing here in Calvin?"

He forced out the words, though they cut his throat like glass. "I live here."

Moments before reaching her friend Merritt's house, Elsie Atchison had leaned into the wind working against her and shoved the letter deeper into her pocket.

I'd hoped to tell you in person, but I can't wait any longer. I love you.

Love her? How could Arnold Nelson love her? He didn't even know her. Not the real her hidden beneath layers of expectations she worked hard to meet.

Snow soaked through her boots, freezing her toes. She forced them faster toward Merritt's.

She'd left the empty schoolroom, but her feet hadn't turned toward the room she rented in the family home of one of her students. The family had left to visit a far-off daughter for Christmas. The house would be entirely too quiet. Elsie needed to talk through this disaster. Needed to find a solution.

Merritt would help. She was her sister Darcy's friend, Elsie's by proxy. She might even be able to tell Elsie how to fix this mess.

The letter crinkled as Elsie hugged her middle.

Love? How had these letters gotten so out of hand? She'd only agreed to the correspondence to avoid disappointing her parents. She'd known Arnold forever but had never felt that way about him.

The thought of marrying Arnold closed in around her as if smothering her. She wanted to teach. Not marry. Her mother couldn't understand how Elsie felt. Pretended she didn't hear when Elsie brought it up.

Arnold was an attractive, polite gentleman that most women would welcome as a suitor. But his charm did nothing to make Elsie's heart beat faster.

Her classroom was a refuge. It was steady. Day in and day out, *she* planned the day for her students. *She* created the rules.

There, she didn't worry about betrayal leaving her raw and vulnerable.

She reached Merritt's house and climbed the porch but stopped in her tracks. Beside the door sat a beautiful dog with shaggy, spotted fur and intelligent blue eyes.

She held out her hand for the dog to sniff. "Well, where did you come from?"

The dog nuzzled into her hand, and she scratched its ears. She hadn't known Merritt liked dogs.

With a final pat, she straightened and stomped the snow off her boots, then after a short hesitation, opened the front door.

When Elsie had first arrived in Calvin, Merritt had taken her under her wing, insisting they were family. And family didn't stand on formalities like knocking on the front door.

A wind gust blew a dusting of snow across Merritt's floor as Elsie practically tumbled in, almost knocking her friend over. "Sorry, Merritt!" With her shoulder, she rammed the door closed behind her. "Brr, the temperature is dropping fast."

She fumbled with the buttons on her coat while she turned around. "I really need to talk to you."

Elsie's hands stalled mid-motion. It wasn't Merritt behind her.

Her breath stuck in the back of her throat. Whether from surprise or dread, she didn't know.

Nick. Nick McGraw.

The very man who'd broken her heart five years ago.

He looked the same except for the stubble darkening his jaw. And the new shadows darkening his eyes.

Never had she thought she would see the greatest regret of her life again.

He stepped back, eyes narrowing as if she had become a threat simply by walking through the door.

At his reaction, an echo of her old anger rose in response.

Five years ago, he'd given her an ultimatum.

That night flooded back. She could almost feel the way the winter air had sliced her cheeks as she'd watched him mount his horse. He hadn't even looked back as he'd ridden away. Hurt and betrayal had vied for the most awful sort of win.

Now the air sizzled with the bite of that familiar betrayal. Something hot.

"Nick?" She whispered his name, barely audible above the wind rattling the windows.

His eyes narrowed.

Idly, she noticed that his hair had grown over his ears. "What are you doing here in Calvin?"

He didn't move, his face a mask. "I live here."

He lived here? She knew his *family* lived here. She'd arrived in town full of nerves, breathless at the thought of seeing him again. But it'd been months, and she'd never seen him. "You're not teaching?" It was a silly question. She was the teacher in the one-room schoolhouse. But if he lived nearby, that meant he wasn't a teacher after all.

A muscle in his jaw twitched. "You sent the children home early? You're the teacher?"

How could the simple words, spat out like that, sound like an insult?

Elsie's stomach churned. She gripped her wet skirt to keep her hands from shaking and raised her chin so he wouldn't see the way her lips threatened to tremble. "I am."

"What happened in Elk Creek?"

Her chin notched higher. "I left." She refused to admit how things had worked out. Not to him. "When Merritt retired, she let me know of the opening. And here I am." She spread her hands out to punctuate her sentence.

He remained closed off, revealing nothing. She'd never experienced Nick like this. He'd always been open to her. Until those very last moments together . . .

No, she couldn't think about that.

So instead, she cleared her throat. "It's been a busy semester. The Christmas pageant went well." Except for when one of the school board members had come in and demanded his daughter be the lead.

Merritt's voice rang out from the kitchen. "I found it! Sorry, Nick—"

His head jerked to the left, his eyes blinking furiously

as if he'd forgotten where he was, what he was doing here. "I have to go."

"Nick, wait—"

For a moment, Elsie thought he would shoulder her out of the way.

"Move."

She stepped aside, shaken. The Nick she'd known before would never have spoken so coldly.

She called after him as he went out into the blowing snow. "I've thought about what I might say if we ever met again—"

"I haven't thought about you at all."

She barely heard his mutter over the wind, but the words struck her like a blow from a ruler across the backs of her knuckles. Sharp, shooting pain.

Tears gathered. Different tears than before.

The door snapped closed behind him, and Elsie's chest heaved beneath the hand splayed across her chest.

Her strength drained away. She leaned against the hallway wall and slid down.

She heard Merritt's swishing dress stop beside her.

Elsie muttered, "You didn't tell me Nick lived at home."

Merritt stood over her with surprise in her wide eyes. Obviously, she'd overheard some of Nick's parting words. "What happened?"

Elsie couldn't speak. She'd come face-to-face with the man who'd been a part of the worst moment of her life—and it was like opening a box of stuffed-away pain. Everything came flooding back.

Elsie shook her head.

Merritt sighed. "I thought you and Nick had been friends."

Friends? Oh, they'd been so much more than that. But back then, Elsie had wanted to keep things about Nick to herself.

"Obviously, there's more to it."

Elsie swallowed. Hard. She'd never told anyone what had transpired that night . . . and at this moment, she couldn't find the courage to tell her dear friend. What would Merritt think of how naive she'd been? Her mistakes?

Merritt eyed her. "Maybe you should go after him. Smooth things over."

"There's nothing left to say."

Merritt bent down, eye level, serious. "Surely nothing happened that would jeopardize your post here in Calvin."

The tone of Merritt's voice made Elsie's mouth go dry. She looked away.

No, nothing indecent had happened, but appearances mattered. Morality clauses in teacher contracts mattered. And she knew how quickly rumors could spread.

"Nick is good friends with Adair Benson," Merritt said. "One of the school board members."

Elsie's stomach lurched.

"They go shooting together sometimes."

No, no, no. If Nick leaked anything about what had happened, her reputation would be in tatters. Her job threatened.

He wouldn't do that, would he?

The old Nick, the one she'd fallen for five years ago,

would never have betrayed her trust. But she didn't know him anymore, did she?

Elsie sucked in a breath. "I think I do need to go smooth things over with Nick."

Smooth things over? Beg for his discretion was more like it.

Concern passed over Merritt's face as she helped Elsie to her feet. "Would you like me to go with you?"

The letter crinkled in Elsie's pocket as she fished for her gloves. Her reason for coming to Merritt had been forgotten in the shock of seeing Nick again.

She'd have to deal with Arnold's declarations later.

With a jerky movement, Elsie yanked the door open. "No reason for you to brave the storm."

Then she charged into the storm, following Nick's disappearing tracks in the snow.

Acknowledgments

With heartfelt gratitude—

To my mentor, Lacy Williams, thank you for the countless hours you poured into teaching me how to plot and pace a strong story, write with emotion, and navigate the ever-unfolding journey of the author's life.

To Susan May Warren and the incredible Sunrise Team, thank you for believing in me and helping bring this publishing dream to life.

Above all, to my Lord and Savior, Jesus Christ, the author and finisher of my faith—every word I write is for Your glory.

Also by Lacy Williams

Christmas Bells and Wedding Vows (anthology)

Wagon Train Matches
A Trail So Lonesome
Trail of Secrets
A Trail Untamed
Wild Heart's Haven
A Rugged Beauty

Wind River Hearts series
Marrying Miss Marshal
Counterfeit Cowboy
Cowboy Pride
The Homesteader's Sweetheart
Courted by a Cowboy
Roping the Wrangler
Return of the Cowboy Doctor
The Wrangler's Inconvenient Wife
A Cowboy for Christmas
Her Convenient Cowboy
Her Cowboy Deputy
Catching the Cowgirl
The Cowboy's Honor
Winning the Schoolmarm
The Wrangler's Ready-Made Family
Christmas Homecoming
Heart of Gold

USA Today bestselling author **Lacy Williams** is devoted to bringing her readers heartwarming love stories about cowboys and the women that tame them. She is the author of over fifty-five books, including the acclaimed Wind River Hearts and Sutter's Hollow series. Her books have been nominated for the RT Book Reviews' Seal of Excellence as well as finaled in RT's Reviewers' Choice Awards. She has been a puppy parent almost her whole life and often writes with one of her dogs snuggled in her lap. She is a mom of four and spends her non-writing time buried under piles of laundry and dishes.

Learn more at lacywilliams.net.

Wendy Galinetti grew up in Michigan's Upper Peninsula—the eighth of eleven kids in a town just big enough to have a library (thankfully). After high school, she saved $325, climbed into a small plane out of a cow pasture, and flew to Bible college in Oklahoma, where she met her husband of over 40 years. Together, they planted a church in Grand Blanc, Michigan, where they still pastor and live happily ever after (with a few plot twists along the way). Wendy is mom to four grown children and GiGi to three delightful grandkids. When she's not writing stories or skits, creating Bible studies, leading small groups, or leading worship, you can find her at a local boutique indulging her love for fashion—and solving the world's problems with the kind ladies who shop local. Wendy writes the kind of stories she loves to read: emotional, faith-filled tales about flawed characters who are transformed by truth and grace—and willing to risk their hearts (and sometimes their lives) for love.

Her books come with faith, laughter, a few tears, and a firm belief that faith, love—and really good coffee—can get you through anything.

Discover more at wendygalinetti.com.

BLOOD OF KINGS: LEGENDS

Award-winning author
JILL WILLIAMSON

with Andrew Swearingen,
Kelly Fernlake, & Niki Florica

Return to the world of Er'Rets in an epic
fantasy series brimming with richly woven
tales of loyalty, love, and sacrifice…

We solve the problem of what we read next.   Available on Amazon

YOU MAY ALSO LIKE...

When a blizzard strikes Deep Haven and Megan is overrun with catastrophes, it takes a former Ranger to step in and help. But the more he comes to her rescue, the sooner she'll move out... Come home to Deep Haven in this magical tale about the one who got away... and came back.

Still the One by Susan May Warren and Rachel D. Russell

Grace Howell leaves her life as a ballerina and returns to Heritage, Michigan, to heal. Teaching dance is just a temporary gig, until she finds herself unexpectedly charmed by small-town life and her growing attachment to Seth Warner, a man from her past with a troubled history of his own.

You're the Reason by Tari Faris

Dani Sullivan is determined to revive Jonathon Island's fading charm and reunite her fractured family. Her plan? Reopen the Grand Sullivan Hotel. But without the funds to restore the hotel, Dani's forced to accept help from Liam Stone—a big-city hotel developer whose sleek, modern vision is everything she's trying to avoid.

Meet Me at the Grand by Lindsay Harrel

We solve the problem of what we read next.   Available on Amazon

**WHERE EVERY STORY IS A FRIEND,
AND EVERY CHAPTER IS A NEW JOURNEY...**

Subscribe to our newsletter for a free book, the latest news, weekly giveaways, exclusive author interviews, and more!

@sunrisemediagroup

@sunrisepublish

@sunrisepublishing

Shop paperbacks, ebooks, audiobooks, and more at
SUNRISEPUBLISHING.MYSHOPIFY.COM